Impulses

An Arthur Blake Mystery Novel

by

Richard Davidson

Richard Davidson

Books by Richard Davidson:

Self-help:
DECISION TIME! Better Decisions for a Better Life

Mysteries:
The Lord's Prayer Mystery Series
Lead Us Not into Temptation
Give Us this Day Our Daily Bread
Forgive Us Our Trespasses
Thy Will Be Done
Deliver Us from Evil

Imp Mysteries:
Implications
Impulses

Anthology: (Editor)
Overcoming: An Anthology by the Writers of OCWW

"Impulses," by Richard Davidson
ISBN 978-0-9829160-8-7
An Arthur Blake Mystery Novel

Manufactured in the United States of America.

This book is dedicated to all those people who have too many projects, problems, and obligations to handle at one time, but still manage to cope with their burdens and meet their deadlines.

CHAPTER 1 – AWAKENING

Arthur felt the jostling as he pushed his way through the unruly crowd. Strangers stared at him, menaced him with shaking fists, and aimed sharp fingers at him like weapons. Repeatedly they shouted that opening to Dickens' book, "It was the best of times, it was the worst of times ..." Then the shouts gradually morphed into something else.

"Arthur, wake up. Wake up. You're moaning and shouting garbled words in your sleep."

He forced his eyes open, first the right, then, with some difficulty the left, to reveal Irma shaking his shoulder from her side of the bed. She looked anxious and concerned.

"Your outbursts woke me, and when I looked at you, I saw you sweating. Feel your pajama top; it's soaking wet. You're either ill, or you had a terrible nightmare."

"I don't feel ill, but something in my subconscious is eating at me. I rarely have nightmares, but this one had twisted reality stamped all over it. Everyone around me blamed me for his or her problems and they wanted, individually – not as a single group, to kill me. Their hatred burned into me; that must have been why I sweated so much."

"Are you worried about the outcome of your meeting with the bishop this morning? We both know he wasn't happy about the outcome of your last investigation. Can he fire you as a pastor?"

"Nope. Unless I volunteer to abdicate, the only way they could take back my credentials and keep me from performing rituals and sacraments would be to convict me of something specific in a church court."

"Then what has you so disturbed?"

"That's the problem; I really don't know, but I feel as though the sword of Damocles is dangling over my head, poised to fall if I step out of line."

Irma studied her husband for what seemed like a long time. Then she threw back his covers and pulled him out of bed.

"It's time for us to get out of the house and away from our normal routines. No one can be introspective when an enthusiastic dog is being affectionate. We'll take Rex with us and drive to Parkville for a hike around Mallard Lake and some visiting with our friends there."

"That sounds great, but you're forgetting something. I have to visit Bishop Chandler in his Rockford office this morning."

"Then we'll hike around something in Rockford this afternoon. We'll all drive there together. Then Rex and I will scout out a good hiking spot while you're in your meeting."

CHAPTER 2 – JUDGMENT

Pastor Arthur Blake had enjoyed a successful career as a NASA aerospace engineer before he felt drawn to focus on heaven instead of the stars. He had made a mid-course correction to enroll in Garrett-Evangelical Theological Seminary. Following graduation, he had assisted in several churches and then had attained ordination as an elder within the Northern Illinois Conference of the United Methodist Church. Following ordination, he had served five years in the far-northwest Chicago exurb of Parkville as pastor of Parkville UMC. During this assignment, he had discovered and honed his investigative talents on several occasions when church-related incidents had been criminal in nature and threatening to his flock. Because of his demonstrated knack for uncovering the causes of sinister events, Bishop Howard Chandler had removed Arthur from Parkville United Methodist Church and appointed him investigative troubleshooter for the entire Northern Illinois Conference. Today's summons to Bishop Chandler's Rockford office had resulted from Arthur's having performed too well in his first investigative troubleshooter assignment.

When Arthur entered the lobby of the Bishop's office, the receptionist greeted him and confirmed her memory that he liked his coffee black. She announced that Bishop Chandler was ready to meet with him; she would deliver his coffee during the meeting. Arthur began to feel optimistic when he entered the bishop's office and saw the two wing back chairs and coffee table arranged in front of the fireplace, reflecting more pleasant occasions when

Howard Chandler had used informal sessions to compliment him for his successful efforts. This contrasted with their last meeting, when Bishop Chandler had assigned Arthur to the upright side chair in his downtown Chicago office. That visit had been more of an inquisition than a fireside chat.

Howard Chandler rose to greet Arthur and extended his hand in welcome. Most visitors would have relaxed at this action; Arthur advanced for the opening handshake with all of his senses tuned for peak efficiency. In his mind, he heard the opening bell of a boxing match.

"Welcome, Arthur; join me by the fire. I believe that I have good news for you."

Arthur hesitated slightly at Bishop Chandler's posturing statement, and reached his usual chair just as the receptionist delivered his coffee. He smiled at her and reached for the reassuring hot mug, while taking his seat in the same motion.

"That sounds encouraging, Howard. Our last meeting in your Chicago office ended on a somewhat tense note."

"My temper has cooled since that encounter. You disturbed the Conference's equilibrium by discovering embarrassing historical details during your last assignment, and then I became frustrated when the media published those facts."

"That wasn't my doing."

"I understand that now. Fortunately, the media publishes so many scandalous stories that few gain much credibility. Most people forgot the incident and moved forward."

"Then you want me to continue working as investigative troubleshooter?"

"Let's say that my colleagues on the Board of Ordained Ministry and I would like to see a pause in the internal investigations. I asked you here today to offer you a six-month sabbatical leave for purposes of study or travel, as you wish. During that period, we'll take a census of Conference problems to determine whether continuation of the investigative troubleshooter post is justified. At the conclusion of your sabbatical period, based on the results of our study, you'll either return to your troubleshooter post, or transfer to a new assignment."

"In other words, you want me to disappear for a while, so that you'll be able to delay your decision about my future."

"I certainly wouldn't phrase it that way, Arthur, but I see some merit to gaining the perspective that comes with the passage of time. I hope you'll cooperate with our approach."

"It's unexpected, but it may have some value." ...*but not for the reason you've suggested.* Aloud, Arthur continued, "I accept your offer."

They shook hands, and Arthur left. The meeting had been unexpectedly short. He had time to go to the restaurant where Irma would meet him, and consider his options over a large mug of coffee while waiting.

CHAPTER 3 – IRMA

Irma Custis had been the County Medical Examiner who responded when newly appointed Pastor Arthur Blake had discovered a badly decomposed body in the attic of Parkville United Methodist Church's older building. This event had triggered both his first investigation and a mutual attraction between Arthur and Irma, culminating in their marriage after several years of increasing affection for each other. During and beyond those years, they had worked together to unravel a series of mysteries, assisted by several professional and amateur investigators. Among these were Parkville Police Chief, Bobby Andrews and his wife Renee, herself a former police officer; Joe and Penny Gonzalez from an unpublicized federal agency; plus Wally Sanborn and Jeremy Hadley - members of the Parkville UMC congregation.

Irma's background in forensic pathology meshed well with Arthur's talent for sensing the most logical procedure during any investigation. Irma applied the brakes whenever Arthur formulated a theory based upon insufficient evidence, while Arthur helped Irma to see unexpected consequences of her rigorous measurements and evidence gathering. Beyond their joint efforts during investigations, they were deeply in love. Their marriage would likely have succeeded in the absence of crimes to investigate, but they would have been bored as hell. Criminology stimulated them.

CHAPTER 4 – PLANS

Once they had returned from Rockford to their home outside Amboy, Illinois, Arthur and Irma settled down on the long front porch of their century-old Queen Anne home to assess the options that the six-month sabbatical leave had opened for them. As usual, Irma sat curled up on the couch with her yellow legal pad of paper while Arthur alternated between sitting in the rattan chair and pacing the length of the porch.

Arthur said, "In the past, we've always had a case needing investigation thrust upon us by circumstances. We didn't have to go looking for one. Now, Bishop Chandler has given us free time to tackle something big, but we don't have a project backlog. We don't even have anything from Penny and Joe's federal agency requiring a consultant."

"That's because their whole group is working for Homeland Security on anti-terrorism investigations. We could be like normal people and just spend some time with your parents, or travel."

"You may have a good idea, Irma. Mother and Dad came up with a case for us before."

"There are more reasons for visiting your family than trying to find a new case. You're a bundle of nerves. No wonder you're having nightmares. Do you have any feeling for what's bothering you?"

He forced himself to stop pacing and sat in his chair, but his right toe bounced up and down nervously. "We've been through a lot together. I've handled myself well due to the balance between my spiritual work in the church and the intellectual challenges of investigating crimes and conspiracies. Bishop Chandler first took away the church appointment that served as a focus for me, and now he's suspended all of my connections with the Conference for six months. I'm out of balance. I don't feel useful enough."

Irma reached over and patted him on the knee. "I hope you remember all the conversations we've had over the years, when I told you that someday you might have to choose between your career as a pastor and your sideline life as an investigator of bizarre and criminal events. Every time we discussed whether your criminal investigations slighted your church responsibilities, you laughed it off and delayed any possible choice for some distant future time. Don't look now, but by suspending your church activities for six months, Bishop Chandler has brought you to that decision point."

"You mean that it's time for me to select one career and abandon the other."

She leaned back and stared at his fingers nervously drumming on the arm of the chair. "Abandon's a pretty strong word. If you were a full-time criminologist, you'd still have your personal religion; and if you were a full-time pastor, you'd still check out unusual events that just fell into your lap – you just wouldn't go out looking for them, the way you do now."

"I told you that the lack of balance between my two interests bothers me."

"You were once an aerospace engineer for NASA, and you gave that up. Yet you still use engineering approaches to solving problems."

"Would people think of me differently without my church affiliation?"

Irma smiled. "Aha! You already know which way you would lean if you had to make a choice. Good; that's half the battle."

"I didn't say anything definite."

8

"Of course you didn't, but remember that you don't have to abandon your credentials. You told me that. You can simply convert your sabbatical into an indefinite leave of absence without pay. That would save the Conference money, so they would be likely to go along with it. We can easily live on the consulting fees we've received from Joe and Penny's federal agency and from others."

"Wouldn't it bother you if neither one of us had a steady job?"

Irma stood up, walked to his chair, and kissed him.

"I enjoyed that, but what triggered it?"

"You did, by showing your concern for my feelings; but in case you didn't notice, we've had a very steady diet of investigations for a long time."

"What would I do when we didn't have an active case, like now? It actually sounds nonsensical to debate a full-time investigative career when we don't even have a tiny case for part-time analysis."

"So that's the root of the problem. You're as bad as Sherlock Holmes was whenever he found himself in a fallow period between cases. The lack of something to investigate is driving you crazy."

"Perhaps, but he was just a fictional consulting detective."

"Well maybe at such times you could sit down and start writing a theological treatise or a handbook for amateur detectives."

"I guess that's a possibility. I'll think about your suggestion for a while. My biggest problem would be figuring out how to keep myself occupied between cases."

CHAPTER 5 – MESSAGES

Arthur arrived home following his second visit to Bishop Chandler's office in a much better mood. He found Irma in the back yard, brushing Rex to remove the bulk of the golden retriever's loose and shedding hair. A large pile of blondish tresses covered a newspaper sheet on the ground, and stray wisps, buoyed by the slight breeze, drifted toward the woods at the rear of the property.

"You're doing a great job, Irma. Rex even looks as though he's enjoying it."

"Welcome back, Arthur; I hope your latest discussion with Howard Chandler went well. You appear to have survived it in good shape – and yes, Rex enjoys attention in any form, even when it involves a wire brush."

He hefted a substantial package onto the picnic table and sat down on a white plastic chair. "I expected Howard to voice some resistance to our leave of absence proposal, but he accepted it without debate and ended up endorsing the concept. I think he felt that my absence would relieve him of potential problems. He's conventional and doesn't really know how to deal with me because I don't fit the traditional clergyperson mold."

"I'm glad you're in a better mood. However, Bishop Chandler's ready acceptance of your leave of absence may reflect the fact that you once considered both him and his wife to be suspects in a murder investigation."

"I think he forgave me for that long ago, but I agree that it may still reside in his subconscious."

"What's in that package on the table? Is it a going away present for you?"

"It's actually a gift from Howard Chandler to you. He probably felt that you deserve a reward for taking me off his hands for a while. Why don't you check it out?"

Irma stood, patted Rex on the head, and walked over to the table, trying to read the expression on Arthur's face as she approached the package. "Is this thing going to explode or anything?"

"You'll have to find that out for yourself, but just in case, Rex and I will take cover behind the apple tree."

Irma tore open the wrapping paper to discover a large pulpit Bible. When she opened the book's front cover, she found an inscription. *Irma – Keep Arthur focused on the fact that whether he has a church or not, he is pastor to those around him – Howard Chandler.* She motioned Arthur to join her so that he could read it also.

"That was very thoughtful of Howard, Arthur. Despite you're being an anomaly to him, you're still one of his favorite people."

"We've had our ups and downs. I think he's glad to have me out of his hair, but still wants to have a claim on me because he knows he may need me in the future. That's fine with me. I'll want the legitimacy of Conference affiliation going forward."

Irma looked at him intently. "Are you feeling any more positive with this leave of absence arrangement? You still don't have a case to investigate."

He held her hand. "Thanks for all of your concern. Yes, I feel better. It's a definite step forward. Case or no case, I've committed to something, and that makes it significant. Did anything other than dog grooming happen while I was away?"

"Check the answering machine. I think we may have some telephone messages. The phone rang a few times while I was out here in the yard with Rex."

Arthur entered the house and saw that the machine held three messages. He pressed the button to cue the first one.

"Pastor Blake, this is Annie at Bishop Chandler's office. Howard wanted to catch you before you left on a trip or committed to a project. We've just learned that Pastor Rebecca Klingham, who succeeded you at Parkville UMC, has committed suicide. We don't have any details for you. Bishop Chandler would like you to investigate the circumstances and deal with the police there. He'd also like you to substitute at that church for a few weeks until he is able to arrange for a full-time replacement. Thank you in advance for filling this void. Please call me if you have any questions."

Arthur made a few notes and pressed the button for the second message. "Hi, Arthur – Wally Sanborn here. Our young friend, Jeremy Hadley, apparently decided to look into the disappearance of a roommate, and now he's gone missing too. I've just learned this from his mother, Shirley. She's calm on the surface, but I know she's really upset inside. I'll be trying to determine the circumstances of Jeremy's disappearance. Call me when you can. We'll need your help."

Arthur made some more notes. Shirley Hadley had been his secretary at Parkville United Methodist Church. Wally Sanborn, the Lay Leader and a retired Army officer, was his coffee buddy and one of his best friends. The missing twenty-two year old Jeremy Hadley had assisted Arthur and Irma in several investigations.

He pushed the button for the third message on the answering machine. "Hello, Arthur, this is Mother calling. Your father and I have to go to California because his cousin Ralph has been in a bad automobile accident. Ralph has no other living relatives. We need to ask you and Irma to manage the antiques store while we're gone. Call us as soon as possible. We're booking our flight now."

A few notes and a few sips of coffee later, Arthur returned to the back yard. "Irma, you may not believe this, but our lack of projects is no longer a problem. Our calendar has overflowed."

"As soon as you came out of the door, I knew that you felt happier. You can't function when things are going well. Dreams or no dreams, you thrive when surrounded by people seeking solutions to their problems."

CHAPTER 6 – JUGGLING ASSIGNMENTS

Irma called Arthur's mother, Janice Blake, to tell her that she would drive to Richmond, Illinois, arriving mid-afternoon, and that she would open the antiques store on schedule the next morning, while Arthur would be attending to a couple of assignments in Parkville. He would then join her at the store as soon as he could break free from his local obligations. Janice responded that she and Peter would have already left for California before Irma arrived, but that she would leave the key to the kitchen door under the flowerpot next to the garage. She'd leave the store and front door keys in the center desk drawer in Peter's den, and she'd have bowls set out in the kitchen for Rex's food and water.

Irma and Janice had become close friends years earlier, when she and Arthur had first revealed the onset of a serious relationship while visiting the senior Blakes at their home in Richmond, Illinois. Since that time, The two of them had shared their thoughts and outlooks on many occasions, both by telephone and in person. Janice trusted Irma and welcomed her running the shop.

While Irma and Janice negotiated their arrangements, Arthur called his former secretary at Parkville UMC, Shirley Hadley, to determine the circumstances of Pastor Klingham's suicide and to learn what Shirley knew about events that might have triggered her son Jeremy's disappearance.

"Hi, Shirley; I'm calling to let you know that I'll be arriving in Parkville in a couple of hours to assist with the church situation and look into Jeremy's activities. Would you please contact Wally Sanborn and ask him to be at the church when I arrive. I'll need his assistance."

"It's great to hear your voice again, Arthur. I'll have Wally here for you, and I'll make some notes about recent developments at the church that we may want to discuss regarding Pastor Klingham."

"That sounds as though you have a theory as to why she committed suicide."

"I won't go so far as to call it a theory, but I'll list some intriguing coincidences that might point you in a promising direction for examination. I'd rather not discuss it over the telephone."

"Fair enough, Shirley; I'll see you shortly. See if you can scare up some pastry from your husband's shop so that our meeting will seem like old times."

"I asked Walter to schedule a delivery as soon as I heard you would be coming back here. Drive safely."

Shirley's husband, Walter, operated Hadley's Bakery and Catering Company, and Arthur had long missed the automatic pairing of pastry and meetings that he had enjoyed while pastor at Parkville United Methodist Church. At least that aspect of his inquiries would be pleasant. He didn't know where the search for Jeremy Hadley would lead, but he hoped that he would be able to pursue Jeremy, cover his temporary Parkville UMC obligations, and commute for some portion of the week to the Richmond antiques store too.

Arthur took a deep breath, smiled at the way events had accelerated, and prepared himself for a period of spreading himself very thinly over his several challenges.

CHAPTER 7 – PARKVILLE

A wave of nostalgia engulfed Arthur as he pulled into his favorite space in the lower parking lot at Parkville UMC. The church, facing the X-shaped intersection of Main and Jeffers Streets, straddled a hillside, so that it had an upper level parking lot on Main Street and a lower level parking lot on Jeffers. Arthur traditionally parked in the Jeffers lot, so that he entered the building on the lower Sunday school level and climbed stairs to access the main floor with its offices and sanctuary. He enjoyed the stair-climbing exercise and the fact that this route usually avoided chance encounters with talkative members on his way to the offices.

When he entered Shirley's office, she greeted him with a smile and a hug, both tinged with a sense of relief. In her mind, Arthur could fix anything.

"Welcome back, Arthur; Wally Sanborn will join us in a few minutes. He took a telephone call from the funeral director who will be transferring Pastor Klingham's body to Chicago, where most of her family lives. As Lay Leader, he was the best person to handle such things pending your arrival. Fresh coffee is in the pot, and I have one of your old NASA mugs on the table."

Arthur always worked better with a mug of coffee in hand, so he poured himself some steaming brew and returned to the conversation. "Thanks, Shirley; I agree with your comments, and it's good to be back, despite the circumstances. I know that you're most concerned with your son's disappearance, but I'm going to have to heed my official orders and give priority attention to the circumstances of Pastor Klingham's death. Is that acceptable to you?"

"I understand, Arthur. Jeremy's resourceful, as well as a criminology graduate, so I'm still hopeful that his adventure will have a positive ending. I'm good for talking about Rebecca's suicide first."

Arthur patted her shoulder to reassure her. "I met Rebecca Klingham only once at Annual Conference, and our conversation was brief. What can you tell me about her?"

Shirley relaxed against the back of her chair. "Pastor Klingham was about forty-two years old, a little younger than you, and she had been through two divorces, neither one of which had been amicable. She had a son, John, during her first marriage to Bruce Wenger. John Wenger is just about the same age as Jeremy, twenty-two. Rebecca confided to me that Bruce secured custody of John after the divorce because her drug problem had wrecked their marriage. She later licked that addiction and married Ralph Klingham while they were in seminary together. That marriage lasted only two years because he was very evangelical and somewhat abusive to her, while she was too liberal in her outlook for him."

"It sounds as though you've completed a good part of the investigation for me. Please continue."

"It is true that no one can be around you very long without picking up some detective skills, but I started noticing coincidences long before Rebecca took her own life."

"What kind of coincidences?"

"During Rebecca's time here, four older women who had illnesses or recent operations died shortly after Pastor Klingham visited them."

"Were those hospital visits?"

"No, the women had been patients at two different hospitals, but she last visited each of them at Parkville Rehabilitation Home."

"So, they died despite the presence of professional staff to treat them. Do you have the dates of their deaths?"

She handed him a sheet of notepad paper. "I wrote them down for you so that you'd be able to check for anything suspicious."

"And how did Rebecca Klingham die?"

"Bill Martin, our head of the Trustees Committee, found her dead in her garage at the parsonage. Her car engine was running, and a hose taped to the exhaust pipe fed into the car through her rear window. She had a paper on the seat beside her."

"What was written on it?"

"The wording was *time to say goodbye*, and before you ask, I'll tell you that it was definitely her handwriting."

Arthur gave Shirley a thumbs-up gesture. "That was a very good summary, Detective Hadley. I've made my notes, and I'll keep you posted as I investigate further."

Wally Sanborn knocked on the doorpost as he entered the room. "Hi, Arthur; it's good to see you. Now I won't have to be the one responsible for sympathizing with a grieving mother."

Shirley gasped.

Wally's face went red. "No, Shirley; forgive me. I was talking about Rebecca Klingham. There's absolutely no reason to think that anything happened to your son Jeremy. I need to think about the potential effects of my words before I voice them."

CHAPTER 8 – JEREMY

Wally Sanborn, Arthur, and Shirley sat around one end of the oversized table in the conference room, Shirley having activated the voice mail system to avoid interruptions for answering telephone calls. A carafe of coffee and a tray of assorted pastries highlighted the other end of the massive oak slab.

Shirley initiated the discussion of recent events in her son's life.

"Jeremy started dating Michelle Caspar a few months ago. They both went to University of Wisconsin, Platteville, but Michelle was a graduate student when Jeremy was an undergraduate. She's about five years older than Jeremy, but he was friends with her younger brother, Kevin, and as they spent time together in groups with other friends, something clicked between Jeremy and Michelle."

Arthur gestured an interruption with a slight wave of his hand. "I know the whole Caspar family. Michelle and Kevin studied Political Science under Professor Edward Middlemiss at Platteville. Wally, have you continued to keep in touch with Edward?"

"Not as much as I should, Arthur; I suspect that checking on Jeremy's relationship with Michelle will give me a good reason to contact him."

Shirley continued, "Anyway, Jeremy and Michelle dated for a month or so, and then they got serious enough that they decided to live together. That's not exactly what the church recommends, but young people today have manipulated the standards to suit their desires."

Arthur said, "There's no cause for concern so far. They're both intelligent and trustworthy people."

Shirley nodded, a little impatiently. "As I was saying, they moved to Madison to be near the main campus of the University of Wisconsin. They found a neat little apartment there. I visited them, and went shopping with Michelle for some decorations to liven up the place."

Wally asked, "When did things start to unravel? As I understand from our earlier conversation, Michelle left on some kind of quest; is that correct?"

"I can see that both of you men want to move past their contented time together and get to the mysterious events. Fair enough, I'll skip ahead in the story.

"Jeremy told me that Michelle found some books in the library that intrigued her and stimulated her to do some additional online research. At the end of this effort, she wasn't entirely satisfied, so she decided that she needed to take a field trip to learn more than she could through her computer. Jeremy hadn't paid much attention to her studies because he deemed them casual, rather than carrying a deadline. He went back to the apartment after work one day and found a note from Michelle saying she had gone out of town to pursue her research further. He expected her to call with more details within a few days, but she didn't."

Arthur said, "Jeremy must have been worried and wondering whether something had happened to her."

"That's exactly how he felt, so I asked Wally to go to Madison to visit Jeremy and help him discover more about Michelle's intentions when she left."

Wally said, "That's what I planned to do, but I failed to tell Jeremy I was coming, and he decided on a plan of action before I arrived in Madison. He left to track Michelle without leaving any clue to his theory regarding her whereabouts. Now we have two people missing instead of just one."

Arthur said, "I assume you had access to the apartment and gathered any computers, books, or notes that were there for further examination."

"I would have, Arthur, but they took their computers and everything connected with Michelle's research. Their apartment looked as though it had been picked clean by a search warrant crew."

CHAPTER 9 – PASTOR KLINGHAM

Rebecca Klingham knew that her background, including two divorces and drug addiction, was highly unusual for a preacher in a small-town church. Despite these black marks on her record, or perhaps because of them, she believed that she would be an outstanding pastor for Parkville UMC. She could relate well to people with personal or health problems because she had suffered through similar difficulties herself. Too many spit-and-polish preachers knew every chapter and verse of the United Methodist Book of Discipline, but had no empathy for the problems of people in their flocks. She had even heard of pastors who tried to delegate hospital visits to lay assistants rather than making personal calls on ill patients.

The first few months of her service in Parkville had gone very well. Her revisions to worship and administrative procedures had set well with both the staff and the congregation. She had made it clear from the day of her arrival that she was not Pastor Arthur Blake and that she was not going to imitate him. Everything had gone well until church members started to die so frequently.

Every church had unhealthy older people, but there had been something creepy about the sequence of events here. Four times, she had visited female church members at Parkville Rehabilitation Home, and all four times those women had died within a week or two of her visit. They hadn't even had similar diseases or problems. One had endured complex back surgery, one had complications of diabetes, one had undergone hip replacement surgery, and one had suffered a minor heart attack. Why had they all died at that rehab place?

Rebecca knew that people had started to murmur and gossip about her in the wake of these unexpected expirations. A few had suggested that she had assisted in suicides of these unhealthy women. Others hinted at witchcraft or labeled her as bringing bad luck wherever she went. Rebecca knew that several recent hospital patients had waited until they were home after treatment before they had informed her of their health problems.

These coincidences had affected her interactions with members of the congregation and staff. She could see questions in their facial expressions. With increasing frequency, she noticed herself hesitating before making major decisions. At times, she wondered whether she had started to succumb to some kind of mental breakdown.

CHAPTER 10 – BLAKE'S ANTIQUES

Irma didn't recall the normal business hours at Blake's Antiques, so on her first morning in Richmond, she showered, had a quick cup of coffee, fed Rex, and then restricted his travel to Peter's den and the enclosed porch next to it. Preparations completed, she left for her new assignment, arriving at the shop promptly at eight o'clock. The sign on the door indicated the business hours as ten o'clock to five o'clock, so she reversed course and headed for the Cubby Hole Café and a more substantial breakfast. While there, she chatted with her server, Carol, and learned that the antiques tourist trade had declined during recent years, and that those visitors who continued to come sought unique items likely to increase in value, rather than nostalgia items such as old product packaging and tools. In response to Irma's expression of surprise at her detailed knowledge, Carol admitted that her parents had operated a Richmond antiques store for twenty years before they had retired and moved to Florida.

As Irma left the Cubby Hole, she made a mental note to consult Carol if she ran into difficulties dealing with customers during her shop-sitting stint.

Irma always enjoyed entering Blake's Antiques because she felt as though she was stepping through a portal into the past. The items that surrounded her stimulated her to feel close to her parents, grandparents, and earlier generations that she had never met. It had always felt like entering a private museum. Once inside, she put her laptop computer onto Peter's oak desk and draped her light jacket over his matching pole-style hat rack. Then she changed the sign in the window to *OPEN* and prepared to greet any customers who might descend upon the shop. She would use those intervals without customers for browsing the inventory to gain familiarity and for sorting related items into displays to enhance their appeal to shoppers.

It didn't take long for Irma to realize that customers in this country village would be infrequent, especially with the summer tourist season well behind them. During the first two hours, two middle-aged women circulated through the shop on separate visits, and a portly man entered to ask for directions that she was unable to supply. Approximately three hours into her day at the shop, the back doorbell rang. It took Irma a few minutes to determine the source of the insistent jangle. Then she pulled back the freight door's slide bolt latches and pushed the button to power it upward. As the door rose, she found herself facing the back end of a large truck.

The truck driver waved his gloved hand. "Hi. I have a crate on a pallet for Peter Blake. I assume that's not you."

"I'm here to give Peter the day off. I'm also new to the shop, so I don't know whether we have a ramp for you to use for wheeling the crate inside."

"That's not a problem. I carry my own ramp and a pallet mover. There's only a slight incline. Figure out where you want me to put it, while I set up the ramp."

The back room had very little open space. Irma calculated that the large crate, a cube three feet on a side, would fit if she moved two chairs and some small cartons into the sales area. She proceeded to do so, finishing her task just as the truck driver completed his unloading.

Irma signed for the shipment. The paperwork indicated that it had come from someone named Katie Flanagan in Boston.

After the driver departed, Irma returned to the sales area, where she found a young married couple examining a small desk. She casually observed that it resembled one that her father had owned and that it appeared to be in very good condition. With the added weight of that endorsement, the couple purchased the desk and loaded it into the back of their minivan.

After they left, Irma found Peter's toolbox and prepared to open the crate in the back room. Before she could do so, the telephone rang. She answered it, remembering to have a salesperson's smile in her voice.

"Blake's Antiques – how may we help you?"

"Hi, Irma; it's Peter on this end. I wanted to be sure that you weren't having problems at the shop."

"I'm doing pretty well. I sold a small desk, and I'm about to uncrate the shipment that arrived today."

"Congratulations on the desk sale. I think I know the one you sold. Did it have a pull-down writing surface with supports that come out as you open it?"

"That's the one."

"That's a welcome sale. That piece has been in stock for a couple of months. I didn't quite understand your comment about the shipment. I don't have anything on order."

"Well, Peter, you received a crate that is a three-foot cube. From the truck-driver's grunting, I'd say that it must be heavy."

"It will be interesting to see what it contains. The only thing that would make sense to me would be if someone's estate sent me antiques to sell on a consignment basis. Let me know what you find when you open it."

"There was a sender's name on it. The crate came from someone named Katie Flanagan in Boston."

"I don't know her. Hopefully, she included some paperwork explaining the shipment."

"How's Cousin Ralph doing?"

"That's the other reason for my call. Ralph died today. His injuries were too severe for the doctors to save him. The funeral will be in three days, and then Janice will fly home, while I stay here to inventory and dispose of his possessions. He lived frugally, so we'll donate most of his things to charity. You live a long life, and shortly after you go, there's little evidence that you were ever here."

"The evidence is in people's memories, Peter, not the physical leftovers. The dead continue to dwell with us so long as we remember them."

CHAPTER 11 – MICHELLE

My brother Kevin has always been easy to get along with, but he's an external person. Unless you're talking about something he can see, hear, feel, taste, or smell, he's not interested. The poor guy never had much of an imagination, and he won't try to think or talk about something that's abstract. If he were to take one of those tests that's supposed to help you pick your career, his least likely choice would be philosopher. *How can a brother and sister be so different?*

Jeremy's more my type. I can talk about deep things with him. I don't think he completely understands my feelings and my need to get inside my soul, but at least he tries to follow my thinking and my theories. It's hard to cope with the day-to-day physically repetitive world when you're more concerned with concepts that go beyond it. For that matter, is the physical world even real? It may only exist in my mind. I've wondered all my life whether the world will end when I die. If I weren't here to perceive it, would the world exist at all? Are there other worlds? Are we like characters in a book who don't know the world of the reader? There has to be more to life than selecting a wardrobe and being sure to get enough to eat.

I'm not smart enough to work out these ideas by myself. I read that we use only a tiny portion of our brain's capacity. My goal has to be to use more of that organ's potential in order to understand better how I relate to the several worlds around me. I'm not even sure that Jeremy will be able to keep up with me on this journey. I expect that it will be a lonely quest and that I won't be successful at convincing others to accept my conclusions.

CHAPTER 12 – BOBBY ANDREWS

Sergeant Al Gomez looked up from his paperwork and smiled as Pastor Arthur Blake entered the Parkville Police Station. "Hello, Arthur, I haven't seen you around here for quite a while."

"I've missed you folks since we moved to the Amboy area. You'll have to come down for a visit sometime, Al."

"I just might do that if I find myself down that way. Are you here to see Bobby?"

"I am, but he doesn't expect me. Is he in his office?"

"He is. Do you want me to let him know you're here, or would you prefer to surprise him?"

"I'll take the surprise route. I might as well have some fun with him." Arthur opened the door to the inner offices and left the lobby.

Parkville Police Chief Bobby Andrews had worked with Arthur Blake in solving several mysteries that had occurred during Arthur's term as pastor of Parkville UMC. During the course of those investigations, they had become close friends and sounding boards for each other on family matters. Bobby, a massive African-American man, had obtained his police training while serving with the Military Police in Kosovo during the hostilities there. He had become very family oriented after he married one of his officers, Renee Weems. Renee and Bobby's young daughter, Thelma Lou, was the center of attention at every social gathering she attended.

Arthur knocked loudly on Bobby's doorpost. "Hello, Stranger."

Bobby rose to greet his friend with a bear hug. "Hello, Stranger, indeed; I was afraid your interests and casework were going to keep you away from Parkville on a permanent basis. It's good to see you, Arthur. Have a seat, and tell me why you're in town."

"I'm here because Bishop Chandler wanted me to review the circumstances of Pastor Klingham's death and to serve as interim pastor until a permanent replacement is appointed."

"Then this is an official visit, rather than a social one?"

"It's both, of course, and I'll treat for lunch after we finish here. I haven't been to House of Ming for a long time."

"You're on for that one. Turning to the business end of things, Rebecca Klingham committed suicide by carbon monoxide asphyxiation due to feeding exhaust fumes into her car while running the engine in a closed garage. It is a simple and tragic story."

"How thorough was your team with the crime scene investigation?"

"Arthur, I told you it was a simple suicide. It wasn't a crime scene."

"The last time I looked, it was illegal to kill yourself. Therefore, the garage was a crime scene, and I have a few questions. I hope your team has answers."

"Having worked with you before, I know you're debating our findings. What do you want to know?"

"First, what kind of hose was used to feed the exhaust fumes into the car?"

"It was a flexible hose from a shop vacuum cleaner. It wasn't anything unusual."

"Did you find a shop vacuum cleaner in the parsonage garage? There wasn't one when I lived there."

"Let me look through the case file ... it doesn't say that they found one, but I'll check with the people who were there. What else?"

"Keep your file handy. How was the hose attached to the exhaust pipe?"

"With duct tape, of course ... that's pretty normal for such a thing."

"...and did you find the roll of duct tape there?"

Bobby again consulted the file. "It doesn't say anything about having found it."

"Then I have to question why someone who was about to commit suicide would take the tape out of the garage and put it somewhere else. That's in addition to the question of the location of the shop vacuum that goes with the flexible hose. This starts to look like a homicide where the murderer brought his or her own supplies, staged the suicide, and then took the remaining tape away for later use."

Bobby stood and stared at Arthur. "You're saying that we dropped the ball on this one. You think we assumed suicide and didn't check for other possibilities."

"Sometimes, crime scenes look simple and obvious when they aren't. Was there an autopsy?"

"Pastor Klingham died just a few days ago. It was an obvious suicide, and the pathologists were busy in Rockford, so we all agreed to release the body to the family. They're in Chicago."

"So, there hasn't been an autopsy. I suggest that you arrange for a private postmortem examination in Chicago. There are pathologists available. Red tape and backlogs would make it difficult to arrange an official autopsy there."

"You're asking us to tell the family we may have overlooked something and to come up with funds to pay for a private autopsy. What do you expect to find?"

"I suspect that Pastor Rebecca Klingham was put into that car unconscious and then asphyxiated by some unknown person, who staged the whole event."

"You're saying that we didn't investigate thoroughly and that the coroner didn't think an autopsy was important enough."

"Yup."

"What if we just marked this case closed and declined your request?"

"Then I'd have to inform the family and Bishop Chandler that there are questions about the cause of Pastor Klingham's death and about the quality of the investigation."

"I think I'll skip that lunch outing, Arthur."

CHAPTER 13 – SUMMONS

As Arthur started to drive away from the police station, his cell phone rang. He pulled into a different parking space and took the call.

"Hello, this is Pastor Arthur Blake."

"Hi, Arthur, it's Irma. I need some assistance. We've received a mysterious shipment at Blake's Antiques that your dad says he didn't order. It's a large crate. I'd like you to be here when I open it, so that we can check with each other as to the significance of each item contained inside. I also want a second person present in case anything legal comes up as to what we did or didn't receive. It came from someone in Boston your dad doesn't know. Peter speculated that this could be a consignment for him to sell over time. If so, we need a witnessed inventory of the shipment's contents so that nobody accuses him of a shortage later."

"Your shipment sounds intriguing. I'm leaving Bobby's office now. I can arrive there in three hours, allowing for lunch along the way. If that's too long, I'll skip lunch, and you can have a sandwich waiting for me when I get there."

"Three hours will be fine. Drive safely. Peter said his cousin Ralph died from the injuries he suffered in his accident."

"Sorry to hear that. You can give me further details when I get there. I'd like your input on our cases here too. While you're waiting, pick out a special antique for the den. We have to support the folks' business. I'll see you soon."

When Arthur arrived at Blake's Antiques, he found Irma standing outside the front door, talking with a young woman. He parked and joined them.

"Either business has overflowed the premises, or things are so bad that you're grabbing people as they walk past the store. Hi, Irma. Who's your friend?"

"Arthur, I'd like you to meet Carol, who works at the Cubby Hole Restaurant. Carol, this is my husband, Arthur. He'll pop in to assist me from time to time during my temporary assignment here."

Carole and Arthur shook hands and murmured greetings.

Irma said, "Carole is the daughter of a former competitor in the antiques business here. Her parents retired and moved to Florida."

"What was the name of their store, Carol?"

"It was called The Brass Rooster."

"I remember that one. I bought my desk set and blotter pad there. Your parents had some interesting pieces, including some old mechanized banks that fascinated me when I was young."

"I remember those. I played with them whenever I had extra coins."

Irma said, "Carol stopped to see me on her way to work. I met her at breakfast yesterday, but she has the late shift today."

Carol laughed. "You have to be flexible in the restaurant business. I'll go now, so that I won't be late. I'm glad to have had the chance to meet you, Arthur."

Once Carol had left, Irma and Arthur went into the shop, where they gave each other a proper greeting. Then they went to the back room to view the unexpected shipment.

Arthur examined the crate. "It's the right size and ruggedness to contain one or two bodies curled up under a top layer of miscellaneous items."

"It may be the right size, but you're talking to someone who has a long history of examining corpses. By now, I would have noticed the smell of death in this small room. Your corpse theory is suitable for this time of year, a few weeks before Halloween, but I'll bet against it."

"Instead of betting at all, let's open the crate and inventory the contents."

"Let's pull it closer to the storage room. I assume that we'll put everything in there until your dad returns to examine and price each object."

"That's a good plan. Stand by for surprises."

After sliding the crate into its new location, Arthur removed its top by prying each edge upward with a crowbar. Then he removed the square plywood slab and shined a flashlight into the open container.

"My first observation is that this crate was not packed adequately to cushion the individual objects inside it. The person who packed this was either unprofessional or didn't care about protecting the contents. If we find items that Dad is supposed to sell, we'll have to indicate their condition. It's likely that some will have suffered damage during shipping."

"I agree. There's a sizable air gap above the brown blanket on top. It's possible that the person preparing the shipment thought he or she had it packed well, but that the contents settled during shipping. Let's each grip the blanket in the corners of the crate and see if we can pull it out without damaging anything further."

Arthur and Irma each pulled gently on the blanket. The Arthur said, "My side is either snagged on something, or the load is sitting on top of the blanket."

"I'm feeling a little resistance, but my side of the blanket is moving. I'll pull it free, and hand it to you, Arthur. If you drape it over the side of the crate, we'll be able to see what's underneath."

Gradually, they eased the one end of the blanket upward until they reached the free end. Then they let it hang over the crate wall at Arthur's side and peered downward.

Irma reached down and touched several items. "I think we have a crate full of books. Everything I touch feels like a bound volume."

"Let's pull all the objects out and line them up on the floor."

Soon, they had more than two hundred and fifty books of varying sizes lying flat on the floor, some of them cushioned in wrappings and others without surface protection. Arthur examined two of the unwrapped books. "They're apparently all quite old. The unwrapped volumes look significant and valuable. I assume that the shipper wrapped the rarer books. If the cushioned volumes are more valuable than the loose ones, we have something very significant indeed."

"I agree, Arthur. It appears that we have a collector's library."

"I can reach one conclusion about it."

"What's that?"

"Someone must have guarded and cherished this collection for many years. Even before removing the protective wrapping from the more valuable books, I see complete sets that are well over one hundred years old."

CHAPTER 14 – JEREMY HADLEY

He didn't completely understand Michelle, but she was like a breath of pure oxygen to him. Jeremy Hadley had always assisted other people, whether his father at the family bakery and catering business, Pastor Arthur Blake and Irma when he was the junior member of ABC Consulting, or Police Chief Bobby Andrews when he was an intern trainee. Michelle had never wanted to be anyone's protégée or apprentice. She would select a goal or a task and teach herself how to accomplish it. By taking this approach, she had frequently lagged behind others who sought help along the way, but she had earned the benefits of self-sufficiency and initiative. At this stage of her life, no one would bet against Michelle Caspar's being able to achieve any target goal.

Jeremy had felt himself growing as he learned the benefits of Michelle's independent approach to any challenge. At first, he had only admired her capabilities from a distance, but he had gradually convinced himself that he too could be self-sufficient. His communications with his family and friends diminished as his self-confidence neared that of Michelle. He grew in independence to the point where he thought that he and Michelle, as a team, could accomplish anything, so long as he could keep up with her.

She had a new project that she had promised to share, but so far had not. It had something to do with her research at the UW-Madison Library. She couldn't take home the reference books and documents she had been studying, so Jeremy had not been able to monitor her efforts. He expected her to give him at least a summary of her work soon.

On the way back to their apartment, he stopped at the supermarket and bought all the ingredients for her favorite dinner, shrimp Creole, along with a bottle of her favorite wine. Tonight, he would seduce Michelle into sharing information about her project.

When he arrived home, he found an envelope bearing his name propped up against a candlestick on the kitchen table. As soon as he opened it, he knew that he had implemented his seductive meal plan too late. Michelle had started her quest without him.

CHAPTER 15 – FOLLOW-UP

The uncrating and inventorying of the book shipment on Arthur's second day at the shop came to a halt when his cell phone rang. He answered it after seeing that the caller was Parkville Police Chief Bobby Andrews. Irma took a break and left him alone to talk.

"Hi, Bobby, what can I do for you from a distance? I'm in my dad's antiques shop in Richmond."

"You can give me a rain check on that lunch I turned down, and this time I'll be picking up the check. We have the results of that private autopsy."

"I'm impressed, Bobby; you set that up quickly."

"Your analysis was correct as usual. Pastor Klingham didn't commit suicide. Her death wasn't even due to asphyxiation from the car fumes. It was all a misdirection play and we fell for it. Rebecca actually died from manual strangulation. Someone used a carotid sleeper hold on her from behind, probably as she entered her garage. Ordinarily, this hold leaves very little evidence, but this perpetrator applied the hold so viciously that he or she compressed and cracked some vertebrae."

"That sounds as though the killer was extremely strong and aggressive, but not a professional, because of the vertebrae damage. Have you checked the databases for other similar crimes?"

"We're doing that now, but I don't expect to come up with anything. I have the gut feeling that this was personal. I'm going to check people in her background. She'd had two divorces and an earlier drug habit. There could be former husbands or drug dealers interested in eliminating her."

"Those are reasonable possibilities, Bobby. Email me your search results if you come up with anything promising. You may want to check the possibility of a former spouse who still carries insurance on her or who is a beneficiary on her policy. I'll be here for a while longer, but I'll let you know as soon as I get back to Parkville. I have to get back at least by the weekend, because I'm on temporary pastor duty until they get someone permanent for Parkville UMC."

"I'll see you then. For once, you're on the sidelines minding your dad's store while I lead the investigation of a crime connected to your old church."

CHAPTER 16 – SEEKING HELP

Jeremy had always believed that everything we do has its purpose. Because of his feelings for Michelle Caspar, he investigated her borrowing and reference reading history at the University of Wisconsin's Memorial Library in Madison. Official records did little to uncover the subject matter at the center of her recent research binge because Michelle had not had the luxury of checking out the reference volumes. She had simply copied individual pages and taken them with her. Jeremy's efforts to detect Michelle's interests had failed. As he sat at a user desk debating his next move, he felt a tap on his shoulder. He turned around to find himself facing Debbie Danforth, a library staff worker with whom he had frequently flirted prior to getting serious about Michelle.

"Hi, Jeremy, you look either lost in thought or just plain lost."

"Good to see you, Debbie ... it has been a while."

"We could remedy that pretty easily. I'm free tonight."

Jeremy hesitated before responding. "You know that I've been dating Michelle Caspar lately. That's why I haven't been around here as much. Anyway, she spent a lot of time here in the library working on a project that became an addiction for her. Then she left Madison to follow up on it somewhere else. I have no idea where she went, but I think the key must lie in tracking what she researched in this building. Would you be willing to help me learn more about her work here?"

"You're asking me to help you find information so that you'll know where to go to follow Michelle. You do realize that I'd rather flub that assignment so that you'd stay here with me."

Jeremy held her right hand briefly and then released it. "Debbie, I do like you very much, but we've only been playful with each other, not serious."

"Maybe you were too blind to notice it, but at least one of us was serious."

"I'm sorry. What can I do to make it up to you?"

"I'll help you trace Michelle if we can have one serious weekend of dating first. I want my chance to show you how I feel. Then, I'll help you, even if I can't get you to look at me differently."

"Fine, Debbie ... I'll meet you outside the library after work."

"That will be at six o'clock, and I'll expect you to take me seriously, starting with dinner at a classy restaurant."

"I'll give you my full attention for two days, but after that you promise to help me trace Michelle, regardless of how well our relationship grows."

"I can't ask for a better deal than that. Thanks, Jeremy."

CHAPTER 17 – EX-HUSBANDS

Sergeant Al Gomez stuck his head through Bobby Andrews' open office door. "Are you busy, Chief?"

"Come on in, Al. I need a break from preparing our budget for the higher-ups."

"I'm glad you have to do that and not me."

"What's up?"

"I checked out Pastor Klingham's ex-husbands, and while they wouldn't make a good character reference for anyone, they don't appear to have been involved in her death."

"What led you to that conclusion?"

"Neither one of them was within four hundred miles of Parkville on the date of her death. Bruce Wenger, her first husband, now lives in Cleveland, Ohio, and he was in court there on a DUI charge when Pastor Klingham died. Ralph Klingham, husband number two, was in Austin, Texas at a conference on banning adoptions by homosexuals. Before you ask, I did check that he was actually there. Klingham was on one of the discussion panels that day."

"What about the insurance angle? Did either of them stand to gain monetarily from the pastor's death?"

"I haven't been able to discover any insurance on her at all, except what she gets from the Methodist Church Conference as an employment benefit."

"That's something, Al. Who's the beneficiary?"

"No one who would be out to get her … she left the insurance proceeds to her mother. I checked, and Rebecca Klingham's mother is in a retirement home in

Pennsylvania. After her second husband died, she moved to Wyomissing, Pennsylvania from Ohio."

"You've been thorough. That's good police work. Now we'll be able to concentrate on strangers or local people as being responsible."

"That statement is almost right, Bobby."

"What do you mean by almost?"

"I don't know where Pastor Klingham's son, John, was when she died."

"Do you think her son's a suspect?"

"You taught me that everyone's a suspect until eliminated from consideration."

"That does sound like something I would say. Check on John Wenger's credit card usage. We might be able to eliminate him that way."

"I'll get right on it."

CHAPTER 18 – DEBBIE DANFORTH

Jeremy had lived up to his promise. They had enjoyed a steak dinner accompanied by wine and onion rings at Delaney's Steaks and Seafood. Then they had walked along the shore of Lake Mendota, pausing three times to sit on benches, where they had enjoyed some light-hearted necking. As his car approached her apartment house, Debbie was thankful that Jeremy hadn't insisted on going to his place, where his memories of Michelle would have haunted their developing relationship. As it was, Debbie knew that she had only a small chance of converting short-term passion into long-term love. Whatever happened in the future, she would enjoy this weekend to the fullest.

Once inside her third floor apartment, Debbie suggested that Jeremy open a couple of cold beers for them while she prepared some accompanying snacks. Jeremy nodded and selected a Leinenkugel Summer Shandy for Debbie and a Samuel Adams Boston Lager for himself from the large assortment of bottles on the bottom shelf of her refrigerator. By the time he had carried the two open bottles to the coffee table in front of her couch, she had prepared a tray full of assorted sliced cheeses and crackers and delivered it to the same table.

"See, Jeremy, we're a good team. Everything's ready at the same time."

"It has been an enjoyable evening. I really know you only from the library, Debbie. Tell me more about what you want out of life."

"Wow, there's a deep question. I'll say that I want to learn as much as I can about a wide variety of subjects …

hence my attraction to the library. I also want to try my hand at some kind of art, and I'd like to travel with a male companion. Applications are now being accepted for that position if you're interested."

"You're broad-brush as far as your art interest. Can you narrow it down or name a specific interest? Also, why are you sure you don't want to travel with a female friend?"

"Remember, Jeremy, I responded to your spur-of-the-moment question and hadn't thought about these subjects in advance, but I'll try to refine my statements. As to the art, I've always had demands on my time for academic subjects and jobs to support myself. I might be good at art, but I've never given it enough time to find out for sure. Therefore, I'd like to sample several creative pastimes. I may be good at none of them, or some type of art might resonate with me. I've given a little more thought to the idea of traveling, and I've decided that I would have a lot more freedom with a male companion, because I'd feel more secure. A woman traveling alone has to be alert at all times for possible predators."

"In other words, you're looking for a bodyguard."

"Don't be ridiculous. I'm looking for a lover. Now come over here, and apply for the job." Debbie reached over and pulled Jeremy's arm so suddenly that he almost spilled his beer. He managed to place it on the edge of the coffee table while she dragged him toward her.

CHAPTER 19 – INPUT FROM PETER

Irma placed a phone call to Peter Blake while Arthur reread the letter they had found in the crate of antique books. He had some misgivings about unstated implications of its message. While appearing to concentrate on his own analysis of the situation, he focused on listening to Irma's end of the telephone conversation and on extrapolating Peter's portion of the discussion from her words.

"Hello, Peter; it's Irma again. Arthur and I opened the crate and found that it contained a large number of old books, carefully cushioned and with the more valuable volumes wrapped. There was some settling during the crate's journey to your shop, but we didn't see any significant damage to the books. ..."

"They were sent by someone named Katie Flanagan in Boston. According to a letter we found in the crate, she's the daughter of Maria Svenson, whom we met at the Antiques Fair at the Parkville church several years ago. Maria was the previously estranged daughter of John Hendrix, your co-judge at the event. ..."

"The letter said that Maria died in a car accident, John Hendrix having predeceased her, and that these books had come from their combined personal libraries. Maria had left instructions in her will to send them to you as an antiques dealer to sell, with her share of the proceeds to go to an appropriate charity of your choice. It also asked that you give Arthur his first choice on any books he wants for his own library, as a token of thanks for his part in reuniting Maria with her father. ..."

"Yes, we know that there may be questions as to how John Hendrix obtained some of these books. I'm sure that underlies Maria's instruction to give her share of the sales to charity. ..."

"You won't believe their quality and age. Some of them date back to the 1700s. Arthur has his eye on the French and English first editions of *The Autobiography of Benjamin Franklin*. The original editions had slightly different titles from that. The French version came out in 1791, and the English version came out in 1793. ..."

"Yes, I know it will be difficult to determine the history of each book, but Arthur feels we'll be able to approximately sort books that John Hendrix purchased with questionable funds from those that came from the libraries of Maria and her deceased husband. ..."

"So, you'll stay and handle disposal of Ralph's belongings, while Janice returns ahead of you. That's fine. I'll be there to meet her. Call us if you need any additional support. We'll leave the books untouched for your examination. We'll see you soon. Goodbye."

After she disconnected, Irma said, "I'll meet your mother's plane when she returns from California, and then stay in Richmond with her to keep the shop open. She has background as an art historian and may want to examine these books."

"That will mesh with my responsibilities. I'd better get back to Parkville to see how Bobby's doing with his investigation of Pastor Klingham's murder, handle activities at the church, and prepare my sermon for Sunday. Two questions bother me."

"What are they?"

"First, how many of these books did John Hendrix purchase with funds from art treasures stolen by the Nazis? Second, what's the best charity to use for donating book sale funds so that some money gets back to the families of Nazi victims?"

Impulses

"I have a third question. How is Shirley Hadley going to feel when you tell her that you're investigating the origin of these books and the Pastor Klingham mystery, but that you haven't done anything to find her missing son, Jeremy?"

CHAPTER 20 – PARKVILLE

When Arthur Blake arrived in Parkville, he headed for the parsonage and installed himself there as a temporary resident. He would sleep on one of the couches, because he didn't want to disturb any of Pastor Rebecca Klingham's belongings. He felt it likely that a careful examination of her personal effects would give him additional ideas for investigating her murder. From the parsonage, he would travel first to the Parkville Police Station to discuss the Klingham case status with Bobby Andrews, and then he would follow Irma's implied suggestion and spend time with Shirley Hadley discussing Jeremy's disappearance.

Arthur found Bobby Andrews in the police station lobby, completing a conversation with Sergeant Al Gomez. After Al left the room, Bobby said, "We need to talk. Let's head into the conference room so that we'll have privacy."

The abruptness of Bobby's comments alerted Arthur to the possibility of a problem, but he followed Bobby into the conference room without hesitation or comment. Once they had both entered, he closed the door.

"What's up, Chief?"

"I thought your suggestion to check out Rebecca Klingham's ex-husbands and son would lead to something worth pursuing further, but none of those people could have committed the crime. The two ex-husbands were more than four hundred miles away from Parkville when someone murdered Rebecca, and her son used his credit card in Indiana on that day to pay for dental surgery with heavy anesthetic that wouldn't have worn off for several hours. I checked with the dentist. She said that she had replaced several of John's teeth with implants and that he had reported substantial facial swelling that afternoon. It was still bothering him when she gave him a follow-up examination the next morning."

"I guess we'll have to generate and pursue a different theory."

"That's the problem, Arthur. We're not working as a team in this investigation. You come up with a theory, and I have to investigate it along with my small-town force. We once worked together on Parkville crimes, but now you're off somewhere else and only passing through here occasionally."

"Bobby, try to be patient. I'm in a situation where I'll have more time for investigation work in the future, but right now, I'm committed to working on three cases at the same time."

"There's not enough of you to handle all that, Arthur. Why don't you cut back on one or two of those cases?"

"Fine, but I can't cut back on your case, because Bishop Chandler assigned me to determine what happened to Pastor Klingham. I'm sure you wouldn't suggest that I not help Shirley find her son, and Jeremy worked for you a while back. Then, there's the case of a shipment containing old books, possibly purchased with funds from art stolen by the Nazis during World War II. Should I turn my back on my father? I have to keep juggling these cases, or I'll hurt someone who's important to me."

Bobby stared at Arthur for several seconds and then shook his head. "You are in a messy situation. Well, at least I have your attention for right now. Please dream up a new approach to my investigation of Rebecca Klingham's murder. I've run out of suspects to check out."

"Let me have a day or two to come up with something. I'll spend tonight going over her personal papers at the parsonage. I'm hoping to find something there that will reveal her state of mind and give us a clue. It's the best I can offer for right now."

Bobby put his hand on Arthur's shoulder. "Fair enough – I'm still your friend, even when I get frustrated with the way a case is going. I'd try to help you with your other two quandaries, but I'm afraid they're outside of my jurisdiction. A small town cop is tied to his town and not much outside of it."

"I'll get back to you as soon as I have something, Bobby."

When Arthur entered Parkville United Methodist Church from the lower parking lot, he headed directly for Shirley Hadley's office. He had to assure her that he would be giving priority to her son's disappearance. He pulled the side chair into the open space next to her desk and sat down.

"Hi, Shirley, have you heard anything from Jeremy?"

"Not a thing, Arthur ... I haven't even heard from Wally Sanborn. He went off to check on Jeremy in Madison, Wisconsin. I wait to hear from them, and I wait to hear from you. My patience is starting to run out. Do you have any information for me?"

"I'm afraid it's too early for me to have anything but hope for you. Irma called me off to my dad's shop in Richmond, Illinois because of an emergency there, but I'm back now. Jeremy's disappearance gets my full attention today."

"I wish I could accept your attempt to reassure me, but I took several messages from Bishop Chandler's office in your absence. You're to call him right away. Hopefully, he won't send you on still another quest."

Arthur took the message sheets to the pastor's office and study, his former headquarters and his temporary station while he subbed for deceased Pastor Klingham. He would have to request that Shirley reinstall his coffeepot and associated supplies. He placed a clean yellow legal pad of paper on the desk and keyed the Bishop's number into his telephone.

"Hello, this is Arthur Blake calling for Bishop Chandler. He has been trying to contact me."

The receptionist put his call on hold while she located the bishop. A minute later, Arthur heard that familiar voice.

"Arthur, thanks for calling in. I realize that you have multiple responsibilities right now, but I wanted us to communicate on a regular basis. We failed to keep in touch while you investigated that Amboy Church fire, and it caused some problems. What do you have for me on the aftermath of Pastor Klingham's suicide?"

"The main piece of information I have to report is that Rebecca Klingham's death was not a suicide. There is no doubt that someone murdered her and tried to make it look like a suicide."

"That is disturbing news. The police officer I spoke with right after Pastor Klingham's death indicated that it appeared that she took her own life. Something must have happened to lead them to change their minds. Did you have anything to do with that development?"

"I did point out that several items at the crime scene were inconsistent with suicide."

"I suspected as much. Arthur, why is it that any simple investigation becomes complex when you're involved in it?"

"Respectfully, Bishop, you do want to learn the true cause of Pastor Klingham's death, don't you?"

"Of course I do, but this time, please try to keep the church from getting involved in a scandal when the facts are published."

"As of now, I have no reason to suspect that anything scandalous will turn out to have been involved."

Richard Davidson

"Let's keep it that way; and keep me advised on developments in the case, Arthur."

"I'll definitely do that, Howard, and please keep confidential the information that Pastor Klingham did not commit suicide. We don't want to stimulate rumors within the congregation, and secrecy may assist the police with their investigation."

Arthur placed the desk phone back onto its cradle. Then he opened and closed each of the desk drawers, looking to see how neat Rebecca had been and searching for anything that might be of value to the case. He found a black bound notebook in the upper right-hand drawer, leafed through it, and put it into his jacket pocket. Then he returned to Shirley's office.

"So much for the required check-in with Bishop Chandler ... sometimes I think he doesn't care for me."

"Oh, but he does. He once told me that you're one of his favorites, but that you frustrate him. The problem is that he wants the world to be simple and ideal, and you keep demonstrating that it isn't."

"It also isn't static. There's a continuous stream of new and often disturbing developments. Let's talk about Jeremy's relationship with Michelle and about your impressions of Michelle. A mother sees things that others miss."

"Thanks for the compliment, Arthur, but I also know that a mother's views are subjective and colored by her relationship with her son. I'll try to be factual, but you'll have to filter out all of that relationship stuff."

"That's what I do. I get inputs from everyone associated with a case, and then I try to make coherent sense out of them. Just say anything that comes into your mind, and set the phones to take messages so that we won't have interruptions."

"I'll start with Jeremy, because I know him a lot better than I know Michelle. You've had a major influence on him

54

as he has matured. He wants to help people solve their problems. He also prefers involvement to passive observation. For this reason, I had reservations about his professing his love for Michelle when they moved in together. I don't know whether he truly loves her, or if he wants to live with her so that he'll be nearby when she needs assistance."

"That's an interesting observation. Do you think that Michelle loves him?"

"I've only spent time with her on a few occasions, but I think that while she appreciates everything that Jeremy does for her, she has too much of a focus on her goals in life to love him. Please promise me you won't repeat anything about my reservations to Jeremy when you see him. He thinks he's in a two-way love affair."

Arthur noted Shirley's confidence that he would be seeing Jeremy soon. "Here's a key question, Shirley. Do you have any insights into what Michelle's goals are?"

"I'll start by backing up to my overall impressions of Michelle. She comes from a good solid family, but one that trained the children to be open to both conventional and unconventional thinking. I don't see her as wanting either an early marriage with children or a career followed by a marriage and children after the career. I see Michelle as a seeker. She will get interested in a particular subject or hobby, and she'll pursue every aspect of it until she feels that she won't learn enough more to justify continuing her efforts. Then she'll move on to a new center of interest."

"Was Jeremy a center of interest for her?"

"I'm afraid he was, and now she has probably lost interest and moved on, while he is playing the fearless knight, intent on rescuing the damsel in distress."

"I'm impressed with your observations, Shirley. I hear you saying that Michelle is in no danger, but has disappeared because she has moved on to another interest, while Jeremy doesn't realize the situation and has followed her trail in order to help her, when help may not be appropriate."

"That's my outlook, Arthur. My Jeremy is a Don Quixote, out to right wrongs that may not exist. The problem is that he could still stumble into danger during that process. I need you to find him and lead him back to reality. He respects you and will follow your lead."

"In other words, you don't see a crime involved in the disappearances of Michelle and Jeremy. Two supposedly mature young adults have voluntarily gone away, one following the other. I'm not at all sure that I have any business interfering with them. Given the other criminal and ethical matters facing me, I don't see how I can do anything but let Jeremy and Michelle pursue their destinies until an actual problem arises."

"But, Arthur, we won't know about a problem unless we know where they are. You're my only way to monitor Jeremy's safety. As a mother, I know he'll need you soon."

"As a pastor, I know that he and you should look to God for guidance. I'll be available if we learn of a specific danger, but my abilities have limits, and I have other promises to keep in the immediate future."

CHAPTER 21 – RECURRENCE

That night, it happened again. Arthur slept, but more fitfully than usual, tossing and turning, trying to get comfortable on the parsonage couch, and as he did so, the dream images returned. The same crowd of people pointed and jeered at him. The shouts and catcalls were even louder than before. Then Arthur, in his dream world, noticed something different in the drama. The figures were less anonymous. He started to recognize faces, first Bobby Andrews, then Bishop Chandler, then Shirley Hadley. The shock of that recognition awakened him, and he sat upright with his eyes open and slowly focusing.

I thought I was going crazy, but now it's starting to fit. People are expecting too much of me, and I'm tortured because I can't give them what they want when they want it. Investigating crimes and mysteries isn't like making products. Breakthroughs happen when you least expect them, not on a schedule. I have to discourage the inflated expectations of others and especially myself. There will be failures. If I can facilitate the solving of a case, I will, but I won't always be successful. I can't expect perfection.

What does the dream mean for declaring my plans for the future to the Bishop? Should I keep the investigations as a sideline rather than a profession? I seem to care more about people's opinions of me than I thought. I need friends and don't want to disappoint them, but I won't do them any good if I can't think clearly. Let the dice roll as they will. I need to let God lead my thinking. I can't force results to please people.

Arthur lay back on the couch, feeling just a bit vindicated and more relaxed. As sleep engulfed him, the clamor of the dream eased out of his consciousness. Tomorrow would be a blank slate, with no commitment to achieving anything.

CHAPTER 22 – VIRGINIA

The desk clerk at Charlottesville's Budget Inn, adjacent to the University of Virginia, studied Jeremy Hadley's face, trying to determine whether he posed a threat to her or to the Inn's residents. She decided to be uncooperative until she learned more about this tall young man.

"I'm sorry, but it's our policy that we don't give out any information about our current or past guests."

Jeremy had prepared for such a response. He had found and placed in his wallet's identification window his identity card from when he had worked with Arthur and Irma in their ABC Consultants group. The card indicated at the bottom that ABC was an affiliate of a federal government investigative agency. Jeremy had no authorization to claim that his inquiry was a matter involving that agency, but the card sufficiently impressed the desk clerk that she decided to be more open to Jeremy's questions.

"You'll have to let me copy your credentials for our files, but after that step, I'll answer your questions if I have the information."

Jeremy agreed and gave the clerk the card to copy. "Thanks for your assistance, Mary. I see that's your name from your badge. I'm trying to locate a missing person named Michelle Caspar. She disappeared in Wisconsin without notifying any friends or relatives, but some of the library materials she had studied suggested that she might be on a trip to the University of Virginia. Is she staying here, or has she stayed here recently?"

Mary's fingers danced across her computer's keyboard. "I do have something for you. Michelle Caspar stayed at our inn for two days, but she checked out five days ago. Our records show an address for her in Madison, Wisconsin, but nothing local. I also have an indication that she paid her bill with cash. That's all the information I have for you, Mr. Hadley. If you leave me your telephone number, I'll be happy to contact you if she comes in again."

"Thank you, Mary; I'll have to check with the university administration to determine whether she had any official contacts with them. I expect that to take a minimum of two days, so If you have a room available, I'll take one for that period."

"Room 107 is available. It's a single with a queen-size bed. Here's your key card, and a brochure about our Budget Inn services. I've noted my personal telephone number on the brochure in case you require more information when I'm not on duty here. I'm a graduate of the university, and I'd be pleased to assist you in contacting key people in various departments."

Jeremy's facial expression displayed surprise and thanks.

CHAPTER 23 – A NEW APPROACH

Chief Bobby Andrews picked up his telephone on the second ring and heard Arthur Blake's voice. "Hi, Bobby, if you're not too peeved at me to listen to another suggestion for investigating the Pastor Klingham case, I'll treat for lunch."

"I'm not upset with you, Arthur. I get cranky about expensive investigations every time I have to construct an annual budget and justify it. A police force in a small village can live within its budget only when there are very few crimes. Since you first came to town, we've had enough investigations for a much larger force."

"I didn't generate any of those crimes. I just drew your attention to them. Anyway, I'm about to suggest that you may have more crimes than you thought you had in Parkville right now."

"Thanks for that input. I'll double my proposed budget and ask you to justify it to the top brass."

"Where do you want to have lunch, Bobby?"

"If you're buying and giving me more budget worries, we'll go to McNoonan's Steakhouse. I'll need the Irish atmosphere and libations to quell the indigestion you're going to give me."

"That's fine, but if you don't mind, we'll meet there rather than driving together. I'll be leaving from the restaurant to head back to Richmond and the mysterious shipment at Dad's shop there. I'll fill you in on the details while we're eating if it won't spoil your appetite."

"This cop has heard just about everything, so I'll look forward to it."

They arrived at McNoonan's at the same time and walked in together. Bobby was in uniform, so the host automatically seated them in a back booth in case some of the other diners had an aversion to having the police overhear their conversations.

Once the server had brought them each a pint of Guiness, Bobby offered a toast. "To continuing friendship and appreciation of each other's gifts … may we continue to work and socialize together for many years to come."

"Thanks, Bobby, I hoped that I wasn't rocking the boat too much during our joint efforts on this case."

"I have to put up with you because you see things that I don't. Sometimes that does bother my ego, because I'm supposed to be the professional investigator, but I know that you could never handle the political and diplomatic side of running an official department."

Arthur raised his glass. "I'll drink to my never having to serve within an official hierarchy. I have enough problems keeping the Bishop off my back."

"Has he been after you again?"

"He wasn't happy when I told him that Pastor Klingham's death was murder rather than suicide. He had already asked me to take a sabbatical while he thought about my future in the church, and I had countered his proposal with a request for a leave of absence so that I can spend more time on investigations and consulting."

"But he called you in to sub for our deceased pastor at Parkville UMC?"

"Yup; he can't live with me, and he can't live without me. It sounds like a marriage."

Bobby leaned back, his massive shoulders blocking most of the booth backrest. "I guess we both have the same kind of pressures from above. The difference is that I'd never have the guts to tell them off and become a private investigator. Once you have a child, you feel more responsible and less likely to take a new path. Anyway, you said you were going to give me fresh insights on the Klingham case."

"I'll do that, but I see our food coming, so let's eat before I cause you indigestion with my new input."

They finished eating, and Bobby moved his plate toward the edge of the table to make it more accessible for pickup by the server. "That was good. Thanks for treating. Now let's talk shop about the Klingham case. What have I missed?"

Arthur similarly moved his plate aside. "You haven't missed anything. I'm bringing new information. First, I noticed that my old black-handled scissors with a broken tip on one blade were missing from the parsonage garage. Rebecca may have thrown them away, but it's also possible that the murderer took them after cutting the duct tape that attached the hose to the exhaust pipe. By the way, you do have the hose and the duct tape that attached it in your evidence locker, don't you?"

"Yes, we're methodical. Even though I originally judged Pastor Klingham's death to be a suicide, I had the troops save the tape and the hose as evidence. They may have one or two other things in the carton for this incident, but I'm sure they didn't include your scissors. What other new information do you have?"

"Shirley had told me when I first returned to Parkville that four women from our church who had been patients at Parkville Rehabilitation Home died shortly after Rebecca Klingham visited them there. I don't like coincidences. I didn't discuss this aspect of the case with you earlier because I didn't know how seriously ill those women were. They might have been close to death when she visited them."

"Agreed ... people die of natural causes in hospitals and other health facilities."

"Then, I looked through her desk drawers, and I found her daily journal notebook. In it, she had notes regarding the condition of everyone she visited because of illness. Shirley had previously given me the names and dates of death of those four women, and Rebecca's notes indicate that in each instance when she visited them, they appeared to be recovering well and optimistic about going home soon. She also had notes in there from a later date, indicating how people were associating her visits with the women's deaths and wondering whether she had somehow caused those tragedies. Her notes speculated on how she would be able to regain their confidence and support. The Rehabilitation Home deaths definitely bothered her and were affecting her other work."

"Are you telling me that you think those women's deaths were homicides too – that we have a total of five murders to solve?"

"I'm saying that it's a definite possibility. The four deaths at Parkville Rehabilitation Home were likely homicides, because coincidences like that just don't happen, but that prospect may actually make it easier to catch the murderer."

"You have my full attention. Explain your perceptions to me, Sherlock."

"In this case, it's not Sherlock, but Hercule Poirot who is pointing the way."

"In other words, you believe that we can solve our case based on something a fictional detective did?"

"Not so much the detective, but the details of a case that might be similar. Agatha Christie wrote about a seemingly crazy murderer who killed a series of people at different stops along a railroad. Everyone thought these were senseless arbitrary killings until Poirot figured out that one of them tied to a person who had a motive. In summary, the killer murdered random people at the start of the series, but then killed a person he planned to murder, but made it appear senseless rather than intentional because of the other killings."

Bobby nodded. "I get it. You think one of those four women may have been an intentional victim, and the other three died just so that the killer would confuse the police."

"It's worse than that. In the Poirot case, everyone knew that someone was committing murders. In our case the women appeared to die naturally, but a visiting preacher was common to all of them."

"And then the plan was for her to appear to commit suicide as an admission of guilt."

"That's it, Bobby. If we had accepted Rebecca's death as a suicide, the gossipers would have convicted her of four murders without a trial."

"And with her dead, there never would be a trial to disprove the rumors."

"Correct."

"I think you're going to owe me a second fancy lunch. Now I have to find out everything there is to know about those four women who died in the hospital and all the people connected with them who might have had a motive for murder."

"I didn't suggest that it would be easy."

"Thanks, Arthur. Expect to take part in the analysis of facts we dig up. I thought I was being generous, when I suggested that I'd need to double my budget. This could be even worse."

CHAPTER 24 – INTERVIEW

When Michelle first entered the department offices, she sensed a different ambience from anything she had previously experienced at either UW Platteville or UW Madison. The difference was silence and a noticeably higher air pressure than that of the outer hallways.

The floor, walls, and ceiling of the suite all had soft surfaces, obtained with various soft materials in several neutral tints. The open area of the first room had a comfortable-looking couch and two reclining chairs facing it. A single office door opened onto the common area, and a winding passageway led to the rest of the suite.

Michelle approached the open office doorway, studied the bare bones furnishings inside the empty room, and decided to opt for the winding passageway. Three gentle turns later, she found herself in a second open area, identical to the one she had seen earlier, but the mirror image of it. The suite designers had mirror-imaged not only the office and passageway entrances, but had also flipped the arrangement of the identical pieces of furniture. Michelle had the feeling that she had entered a movie set and started to look around for cameras.

She felt as though she was Alice and this was Wonderland. A middle-aged woman with bushy gray hair and an official-looking yellow lab coat stepped out of the office to greet her. Michelle half-expected her to say, "Off with her head!"

Instead, the woman extended her right hand toward Michelle and said, "Welcome to the Division of Perceptual Studies. I assume that you found your way here intentionally and not by accident. I'm Doctor Rosemary Swinton; how may I assist you?"

Michelle shook the woman's hand. "I'm Michelle Caspar. Everything was so quiet that I thought the suite was empty. You surprised me when you emerged from your office. Your suite is quite unusual. I'm looking for the place where they study memories of prior lives. Is this it?"

"Yes, it is indeed. I was equally surprised to see you because these are our interview rooms. We do have normal offices on the other side of the building. Does your child have memories from another life?"

"Not quite, Doctor – I have no children. I'm here to discuss my own recollections."

Doctor Swinton stared at Michelle. "Do you still have memories of a prior life from when you were a young child? How old are you? Generally, those memories start to fade away by the age of five or six."

"That's the frustrating part. I had some past-life memories as a child, but they faded after I entered elementary school. I'm now twenty-seven years old, and just this year, I've become immersed in the details of a different past life."

CHAPTER 25 – CHURCH AND SERMON

Pastor Arthur Blake approached the familiar pulpit feeling as though he had stepped backward in time. He had first preached from this raised platform six years earlier, introducing himself following the sudden death of Pastor William Middlemiss. Now he was about to repeat that introduction for new attendees with his interim appointment following the supposed suicide of Pastor Rebecca Klingham. At this stage, he would not reveal her true cause of death.

He reached the pulpit, where his sermon papers lay in a file folder, and nodded to a few familiar faces as he opened the folder.

"Good morning. It's good to be back among so many friends and to meet those of you who joined this congregation after I left. Once again, I have the assignment of filling in for a deceased pastor here at Parkville UMC. This time, I expect that it will be a shorter stay. Bishop Chandler will soon appoint a long-term pastor.

"The title of my sermon for this morning is *Sitting on the Sidelines*, and it is based on a recent conversation I had with Police Chief and church member Bobby Andrews. Bobby suggested that because Bishop Chandler had recently granted me a sabbatical leave, I would not make active contributions to my church and community during this period. This morning, I want to assure you that we never sit on the sidelines, even as God never takes a vacation from watching over us all. Sometimes, we are closest to Him when we step away from the rush of everyday problems and listen for that *still small voice* described in the Bible. ... Now that I am back with you in Parkville, I assure you that my door will once more be open to discuss any topic you wish, or any problem you desire to share in confidence. This is a difficult period for this church and its members, but together we will endure whatever hardships face us and find the shape of our new future. I ask your prayers for the family of Pastor Klingham and your thanks for her time spent here with you. Amen."

Following the closing hymn and blessing, Arthur stood at the rear of the sanctuary to greet departing worshippers and then moved into Fellowship Hall to share coffee, cookies, and informal mingling in small groups. As he entered that large room, he saw Irma standing by the far window talking with Shirley Hadley. She had driven back from Richmond to be in church for his sermon without alerting him of her plans. Irma's thumbs-up sign told him he could get his coffee and then relax. He would be free to chat with old friends and with people who had arrived at the church after he had already transitioned from pastor here to the position of investigative troubleshooter for the Northern Illinois Conference.

Coffee was an elixir for Arthur Blake. It sharpened his senses to the point where he sometimes felt he could hear the thoughts that underlay conversational exchanges. It also relaxed him while unleashing his considerable powers of logical thought. He excused himself from a passing conversation with the organist to get some of the caffeinated brew before others emptied the pot. Drawing upon their history of frequent coffee sessions when he had earlier served as pastor here, Arthur filtered his way through the small groups of people to join Wally Sanborn, retired Army officer and now the church's Lay Leader.

"Hi, Wally; did you have any success in tracking Jeremy Hadley in Madison?"

"Now there's a casual opening line. It's good to see you too, Arthur. I did appreciate your sermon. You had the right blend of reassurance and optimism, while reminding people that God leads and we follow."

"Thanks, Wally, and I apologize for starting our conversation with an investigation question. Feel free to pass on answering that one until we're alone later."

"No need to bypass it; I expected to catch up with Jeremy in Madison, but he had already departed, tracking his friend, Michelle. I did check in at the library and discovered Jeremy's second female friend, who confirmed his tracking mission. I also stopped in at the Wisconsin State Capitol building to chat with some officials and old Army buddies."

"How were you received there? Do they get beyond politics and engage in practical conversations?"

"Some of them do, especially when there's no sign of the media watching or listening to them. All of your questions have the flavor of checking my skills at fieldwork. I received hints from Irma earlier that you might be shifting your priorities toward full-time investigation work. If so, tell me where I go to enlist as support staff."

"How serious is that inquiry?"

"It's real. Too many times, I've observed you working on cases without being invited to participate, or provided only minor assistance. I need some action. Retirement doesn't suit me well."

"You're more than welcome to join up, as they say, but there's not likely to be much by way of money, and you could get into dangerous situations."

"Those things don't bother an old military type like me. I'm in, and I can tell from your phrasing that you're serious about increasing your casework too."

"Don't say anything to Irma yet, and for the duration of my temporary assignment here, my priority is to be Pastor Blake."

"Understood, Sir."

"Stop that Sir stuff, and completely eliminate any idea of saluting from your mind. We'll be as non-military as possible."

Wally smiled, nodded, and whistled *Onward, Christian Soldiers* as he walked away.

For the balance of the coffee hour, Arthur exchanged greetings with old and new members of the Parkville UMC congregation who bestowed upon him many expressions of satisfaction that he was back in charge. Irma spent most of the same period chatting with Bobby Andrews' wife, Renee, while the two of them tried to keep track of little Thelma Lou Andrews as she played the game of running through gaps in the crowd of big people.

CHAPTER 26 – MICHELLE'S STORY

Dr. Rosemary Swinton invited Michelle to join her in one of the quiet interview rooms to discuss her background and the steps that had led her to the University of Virginia and the Division of Perceptual Studies. Dr. Swinton offered Michelle her choice of the couch or a reclining chair. Michelle selected one of the chairs and immediately leaned it backward to the first stop.

"This feels comfortable. We used to have one of these at home, and Dad would head for it after a big holiday meal. He'd call it his *sucker seat* because he'd quickly fall asleep in it. I'll do my best to remain awake and alert, Dr. Swinton."

"Call me Rosemary, and I'm sure you didn't come all this way to fall asleep. Why don't you begin by telling me a little about your background? I'll have this little recorder turned on, so that we'll be able to remember our discussions."

"I grew up in Iowa and then went to college at the University of Wisconsin at Platteville, where I majored in Political Science. I have a younger brother, Kevin, who followed the same educational path and very creative parents who are comfortable facing any situation. Earlier this year, I moved to Madison, Wisconsin with my boyfriend, Jeremy Hadley, but I'm not yet sure how serious I want our relationship to get. That leads me to my desire to contact your department."

"Go ahead, Michelle; tell me your story the way that feels easiest for you. There's no structure to our interview process."

72

"Thanks, Rosemary ... see, I'm feeling at home already. I learned about your work when I read some of the books and papers generated here regarding children who remembered living a prior life quite different from the one with their present family. That happened to me. I remember that when I was small and didn't know much about other places and cultures, I would tell my mother that my name was Ruby and that I was a cook in a restaurant in Ireland. I was too young to have tried cooking at home, but I told my mother about a few of my recipes, and she later tried following them with good results. There were a lot of memories of Ruby, but they faded out when I reached the age of five or six, and I forgot about them until about a year ago."

Dr. Swinton paused her note taking. "What happened a year ago to bring the memories back?"

"You're probably not going to believe this."

"That's what we're here for. We listen to many stories of individual experiences and memories, and we find patterns in them that tell us more about our minds and perceptions of unusual things. Please continue."

"Well, as I said, it started about a year ago. I sensed another presence within me. I had the memories of a man who had been a youth in Austria during the Second World War."

"Have you ever read anything about such a person from that time period in Austria?"

"No, I never did. I studied the major battles of that war, but I never thought about what it would have been like growing up there. I still don't know much about Austria, beyond waltzes and the story of *The Sound of Music.*"

"What kind of memories did you have?"

"I had been a student in a school that was in part of a castle that the government had taken over. The walls were thick and made of stone, and the ceilings were so high that they made me think I was in a big cave."

"What else do you remember?"

"I was a very tall boy and I felt awkward when they had a dance with girls from a separate school in the village."

"Did it bother you that you were a boy in these memories?"

"It did, because I had never seen things from a male point of view before."

"Before these memories came to you, were you pleased with being female?"

"Of course I was. That's why the thought of having once been male was so disturbing."

Rosemary's comments and jottings now took up several pages in her notebook. She wondered to herself whether she would have enough blank pages left for the complete interview. "Has the memory of having once been male permanently affected your self-image?"

"I can't see into the future, so I don't know whether it will be permanent, but as of right now, I'm sexually confused. That's why I left Wisconsin without telling my boyfriend, Jeremy. I don't know how long we'll be able to remain a couple. It's been awkward even during the months we've already been together."

"Let's get back to the male Austrian life you remember. What was your name?"

"I was Kurt, but I don't remember the family name. In my memories, we called each other by first names only."

Rosemary wrote as rapidly as she could. She hadn't been sure this interview would be worth using the electronic recorder, but she was very glad she had switched it on at the beginning of their session. "What other incidents do you recall beside that dance?"

"I remember that several of us boys decided that we had to get rid of our Hitler Youth uniforms and swastika badges before enemy troops arrived. It must have been near the end of the war. We buried the clothing and symbol badges near an abandoned autobahn construction site."

"Do you remember anything from when you, as Kurt, grew older?"

"I think I had a wife, but I don't know whether we had children. I also remember a period toward the end of my life as Kurt. I lived in a retirement residence in New York State. It was assisted living, because I had a weak heart and couldn't do very much physically."

"Do you know where in New York it was?"

"They took me there in an ambulance from my home. The retirement home was near a big lake. It was a long ride. I never saw a sign with a city name. They called the residence Destiny something. I thought it was a spooky name. That's the only reason I remember it."

"But you do remember all this clearly?"

"On some days I remember more than on other days. I've looked forward to coming here, so it's clearer today."

"Can you think of anything else?"

"Just one thing more – I remember how I died. Someone pushed my wheelchair down a flight of stairs. I didn't see who did it."

CHAPTER 27 – PETER RETURNS

Arthur climbed out of his SUV, hugged his father, asked about the smoothness of his flight, and then loaded the suitcases through the rear hatch. Once they had settled themselves into the vehicle, he pulled leftward into the steady stream of traffic and worked his way over to the lane that would lead out of O'Hare Airport and onto the Tri-State Tollway. Once on the toll road, the traffic thinned, and Arthur relaxed.

"Dad, if you're not in too much of a hurry, I'll stop at the oasis rest area so that we can have coffee and chat before we get home. I'd like to fill you in on what's happened and get your opinions on a few things."

"That sounds good to me, son. I don't mean to be disrespectful, but once we get home with Irma and Janice, I suspect that they'll do most of the talking. I've tried to think about handling this shipment of old books, but it's hard to figure the best way to determine their individual origins."

They chatted about personal matters and Peter's handling of his deceased cousin's affairs and belongings until they reached the Lake Forest Oasis. Then Arthur drove up the ramp, parked, and they entered the restaurant building that bridged the tollway. Once inside, Arthur went to the bakery for a Danish pastry and coffee, while Peter bought a sandwich and a container of milk at a different food booth. They reconnected at a table in the eating area.

Arthur turned their light conversation toward the current project. "Dad, how do you feel about selling old books that may have been stolen by the Nazis or purchased with funds from the sale of other stolen treasures?"

"I'm relatively alright with it, so long as the proceeds will go to charity. We'd never be able to repatriate actual objects, whether books or art, but once you convert objects into cash, the distribution of the proceeds becomes much more manageable."

"Why do you think Maria Svenson handled disposition of her library in this way?"

"I think she was religious enough to want to leave life without a burden on her conscience. She trusted us to handle the sale and disposition of these antique books so that her children would never have to feel guilty or concerned about the origin of their possessions. We'll have to be true to her trust."

"Thanks, Dad. You confirmed my speculation."

CHAPTER 28 – JEREMY AND MICHELLE

Michelle answered her motel room telephone, expecting it to be Dr. Rosemary Swinton or one of the other people in her University of Virginia department. She was surprised to hear Jeremy Hadley's voice.

"Hi, Michelle; it took me a while, but I finally found out where you had gone. Whatever you're here for, I want you to know that I'm here to support you."

"That's shows a lot of initiative, Jeremy, but you really shouldn't have come. I've moved on to doing something new that is important for me."

"May I come up to discuss it with you?"

Michelle hesitated; then she said, "I'll come down after I finish what I'm doing. Meet me at the Rotunda by the columns in thirty minutes. It's time for us to have a discussion, anyway."

Jeremy wasn't sure that Michelle had indicated that the conversation would be positive, but he agreed.

Thirty minutes later, Jeremy stood by the Rotunda columns looking around expectantly. He was sure that Michelle would come, but he was a little surprised because in the past she had always been the first to arrive at their meeting points. He sensed that something had changed. Maybe she thought he shouldn't have followed her from Madison. He reminded himself to be diplomatic when he spoke with her.

Five minutes later, Jeremy saw Michelle striding across the grass toward him. When she arrived, he put his right arm around her shoulder and tried to kiss her on the lips, but she turned and backed away during the process, so that his lips brushed her cheek. He backed off several feet and waited for Michelle to start the conversation.

"Your call was a bit of a shock, Jeremy. Your criminology experience and training must have prepared you well for tracking someone."

"I suspect that you toyed with completing that sentence with the words ... 'who doesn't want to be tracked.'"

"You're even starting to read minds. I'm not angry with you, Jeremy. It's just that I've changed my outlook on life. I have to find out who I am and how I should approach the future."

"Outside of the fact that we could have had this conversation in Wisconsin, before you suddenly left town, would your new outlook have anything to do with the people at the University of Virginia who study perceptions of prior lives?"

"So that's how you tracked me; you found what library books I read. You really took a chance, because I also read books on several other topics. We've had some great times together, but I have to tell you that I'm not looking for you or anyone else right now. I have to find out more about myself. I'm learning that I'm a more complex person than I ever realized in the past."

"Does this have anything to do with that prior lives business?"

"Don't ridicule it. I believe in the value of those studies, and they are especially important for me. I'm going to stay here until I've completed learning about myself, and then I'm going to go wherever my studies take me. When I do move on, I don't want anyone following me. I'm not looking to be half of a couple, so please let me go my solitary way. You'll have to find someone else, Jeremy. Sorry, but my mind and my path are set in a different direction."

Once again, Jeremy put his right arm around Michelle's shoulder. This time, he kissed her on the forehead. Then he turned around and left. He didn't look back.

CHAPTER 29 – CONNECTIONS

Chief Bobby Andrews looked up to see one of his detectives, Hank Robbins at his office door.

"Hi, Hank; is it safe for me to assume that the big smile on your face means that you've had success checking on those women who died?"

"We don't have answers to everything, Bobby, but Gene and I have compiled a mega load of data, and we'd like to present some of it to you."

"That sounds promising. Can you do it in here, or does your show-and-tell session require the conference room?"

"We're all set to make our pitch without your needing to move at all." Hank waved to someone down the hall and then stepped into Bobby's office, allowing space for Detective Gene Murphy to maneuver a wheeled cart bearing a computer and a large monitor into the room. Gene nodded a greeting to Bobby as he positioned the equipment next to a set of electrical outlets."

Bobby said, "You guys have actually been listening to me. I've criticized you in the past for not being prepared when you were due to file your reports. This time it looks as though you've worked up a complete dog and pony show."

Gene bowed. "We figured this was easier to analyze than a printed report would be. Hank, are we ready to begin?"

"It's all yours, Gene."

The monitor screen illuminated to show individual photographs of four women. "Bobby, these are the hospital patients who each died within a few weeks after receiving a visit from Pastor Rebecca Klingham. We wanted to show you their pictures so that they'd feel more real than just names on a piece of paper. We arranged their photos in the sequence of their deaths, first Phyllis Landholm, then Janet Cuspin, then Mary Welker, and finally Beverly Mandow. They knew each other from attending Parkville United Methodist Church and a women's circle, which is a church club, there."

"So, they were all in the same club."

"Yes, but we're not sure if that's significant. As far as we could determine, they weren't close friends or anything. They saw each other during church services and monthly club meetings, but they never had contact with each other when they weren't at church."

"How long had they been in the church, Gene? I vaguely remember seeing two of them when I was there, but I don't know their histories."

"Their seniority in the church has a big range. Landholm arrived most recently. She had only been there for six months before her final hospital stay. Cuspin was there for three years, Mandow for sixteen years, and Welker for twenty-eight years. None of them had children, although they had siblings plus nieces and nephews. None of those people were in this area at the time of their relative's death."

Bobby got up and walked closer to the pictures on the monitor. "That tells me that their relatives didn't expect any of them to die, or they would have come to support them and say goodbye. What do we know about the individual backgrounds of those patients? Are there any similarities there?"

Hank said, "I checked that info, Bobby. Before they retired, the four women had different jobs and lived in different parts of the country. Janet Cuspin lived closest to here, in Chicago. She worked in the Accounting Department at Illinois Bell Telephone, back when there was a Bell System of telephone companies. Phyllis Landholm worked in Indianapolis as an attorney in the Business Services Division of the Indiana Secretary of State's office. Beverly Mandow worked as a salesperson at Hall's Department Store in Kansas City, and Mary Welker had been a dancer in a couple of Broadway shows in New York City."

"Thanks, Hank; you did a good job of finding all those details. I don't see any connections in their backgrounds. Arthur Blake suggested that the killer might have been after only one of these women, but that he or she killed the others in order to blame all four crimes on Pastor Klingham. His theory comes from a plot in an Agatha Christie mystery that the killer might have read. If that's what happened, we'll have to look for suspects who had a motive to kill any one of these women."

Gene shook his head. "Don't overlook the possibility that the killer might have had a motive to kill more than one of them."

CHAPTER 30 – FAMILY REUNION

They sat around the kitchen table, enjoying an old-fashioned country breakfast of bacon and eggs with pancakes, assorted fruit juices, coffee, and tea. Janice Blake had just joined them after completing her cooking and serving.

"I always enjoy your coming to stay with us, but even more so this trip, because you brought Rex along. He's an intelligent dog."

Irma reached down to pet Rex, who liked to curl up against her legs. "He's more than intelligent. He's heroic in a crisis, and he helped us solve our last case. I hate to admit it, but I'm probably just as happy having him as a member of our family as I would be with an adopted son. Arthur will be glad to hear that."

"I never said that I didn't want to adopt a child, but I agree that Rex is a full-fledged member of our family." Arthur glanced at his father and winked.

Peter nodded slightly in response. "I think Arthur appreciates Rex even more because we never had a dog here. He asked for one on many occasions, but it just never seemed to be the right time for a pet."

Janice stared at her husband. "Admit it, Peter; we didn't get one because you were afraid that a dog the size Arthur wanted would break some of your precious antiques."

Peter partially raised his hands in a sign of surrender. "I'll confess. I'm guilty as charged. We wouldn't have been able to afford replacing delicate pieces in those days, so I evaded the requests to adopt a dog. Now that I've met Rex,

I realize that the right dog would have worked out well. Every large dog isn't a bull in a china shop."

Arthur laughed. "You don't have to apologize, Dad. I compensated for the lack of a dog at home by always dating girls who had dogs. I'll bet you never noticed that."

"I did miss that one, but while we're discussing the question of being observant, why did you select the French and English versions of *The Autobiography of Benjamin Franklin* to save for your personal library from that shipment of books?"

"Beyond their value as first editions, Benjamin Franklin has always been my personal *patron saint* as being the first outstanding American engineer. Despite my career changes along the way, I still think of myself as an engineer."

CHAPTER 31 – JEREMY

Jeremy knew that he had taken a big chance when he tracked Michelle Caspar to Charlottesville, Virginia. He had hoped that she would be receptive to sharing her quest with him, or at least that she would see the romance of his having followed her that far. Instead, she had wanted neither his affection nor attention. He would have to accept her statement that something had changed in her life and outlook. Her actions had confirmed her words. Now he faced multiple forks in the road. Should he stay in Charlottesville and monitor Michelle's movements? That would make him a stalker, and he didn't feel comfortable with that thought. Should he honor Michelle's status and outlook statements, returning to Madison? Debbie Danforth would be happy if he selected that path. She was a bit quirky, but might be the right medicine for his present depressed state of mind; she did make him laugh. Then, there was the option of remaining in Charlottesville, but pursuing a relationship with that girl from the Budget Inn, Mary. She had made her interest in him obvious, and might help him to blur his focus on Michelle.

He laughed to himself as he reviewed these options. Jeremy had never considered himself a magnet for women, but here he was, assessing his possibilities with three of them. Didn't he have higher priority goals than romance?

His cell phone rang, surprising him because he had a new phone and number, having lost his old phone shortly before he left Madison.

"Hello?"

"Hi, Jeremy; Wally Sanborn here; Arthur Blake asked me to try to locate you. I know you're on a field trip, but is everything under control?"

"Wally, you have many talents. How did you find me? I lost my phone and have a replacement with a new number."

"You do know that before I retired I was tied in with military intelligence and logistics. I found an old friend in Army Intelligence who had contacts with all the phone companies. It didn't take her long to find what number replaced your old one. By the way, whoever found your lost phone made dozens of international calls with it. It's been deactivated by the security people at your provider company, and you won't have to pay for any of those calls."

"I'm impressed. The system works. Why did Arthur want you to find me?"

"The overt reason is because he's on temporary duty back at Parkville United Methodist Church, and your mother is his secretary again. She's worried about you."

"Mom always does worry, even though she tries to hide it. If there's an overt reason, there's probably a covert reason too. What's the real reason behind this contact?"

"There's no official announcement yet, but Arthur Blake will be taking a leave of absence from church duties to concentrate more on investigations. I informally signed on with his new group, and he'll be looking for your assistance too."

"Did he say that?"

"Not yet, but he's thinking it."

"Wow, Wally, you find unlisted telephone numbers and read minds too. Well, it turns out that you called at just the right time to help me make a decision. I'll head back to Madison, Wisconsin to pick up my gear, and then I'll find you in Parkville."

Richard Davidson

"Just look me up at the church. Don't worry, I won't tell your mother you're bringing a new girlfriend with you."
"You are good at intelligence! I'll see you soon."

CHAPTER 32 – GATHERING THE TROOPS

With Peter Blake back at his shop in Richmond, Illinois, Irma and Rex had returned to Parkville UMC and joined Arthur in his temporary quarters at the parsonage.

Irma walked around the front room rearranging the pillows on the couches. "It's good to be all together in one place again."

"I'm glad to have you with me too. I don't enjoy couch-sleeping all that much. Now that you're here, we should work together to inventory and study all of Rebecca Klingham's belongings. After we complete that effort, we'll be able to move into the bedroom for more comfort and privacy. Rex will like the parsonage. It has more room for him than my folks' house in Richmond."

"He did pretty well there. I think he made a convert, and your dad will end up getting a dog for him and Janice."

"That would be both an achievement and a new dog-friend for Rex ... I have to return to the question of my concentrating on investigations. We may be opening up Pandora's box with this move."

"What's bothering you?"

"Up to this point, we've handled our investigations together as a team, basically you and me with an assistant or two, plus the official partners of Bobby's police force and Joe and Penny's federal agency. I think that my change in outlook will affect everyone else in ways that may not be positive."

"What do you see happening, and why would it be negative?"

"Wally Sanborn has already volunteered to work with us; he's felt left out in the past when we worked on cases that took us away from Parkville. He wants to be a member of the traveling team. He also said that when he locates Jeremy Hadley, he plans to recruit him for this team. Part of this is his army background expressing itself through building an organization. I think it's leading toward a diminishing of our working together as the primary team."

"We'll always be working as a team so long as we share our thoughts. We used to fly the flag of ABC Consultants, when we worked first with Renee Andrews and then with Jeremy Hadley. I see the development you described as simply adding Wally as the fourth associate. Am I wrong?"

Arthur pulled a straight-back chair away from the dining area table and sat down on it. "The difference is that we set up ABC Consultants to cover our amateur investigation activities while I was professionally the Pastor of Parkville United Methodist Church. It was a sideline activity, and we weren't overly concerned about paying anyone. Now we're talking about making this a business, and it's growing like Topsy. Wally is building an army that may damage our relationships with the police and our federal friends."

"I'm starting to understand your concerns, but I think we'll be able to work around them. How would you feel if we arranged things in a different way?

Two hours later, the doorbell rang, announcing the arrival of Wally Sanborn and Jeremy Hadley. Jeremy had driven to Parkville UMC, where he had discussed his pursuit of Michelle with his mother, and then he had located Wally for their joint visit to the parsonage.

Irma greeted them at the door. "Welcome, you two; it's good to see you again. Come on in, and join us at the table. I have fruit and cheese if you're hungry."

Arthur greeted them on his way back from refilling his coffee mug in the kitchen. "Hi, Wally – Arthur gestured with his coffee mug. Just like old times; grab a mug, and fill it up. Hi, Jeremy – I'm looking forward to hearing about your adventures, if you're in a sharing mood."

"That would be fine, Arthur, but let's wait a day or two. I'm still trying to decide about the next steps for my journey. Wally said that we would be discussing your path for the future and how we might fit into it."

Irma sat down and motioned for the others to sit also. "Jeremy, you just gave a better introduction to these discussions than the one I had planned. Let's talk."

Arthur said, "Everything seems to revolve around my plans for the future, so I'll present the first comments. I've taken a leave of absence from the Northern Illinois Conference of the United Methodist Church. I did so because I wanted to decide whether my investigation activities should become my primary profession, while I only consulted with the Church Conference. Up to now, I've been operating the other way around, with investigations on the consulting end."

Wally Sanborn said, "That's what I understood when I asked to become part of your new venture, Arthur."

"At this point, I'm going to have to call a time-out, Wally. Irma and I have discussed my feelings, and I'll have to say that there won't be a new venture run by me."

"I hear you choosing your words carefully, Arthur. What exactly do you mean?"

"I mean that I won't run an enterprise. I'll investigate, and I'll consult on church matters, but I won't run an organization and worry about its business problems. If there is to be an enterprise, you'll have to run it. Irma and I would call on your group for support services and participation in assignments, but that group would have to be independent from us, just as the police department and the Gonzalez's agency are independent from us. Can you live with that, Wally?"

"That would make me the boss of this entity, with responsibility for generating other business to keep it going when we weren't working with you folks."

Irma said, "That's correct."

Wally turned to Jeremy. "Would you work for a start-up private detective agency that might run out of funds?"

"I would if you'd let me invest in it and become a partner."

They all stared at Jeremy before Wally spoke. "I didn't think you would have any money to invest at your age."

"Dad made me a partner in the bakery and catering business last year. I'm solvent."

Arthur said, "Now you two will have to flip a coin to see who runs this agency."

CHAPTER 33 – RESOURCES

As Bobby Andrews stepped out of his unmarked police car at the Parkville UMC parsonage, he noticed several other cars parked in the driveway and on the street. *I guess I won't be having a one-on-one conversation with Arthur after all.*

Arthur answered the knock on the door. As Bobby entered, he scanned the room and saw Wally Sanborn and Jeremy Hadley in conversation at the dining room table. *Irma's car was outside. She must be in the kitchen.*

"I'm here as requested, Arthur, but I'd thought we'd be having a private discussion of the church case."

"We'll be discussing that, Bobby, but I'll also be filling you in on some changes in my future that will occasionally affect you."

"That sounds mysterious enough."

"It's really quite simple. I'll be spending more of my time on investigations, and less on church-related work. Once I complete this temporary assignment, subbing for the late Pastor Klingham, I'll be on leave of absence from the church, allowing me to tackle any problem that comes along. I'll have the supporting services of Wally Sanborn and Jeremy Hadley who will be starting their own private detective agency."

"Congratulations, you two; I may want to buy services from you when I'm short-handed. What are you calling your agency?"

Jeremy said, "Thanks for that vote of confidence, Chief. We're calling ourselves The Sandley Agency, using a partial combination of our names, Sanborn and Hadley. We've deliberately omitted the word *detective* from the name, because we want to handle non-crime matters as well."

"That sounds like a well-organized venture. I assume you're here because Arthur wants to hire your services for the case of Pastor Klingham."

Arthur laughed. "That was carefully phrased, Bobby. No, you won't have to pay them. I'll handle it out of the pay I'll be receiving as temporary Parkville UMC Pastor."

Irma walked in with a tray of soft drinks and coffee. Bobby raised his right eyebrow at her as he said, "Hi, Irma; these two guys aren't kicking you out of investigations, are they?"

"Not a chance, Bobby ... Arthur and I will continue to work together."

Wally said, "On this case, I see us following up on the leads your department generates, Bobby. We can check out people in places way out of your jurisdiction."

"That sounds reasonable and appropriate for this case. My guys have checked the backgrounds of the four older women that died following visits from Pastor Klingham. They had backgrounds in Chicago, Indianapolis, Kansas City, and New York City. I'll have Al Gomez prepare a report with all the details for you to pick up at the police station.

"Arthur thinks that three of those women were innocent bystanders, but that one was the intended victim. We'll be investigating whether we can prove that all four were murdered or if the perpetrator managed to disguise their deaths enough that we can't prove they weren't accidental."

Arthur said, "We know that Rebecca Klingham's death was a homicide, so we definitely have a dangerous killer to locate and prosecute. The Sandley Agency will need to get properly licensed and armed as soon as practical."

Wally said, "I'm arranging for Jeremy to get trained in martial arts and marksmanship by a few of my Army buddies. I'll be taking a refresher course too. Give us a couple of weeks to discover anything unusual in these women's backgrounds, and then we'll report our findings to all of you."

Irma asked, "Are you going to have an office, or is it too early to arrange for one?"

Jeremy said, "We'll use the apartment I just rented here in Parkville. My friend Debbie, recently arrived from Madison, will be our secretary and associate."

CHAPTER 34 – GETTING STARTED

Wally Sanborn and Jeremy Hadley decided to keep the beginning of their investigation of the four suspicious deaths as simple as possible. The police had concentrated on the four senior victims and had summarized their findings in the report that Wally obtained from Sergeant Al Gomez. Jeremy and Wally had decided to take a different approach.

The two newly minted private detectives drove to Parkville Rehabilitation Home and asked to see the administrator. The receptionist located her by telephone in the Catering Office, where she had been reviewing meal plans for the following week. Six minutes later, Martha Callahan joined them in the reception area, emerging from a door disguised by paneling that matched the surrounding walls. She extended a welcoming hand toward Wally and Jeremy. Martha's air of efficiency and professionalism impressed the visitors as they exchanged introductions and then followed her down a hallway to the privacy of her office. Once settled there, they declined refreshments and launched into their discussion.

Wally looked very comfortable as he relaxed in one of Martha's upholstered guest chairs. "I always enjoy the opportunity to learn how others approach the administration of a group. I served for many years in the Army doing logistics work, so I appreciate that an organization that functions smoothly does so only because of a very large number of detailed decisions and controls that aren't obvious to most visitors. It didn't take long for me to decide that Parkville Rehabilitation Home is that kind of efficient institution."

Martha smiled. "We emphasize the "Home" portion of our name when we train our staff and deal with potential clients. In order to allow even short-term patients to enjoy that at-home feeling, we aim to meet their needs without any obvious display of effort or discomfort due to special requirements. We even developed a fee structure that appears simple to the patient while masking a second layer of backup details to satisfy insurance companies and government agencies."

Jeremy decided that he could be direct with this professional-sounding manager. "We're assisting the Parkville Police in an attempt to learn more about the circumstances of the deaths of four female patients during a relatively short period of time while they were here. I'm referring to Phyllis Landholm, Janet Cuspin, Mary Welker, and Beverly Mandow."

"Are you suggesting that something criminal might have been involved?"

"Let's say that we're taught in criminology studies to double-check events that involve coincidences. The occurrence of four deaths among a group of women with connected backgrounds within a relatively short period of time certainly raises the coincidence flag."

"I'm quite aware of the four deaths you mentioned. During the rehabilitation phase of an illness or recovery from an operation, occurrences of death should be minimal. Those deaths led some people to question the value of our institution, so I would be quite interested in determining whether something other than coincidence was behind them. How may I contribute to your inquiry?"

Wally leaned forward. "Martha, you are an efficient person, and you run this facility with detailed controls. Would you be willing to furnish us with the names and background information for any employees or consultants who joined your staff within six months before the first of these deaths and for those who left the staff within six months after the last of them?"

"We do have a higher staff turnover rate than I would like, but I don't think it would be difficult to compile the data you are requesting. I would have only one condition for cooperating with your inquiry, Wally."

"What's that?"

"I insist that you let me review the data with you, so that your study will include my subjective impressions from working with these people. They are individual human beings and not just abstract statistics. I'll want to protect their rights and give them credit for their accomplishments here."

"Martha, I think your involvement would add to the value of our inquiry. Don't you agree, Jeremy?"

"I do. Let us know when you have the requested information, and we'll meet with you to discuss it, either here or at some more private location."

"An off-site location will be fine, so long as it's not the Police Department. I wouldn't want any rumors about police interest to spread through our facility. Our walls do have ears, as they say."

CHAPTER 35 – DEBBIE

Jeremy hadn't given her much of an explanation for his suddenly wanting to be her guy and have her move to his hometown of Parkville with him. She had a feeling that his old girlfriend, Michelle, had rejected him, but he had offered no details. Rebound romance or not, Debbie had jumped at the opportunity to latch onto Jeremy. He had looked subdued when he returned from his quest. She would be whatever he needed to restore dynamics to his life.

Debbie was six months younger than Jeremy, but she had experienced a far greater variety of adventures. The daughter of an air taxi pilot and a doctor, she had assisted on medical missions in Haiti and the Dominican Republic and had served as a crewmember for her mother when she flew emergency freight into remote areas in Alaska and the Rocky Mountains. Debbie felt that her upbringing had prepared her for any challenge, and she was certain her new coupling with Jeremy would fit into that category. She had been delighted to learn that he wanted her to provide staff support for his new detective agency partnership, but she planned to minimize the staff aspect and morph into a field operative at the earliest opportunity. She thought Wally was the coolest guy she had met in a long time, but he was too old to be a romance competitor for Jeremy. She'd allocate Wally to fantasy excursions.

Thanks to a generous contribution from Jeremy, Debbie had decorated the front room of their apartment, the designated office space for The Sandley Agency, with photographs of famous movie and stage detectives, including no fewer than eight actors playing Sherlock Holmes. At Jeremy's suggestion, she had added likenesses of famous scientists and engineers to indicate that they were not just acting as detectives, but could solve difficult problems.

The phone on the second-hand imitation mahogany desk rang.

"The Sandley Agency, Ms. Danforth speaking; how may I assist you?"

She smiled at the sound of Jeremy's voice, responding to her. "That sounded so professional, Debbie. I know we're going to be a success."

"Thanks, Jeremy. What can I do for you right now?"

"We're going to be having our first full-fledged case meeting. I'd appreciate your setting up the card table and four chairs. Then order a couple of pizzas for delivery. Wally and I will be coming in about an hour, and we'll bring Martha Callahan, the administrator at the Rehabilitation Home. We'll have a bunch of personnel files to analyze."

"Will I be part of this analysis group?"

"Of course you will. You're our researcher."

"That was the correct answer. You win a one-on-one research session later tonight."

CHAPTER 36 – PERSONNEL MATTERS

By the time Jeremy and Wally arrived at the Shandley apartment, accompanied by Martha Callahan from the Parkville Rehabilitation Home, Debbie had set up the card table for their meeting and had arranged three pizzas on the kitchen table along with plates and utensils. She had ordered each pizza with two half-and-half ingredients so that there would be six varieties available.

Jeremy introduced Martha to Debbie, and then took everyone's jackets while Debbie ushered them into the kitchen for the buffet. It turned out that Martha was a pizza enthusiast, so the small talk while eating became energetic, and the four of them felt like old friends by the time they cleared the dishes and settled at the card table for discussions.

Jeremy handed out notepads and pens. "Welcome all. Martha, I do appreciate your willingness to help us discover whether one of your employees at the Rehabilitation Home may have been behind the deaths of four of your patients."

"Let me make it very clear that I'm coloring outside the lines when I discuss personnel information with you. I'm doing so, only because I feel that the sin of discretely opening up our records will be a lot less than the sin of letting someone get away with having murdered four patients. I did request this off-site meeting to keep the sharing of our records as covert as possible. Please do not jeopardize my career by publicizing what we discuss tonight."

Wally said, "As soon as I met you, I knew that you were a person who believed in taking action when it was justified."

"I'm Irish enough to know that that's a lot of blarney, Wally, but that's to be expected from a military guy like you. Anyway, I'll hold onto the personnel files and sort through them without revealing anything until we isolate one or two people whose actions justify detailed analysis. Is that agreeable to everyone?"

They all nodded, and Debbie added, "As a library researcher, I'll contribute that Martha's suggestion is also a very efficient procedure. We won't get bogged down if we defer looking at details until we have identified the likely suspect or suspects. Jeremy, why don't you kick off the discussion?"

"Fair enough; Martha, will you summarize the sequence of the four women's deaths?"

Martha reviewed her notes. "The four of them died over a period of about nine months. The first death on December 28 of last year, was that of Phyllis Landholm after hip replacement surgery. The second was Janet Cuspin on March 13 of this year. She was recuperating after having had back surgery. The third was Mary Welker on June 5. She had suffered a minor heart attack. The final death was that of Beverly Mandow on August 16. She had undergone treatments for complications of diabetes. Our records show no indications that these women were frail or having problems with their rehabilitations. We expected them to return to their homes facing reasonably healthy futures."

Wally completed his note taking. "Did you have any internal investigation of these deaths, Martha?"

"We review and investigate every death of a patient in our care, but we did not group these four people together in a single examination, because we saw no connections among them. Individually, we found their passings to be tragic but unremarkable."

Debbie asked, "Were these the only deaths during this period of about nine months?"

"There was one more, Jonathan Rubendall, but he was in rehab after two heart attacks, and he suffered a third massive one while he was in our care. His death was not unanticipated."

Jeremy said, "In other words, you never expected him to regain his normal health."

"We have a few cases like that, where the family anticipates a death but wants it to occur in an institution rather than in the home. Some people are superstitious about living in a home where someone has died."

Jeremy said, "I understand, Martha. Let's change our focus from the details of each person's death to the staff members who interacted with them. I assume that they all ate the same food, whether consumed in their rooms or in the cafeteria."

"That's correct, Jeremy, except that visitors frequently bring special food and treats from outside sources. In most cases, our patients are not on special diets, so we permit outside food in the belief that it will raise the patient's morale."

Wally combed his hair back with his fingers. "Let's pause our discussion right there. Documentation of what and where people ate would be important if they had all died from poisoning. I don't have a cause of death listing for any of these women. Did they all die in the same manner? Were their causes of death completely different? Martha, what can you reveal about the ways in which they died?"

"Before I address that question, I should tell you that we have two separate sections within Parkville Rehabilitation Home. One section acts as a Rehabilitation Hospital, where patients receive 24-hour oversight by healthcare professionals. Patients in this section must be able to participate in a therapeutic program for a minimum of three hours per day and should be capable of making functional gains within a limited amount of time. Our other section is a sub-acute program for patients who are not able to withstand three hours of therapy each day and who will require longer-term care."

"Which section were our four women in?"

"Two were in each section, so they did not receive the same type or level of care. Each patient's program matches his or her needs."

Jeremy said, "That's completely understandable and appropriate, but my earlier comments about where and what patients ate were meant to suggest that some functions in the Rehabilitation Home apply to everyone, and presumably involve personnel who render services to everyone, or at least have access to everyone without restrictions."

Martha nodded her agreement. "That's a fair statement, Jeremy. We have a limited number of staff members, so they have functions in both sections of our facility, except for specialists who have explicit assignments."

"That means that we should give priority to checking on staff people who worked with patients in both sections of the facility." Jeremy looked satisfied that they had accomplished something.

Debbie said, "Good approach, Jeremy; that will eliminate some people."

Wally said, "If we look at the causes of death for the four women, we'll see what access to them the killer would have required. May we return to the ways in which they died, Martha?"

"You're like a dog that bites an intruder's pants leg, and won't let go of it. Some of this is our collective professional opinion, because we didn't arrange for autopsies on the first two of these people. Here's the summary. Phyllis Landholm, in the Rehabilitation Hospital, died from asphyxia. She either choked on food eaten in her room or smothered while tangled up in her pillows and blankets. Janet Cuspin, also in the Rehabilitation Hospital, died from electrocution by a faulty vital signs monitor. Mary Welker, in the Sub-Acute Program, died from inadvertently drinking grapefruit juice shortly after taking her heart medication. That effectively turned her normal medicine dose into an overdose. Beverly Mandow, in the Sub-Acute Program, died when someone, probably the cleaning staff, combined her medications with those intended for her roommate."

Debbie laughed. "This sounds like a game of Clue; you're saying, 'The cleaner did it in the shared room with combined medications.'"

They all joined Debbie in laughing.

Then Wally gestured for silence. "It sounds funny, but we're discussing very serious events. If I apply logic to the list of death causes, and we assume murders in all four instances, I come up with a profile of a killer who is relatively strong and understands both medical and electrical attack techniques. That person had to smother Landholm while or shortly after she ate, probably with a pillow or by pinching her nose and mouth shut. He or she had to sabotage the vital signs monitor to deliver a shock to Cuspin while not making the tampering obvious. He or she had to know about the effect of grapefruit juice on certain medications in order to give Welker an overdose. Further, the killer had to know enough about medicines to know which of her roommate's medications would fatally affect Mandow when taken in combination with her own prescriptions. We're talking about a strong, medically knowledgeable, and systematic person."

Martha stared at Wally. "That analysis was very perceptive. You must have been in that part of the Army that thinks on its feet."

"I was a Logistics officer assigned to liaison with Intelligence. That means that I had to understand both things and people."

Martha winked. "I see some commonality there. We'll have to share some private conversations over coffee or more pizza sometime."

Wally smiled and nodded.

Jeremy went into the kitchen and returned with the leftover pizza slices on a tray. "Help yourselves to pizza while we continue talking. If you'll pardon the pun, we'll have to chew into Wally's profile of the killer to see if we can identify one or more staff people who match it."

Debbie groaned at his remark, took a slice of mushroom pizza, and patted Jeremy affectionately on his thigh. "My first observation about Wally's profile is that the killer could be either male or female. At a rehab facility where they perform physical therapy, you'll encounter many strong women."

Martha nodded. "I'll agree with Debbie, but I found the most significant ingredient in Wally's profile analysis to be the suggestion that the killer would require medical knowledge in order to know the effects of one patient's drugs upon another patient. Our security is quite good with regard to avoiding the dispensing of any drug without a prescription, but we have never given much thought to the possibility that a drug, properly issued to one patient, would be used to kill another."

Jeremy said, "Hold that thought for a second. Let's review your personnel records to see what staff members with that kind of medical knowledge left your institution shortly after the death of the final victim, Beverly Mandow, in August of this year."

Wally asked, "Jeremy, don't we also want to know who took a position with Parkville Rehabilitation Home shortly before the first death?"

"You may be right, and we may want to take that approach if this one doesn't reveal any suspects, but by looking for the departure of the killer, we'll include long-term employees, along with recent hires."

"Good thinking, Jeremy; I agree. Do you have anyone who left shortly after the final murder, Martha?"

"Affirmative, Wally; I have three such persons."

CHAPTER 37 – TRIANGULAR THINKING

Irma walked into the parsonage kitchen and found Arthur seated, holding his coffee mug halfway between the table and his mouth, and staring out the window with an intense expression on his face. She stopped and stood quietly for about half a minute before she said, "A penny for your thoughts. That's what my mother would say to me when she found me concentrating on something that wasn't obvious."

Arthur's mug completed its journey to his mouth and tipped to deliver its liquid cargo.

"I've been thinking about our two mysteries and about my relationship with the church. They're all three-cornered puzzles."

Irma pulled up a kitchen chair and sat across from him. "Are you going to explain that comment, or do I have to get my futuristic mind probe from my forensics kit?"

"I may be working this out as I try to examine my thinking, but let's look at each case or situation individually."

"Start with the death of Pastor Klingham."

Arthur leaned forward to kiss Irma across the table. Then he leaned back again, his body relaxed for the first time since she arrived. "In the case involving Rebecca Klingham, we started looking at her background when her death appeared to have been a suicide. Then we looked at the four women who died while at the Rehabilitation Home once we realized that Rebecca had been a murder victim. Then we turned our attention to employees at the Rehabilitation Home to see who would have had the opportunity to kill all four of those women patients. There are three sides to the puzzle, and we even have three sets of investigators, the Parkville Police, Jeremy and Wally's Sandley Agency, and us."

Irma had made a few notes on one of her ever-present yellow paper pads. "I see the patterns, but I'll have to think about whether they're useful. How do you get a three-cornered puzzle out of your interface with the church?"

"There, we have Bishop Chandler trying to figure out what to do with a Pastor who clashes with the normal pastoral stereotype, yours truly as that unruly cleric, and the committees that advise the Bishop. I'm an irritant to those committee people, even more so than I am to the Bishop. I don't match with the *method* watchword of the United Methodist Church."

"John Wesley didn't fit the stereotype of a cleric in the Anglican Church either, so he founded his own church which you now serve. Perhaps you should decide to establish the *Church of Perpetual Inquiries*."

"That's a bit too close to the Inquisition, which was a black eye for Christianity. Besides, I'm not charismatic enough to establish a church."

"I'd follow your teachings, along with a few others I know."

"Thanks, but no thanks to that one. I just want to be myself."

"How does the case of Blake's Antiques receiving the unexpected shipment of antique books fit into your analysis, if we can call that an investigation?"

"We can consider that triangular too. One side is Maria Svenson, giving instructions in her will; the second contains her children, preparing the shipment; and the third is our investigating team, deciding which books have a tainted history and which don't."

"Is any part of this triangular way of looking at things useful?"

"It is, at least from a communications standpoint. By being in the middle, we add legitimacy to Wally and Jeremy's Sandley Agency and encourage communication between them and Bobby Andrews' Police Department. Further, I'll have a much better chance of working out a useful relationship with the church by dealing through Bishop Chandler than I would if I had to negotiate with some governing committee. I'm not sure how much communication we'll need with Maria Svenson's children in the matter of the antique books."

"That all sounds very neat, but what, specifically should we do to help with the Pastor Klingham case?"

We're going to let the Parkville Police and the Sandley Agency interface with the suspects and others involved with the victims, but we'll look over their shoulders to see whose actions and words are not consistent with his or her character.

CHAPTER 38 – QUITTERS

Wally Sanborn, Jeremy Hadley, and Debbie Danforth all stared at Martha Callahan in response to her announcement.

Wally said, "You say that three staff members left Parkville Rehabilitation Home shortly after the last of the four women died. Who were they, and what jobs did they have there?"

"They were in different aspects of our operation. Noel Burnside was an accountant. He worked on insurance company interface matters and was the contact person for setting up payment plans for patients taking responsibility for their own charges. We're still looking for a replacement for him. That's a specialized job. Joanna Diaz was a physical therapist. She worked with both occupational therapy patients and with those recovering from heart and joint operations. The third person, Patrick Hurley was in maintenance. He handled whatever we needed to keep the building and the equipment in it functioning properly. He could repair office and medical equipment plus paint walls and shovel snow. He was very flexible."

Debbie looked up from her notes. "All three are potential suspects. The physical therapist had the strength to force the smothering death and the taking of grapefruit juice with medicine if it wasn't voluntary. The maintenance technician could have sabotaged the vital signs monitor to electrocute Janet Cuspin and then could have covered his tracks by repairing it during his inspection of the device after the event. The accountant regularly circulated among the patients with paperwork and could have switched medications without arousing suspicion."

Jeremy said, "Those are interesting observations, Debbie. Collectively, their skills matched all of the killings. What is the likelihood of the three of them having worked together on these killings?"

Martha shook her head negatively. "I may be wrong, but I can't see that as a practical arrangement. These three people had very little contact with each other during working assignments. Jeremy, I can't even recall having seen them together in the cafeteria or at the coffee machine."

"We'll give that possibility a low priority based on your comments. Is there anyone among these three who couldn't have done at least one of these murders? Can we eliminate anyone?

Wally said, "That's a good approach, but *couldn't* is a tricky word. Given the right circumstances, each one of us can do things we wouldn't normally attempt. Further, we're talking about someone who deliberately murdered people. He or she may have hidden some capabilities to avoid attracting suspicion."

Debbie waved her hand for attention. "I like the elimination approach. I'll suggest that the physical therapist is less likely to have been the killer, because that person would have had to be alone when the opportunity arose to attack a target victim. From what I've seen at the University of Wisconsin hospitals, physical therapists have long scheduled assignments and tend to hang out together in groups."

Martha said, "I could counter-argue that a physical therapist, being a healthcare worker, has more one-on-one access to a patient without arousing suspicion. It looks normal when she goes into a patient's room and closes the door behind her."

Jeremy gestured for attention. "We've just demonstrated that we can argue both ways with regard to the likelihood of any of our three job-quitting candidates being the murderer. However, all of our comments so far have concerned whether one or another of these former employees had the means or opportunity to have committed these four patient murders. The police look for means, opportunity, and motive in determining the likelihood of someone having committed a crime. I suggest that we've taken these personnel discussions as far as we should. All three are potential suspects. Now it's time to research their files, activities, and histories to see whether any suspect had a motive to murder any of the patients. Martha, if you would loan us those three files, we'll use them as input to our motive research."

Martha handed the files to Jeremy. "You may have the files for one week, provided you maintain their privacy and security. I'll want a listing of everyone who accesses each file. I'll also caution you that any one of these three people may have had a very classic motive to kill all of those patients."

Wally asked, "What's that?"

"The disgruntled employee motive ... someone angry enough at the Parkville Rehabilitation Home management might have wanted to create a series of embarrassing failures that would cause potential clients to go elsewhere and put us out of business."

CHAPTER 39 – STATUS REPORT

Irma picked up the telephone, exchanged a few pleasantries with the party on the other end, and then handed the instrument to Arthur, distracting him from his crossword puzzle.

"Arthur Blake speaking; how may I help you?"

"Hello, Arthur; Howard Chandler here; I'm calling to remind you that it's time for an update on progress toward solving the murder of Pastor Rebecca Klingham. It would have been a lot simpler if this had remained a suicide, but we'll accept your conclusion that it was murder."

"Good morning, Bishop, I do have some information for you, but we're a long way from solving this crime."

"That's disappointing. I had hoped for a speedy resolution. What do you have?"

"The Parkville Police and I believe that Pastor Klingham's murderer was the same person responsible for four suspicious deaths of female patients at the Parkville Rehabilitation Home who were members of our church. All four of those deaths occurred shortly after Rebecca Klingham had visited those individuals."

"Do the police suspect her of killing them? That would be shocking!"

"No, Howard, Rebecca was a victim, not a suspect. We think the killer spread rumors about her having had a connection to those deaths, so that Pastor Klingham's own death would appear to be a confession by suicide."

"But you said she didn't commit suicide."

"The killer wanted it to look like a suicide, but he or she made enough mistakes in setting it up that we now know it was murder."

"It all sounds very complex to me. Whether it was suicide or murder, Pastor Klingham's death did not involve the church, correct?"

"I'll agree with that statement. The church is not going to have any bad publicity, but Rebecca's murder still needs a solution."

"Justice is more important than avoiding bad publicity. Continue with your effort, Arthur. I'll await your next report. Goodbye for now."

Irma patted him on the shoulder. "I heard only one side of that conversation, but I think you handled it well."

"Bishop Chandler is relieved that he won't see bad news about the church on the news reports. As soon as we established that, I was off the hook."

"We all have different priorities. Are we making progress on that case?"

"We're gathering good pieces to the puzzle, but it's too early to assemble them and see the resulting picture. Bobby and his people are learning important details about the patients who died. Wally and Jeremy have identified ex-employees of the Rehabilitation Home, who may have been involved, but we don't yet have the killer's motive in each crime. We'll need that information to identify the culprit or culprits."

"So, it's possible that more than one killer might be involved?"

"That's at least one theory."

"That sounds as though you're not buying into that speculation."

"I'm not even sure I'm buying into the division of effort on this case."

She stared at her husband. "Now we're getting into the real problem. Would you care to elaborate?"

"I opened my mind to the possibility of turning my career toward full-time investigation work, but now I'm becoming a consultant who reviews the reports of other groups who are doing the actual investigations."

"You've always had an element of that in your cases."

"That approach worked while I held down a pastor's job as my main commitment, but I need to get more involved in field work now. How can I work on the front line of investigations while opening the door to support from Wally and Jeremy's group?"

"I get it. You can handle consulting to an official agency like the police or a federal entity, where you get to be objective from a distance in support of professionals. Wally and Jeremy are supporting you as you support the official investigators, so you've added another layer to the organization chart."

"The whole concept of an organization chart applied to our work bugs me."

"Let's look at it differently. You can be a hands-on investigator of the antique book shipment to your dad's shop, while directing Jeremy and Wally's Sandley Agency to represent you in handling a second mystery. Studying the books won't take that much of your time, so you'll be free to take on another case, should one arise. You'll have your hands-on work, while keeping additional clients satisfied."

"You came through again, Irma. I can live with that interpretation. We'll use them as the safety valve that keeps me from feeling overwhelmed when too many people want me to work on their problems, but I still get to be in the foreground on at least one case at a time."

"Correction – we get to be in that foreground position, usually working together."

"I stand corrected and appeased."

CHAPTER 40 – DEBBIE AND JEREMY

After a quick outing for a late evening hamburger, they had returned to their apartment. Jeremy had receded into his own thoughts as he sat in a large upholstered chair. Those thoughts suffered the interruption of Debbie lowering herself onto his lap.

"Are you thinking about Michelle?"

"Not really, just about the whole recent chain of events."

"I know you turned to me on the rebound from whatever happened with Michelle, but I don't mind. I have you now, and I hope you'll want to stay with me."

"Don't worry, Debbie, I'm not a ping-pong ball. I usually stick with my choices."

"Do you want to tell me anything about what happened with Michelle?"

"It's probably too early in our relationship for that, and I'm not sure I understand the whole story. I'll just tell you that she had some outlook changes that weren't compatible with our continuing together. In the meantime, I'm learning more about you, and I'm finding myself impressed by talents I'd never seen before."

"You're starting to see beyond sexual attraction, and so am I." She planted a long soft kiss on his lips, and received a similar response.

"That was welcome."

"I don't know whether one of those ex-employees at Parkville Rehabilitation Home will turn out to be the killer, but that person is scary, having committed five murders."

"Don't say anything to Martha Callahan about Pastor Klingham's murder. For now, we're letting the public continue to think that was a suicide."

"Won't she think Rebecca Klingham murdered her patients? That's been the rumor around town."

"That was the rumor at Parkville United Methodist Church. Martha Callahan doesn't go there and doesn't know Pastor Klingham except, perhaps, from seeing her in a hallway. She's also focused on the fact that we're looking at people who worked for her but left the Rehabilitation Home."

"I don't get it, Jeremy. Why don't you want her to know about the fifth killing?"

"If people think only about murders at the Rehabilitation Home, they won't think there's a threat to the public. Rebecca Klingham's murder occurred in a residential setting, so it suggests that the killer might strike anywhere."

"Don't worry, Jeremy, I'll protect you if he or she comes here."

"That's very funny. Let's head for bed; we have a lot of research to tackle tomorrow."

"I like it when you talk romantic."

Jeremy laughed and carried her into the bedroom.

CHAPTER 41 – MICHELLE

Doctor Rosemary Swinton sat across from Michelle Caspar and encouraged her to relax as they started their second interview session. This time she would use both her audio recorder and her video camera to record their exchanges.

"Michelle, yours is an unusual case because of your age. We established last time that you had early childhood memories of having been, in a former life, a woman named Ruby who was a cook in Ireland. You said that those memories faded during your elementary school years. That's typical, based on our past cases. You indicated that memories of a second earlier life as an Austrian male named Kurt emerged within the last year or two."

"That's correct."

"You indicated that you are twenty-seven years old. It is unusual to have new memories at such a mature age. It is also unusual to have memories of a prior life ranging through time from incidents as a youthful student to events in a nursing home for the elderly. You said the latter location was in the state of New York, while the youthful memories stemmed from Austria or Germany."

"The student events may have been in Germany or in a part of Austria close to the border, because there was an abandoned construction site for the Autobahn."

"Your memories are both vivid and lasting, Michelle. Are you sure that you never read articles or watched documentaries about the construction of the Autobahn?"

"I knew that the Autobahn was a German highway without speed limits, but that's all I knew about it. I have never even looked at a map to see exactly where it is located or if there is more than one road called an autobahn."

"There's also the matter of your having been male in this second recollection of a prior life. You said that this gender change affected you. Would you please elaborate on that statement?"

"As Kurt, I was an Austrian boy who had been nervous about having to dance with girls when I was a youth. After experiencing these memories, I became uneasy about being with men because I felt that I had been one. My boyfriend tracked me from Madison, Wisconsin to here in Charlottesville, Virginia, and I couldn't relate to him when he arrived. I told him that I had changed and that I had no interest in continuing our relationship. I sent him away."

Rosemary Swinton made a few notes and then resumed the interview. "Are you being honest with yourself?"

"How do you mean that?"

"You said that when your boyfriend arrived in Charlottesville recently, you couldn't relate to him because you had once been a male. Yet, you said these memories came to you over the past year or two. You certainly must have had a close relationship with this boyfriend before you came here but after you had experienced memories of having once been male. Are you sure there weren't other reasons for sending him away?"

"There may have been other problems, such as the fact that I'm about five years older than he is, and his inability to consider as possible anything that violates his concept of normality. I once mentioned my childhood memories of a past life. He laughed at me and said that I must have had vivid dreams."

"Some people have suggested the dream explanation, and we devise tests of that possibility in each instance when we are dealing with young children. Do you have vivid dreams, and do you believe in paranormal phenomena like ghosts?"

"I don't even remember my dreams in the morning, but I suppose you could call them vivid while I am having them. I usually find flaws in their logic before I drift back off to a sound sleep. As far as the traditional paranormal stuff like ghosts, vampires, and zombies, I've always been cynical about their existence and usually laugh at them. My prior life memories will probably make me more tolerant of the paranormal, but if I had to be open to anything in that realm, I'd look for visitors from planets circling other stars."

"In other words, you would call yourself scientific and objective."

"Yes."

"What did you study in school?"

"Political Science, but I placed emphasis on the understanding of people's behaviors rather than straight politics."

"Did you ever have Austrian ancestors or relatives?"

"No, but I think our family name, Caspar, is supposed to be of Germanic or Polish origin; I looked it up online once."

"Did you do that before or after you started to remember having been Kurt?"

"I'm pretty sure I looked it up after I started to remember Kurt. I wondered whether he might have been my ancestor."

"That's enough for today, Michelle. We'll have another session in a few days. I want you to relax your mind and pursue normal activities, but carry a small notebook with you. If you remember something else about Kurt while your mind is relaxed, please write it down in the notebook, and share it with me next time. Thank you for allowing us to study your recollections. What we learn from you could help us understand other case histories."

CHAPTER 42 – FIELD WORK

Wally Sanborn had led the morning planning meeting at the apartment. As they finished their coffee, he said, "It's time to check out those employees who left Parkville Rehabilitation Home. I'll take the two men, Noel Burnside, the accountant and Patrick Hurley, the maintenance technician. Jeremy, you're a natural for interviewing women, so you contact Joanna Diaz, the physical therapist. Debbie, you keep our office presence going here."

Debbie glared at him. "I won't even bother asking who put you in charge of making assignments, but if you think I'm going to miss all the field fun, you're wrong. I get to be an investigator too. I'll talk with the accountant while you're meeting with the maintenance man. There's no reason for you to interview two people while I stay here and stare at a telephone."

Wally said, "Point well taken Debbie. We're equals from here on. The maintenance guy, Hurley, sounds more like the kind of person who worked for me in the Army, so he's a good choice for me. You'll be in charge of interviewing the accountant. Let's hope they're all still in town or not too far away. We could run into problems tracking them down. If so, we'll come up with a Plan B for getting their input."

CHAPTER 43 – PATRICK HURLEY

Wally had gone to the apartment house indicated in the Rehabilitation Home records, but didn't receive a response to his ringing of Patrick Hurley's doorbell. He was about to leave when he saw a young mother with her daughter. She yelled out to him to wait before leaving.

"Are you looking for Hurley?"

She had an Irish accent, and Wally couldn't resist altering his words to match. "That I am."

"Well, if you want to save an extra trip you'll go to Murphy's Pub around the corner. Patrick's always there this time of day."

"That's a big help." He tipped his hat. "I'll be heading that way then. Thank you."

Wally decided it was a good day for walking and headed for Mr. Murphy's establishment. When he arrived, he found seven patrons inside, six at tables and one at the bar. He approached the bartender for information on his quarry.

"Would you direct me to Patrick Hurley? His neighbor said that he would be here."

"That's Pat at the little round table in the back corner. That's his regular spot."

Wally thanked him and headed for the dark end of the room. Patrick was finishing a sandwich as he approached. Although it was difficult to judge height for someone seated and bent forward, Wally estimated this lanky redhead to be well over six feet.

"Good afternoon. Are you Patrick Hurley?"

An automatic smile greeted this inquiry, as the man looked upward.

"That I am, and what can I do for you?"

"My name's Wally Sanborn. I work for the Sandley Agency, and we're gathering some information for the Parkville Police Department."

"But you're not a cop yourself?"

"No, I'm a retired Army officer. This is part-time work for me."

"At least you've got something part time. Since I left Parkville Rehabilitation Home a few months ago, I haven't found any work at all."

"Why did you leave if you didn't have anything else lined up? Were you laid off?"

"Not at all; they liked my work there. I just started to feel like the place was going downhill, after four of their patients died. In the old days, it would have been unthinkable to have even a single rehab patient die."

"I'm glad you brought that up. I'm here to ask you whether you saw anything unusual in the way staff treated those women who died. Did they have new or untested procedures there?"

"I was a maintenance technician, so I didn't get involved in treatment measures, but I did know that some of their equipment was getting obsolete. I had to keep patching some medical devices that they should have replaced a long time ago. One of those women even died because of a short circuit in a unit called a vital signs monitor. That was another reason for my leaving. I had recommended new equipment, but they said business wasn't good enough to get it right away. When that woman died because of a fault in a device I had wanted replaced, I started to worry that they'd blame her death on my maintenance quality. I decided I'd look for something else, rather than wait around to be the fall guy for patient problems."

"I can understand your stress, Patrick. Was it just the equipment condition that led you to conclude things were going sour over there, or were there other problems?"

"Wally, there were other things, but I couldn't quite identify them. They had new young staff members who didn't take responsibility the way the older ones did. That's just the current trend, like hiring schoolteachers barely older than their students, instead of the long-term professionals who taught you and me. The consulting doctors didn't spend as much time at the Rehabilitation Home as they did in the old days, either."

"It sounds as though you felt that enough things had changed that you had to move on to something better."

"That's exactly it, Wally. I didn't feel comfortable there anymore. Let me buy you a Guinness, and then you can tell me whether you know of anyone who's looking for the best jack-of-all-trades maintenance technician there is. You won't be sorry if you recommend me to someone; I guarantee that."

CHAPTER 44 – BOOKS

Arthur and Irma had joined Peter and Janice at Blake's Antiques. The sign in the window read *Closed for inventory*. They knew that examination of the book shipment would take a significant amount of time, and they didn't want interruptions or suspicions of something unusual transpiring in the shop. They sat in Peter's office, surrounded by carts and shelves loaded with the old books they had received.

Peter said, "Now that Arthur has his precious coffee, we can get started on reviewing this collection of books. I'll start by observing that taken in total, this shipment constitutes an extensive and valuable library of western thinking and literature over the past several centuries. Our job today is to decide how to handle its disposition and sale, primarily for the benefit of one or more charities. Arthur, may we have your opinion?"

"Thanks, Dad. My first observation is that the history of these books is cloudy. They aren't part of the stolen Nazi art treasures once in the possession of John Hendrix, Maria Svenson's father, because he transferred all those physical items to the government agency charged with their repatriation. However, the scope of this collection, plus Maria's desire that we donate her proceeds from the sale to charity, suggest to me that some or all of these books carry a taint. They certainly constitute a more valuable collection than Maria could have expected to accumulate on her own. My guess is that John or Maria purchased at least some of these books with the proceeds from sale of stolen art items, or with investment profits derived from those items. How should we sort the volumes for sale or disposal?"

"May I speak to that point, Arthur?"

"Certainly, Mother; you don't need to ask for permission. Just jump in with your comments."

"From an art history point of view, it would make sense to split this collection into as few groupings as practical. The books are much more valuable as part of a library collection than they are individually. Taken together, the books also tell us quite a bit about the person or persons who acquired this collection."

Irma nodded affirmation. "I looked through them for about fifteen minutes, and my impressions of the collector were introspection, a love of history and science, and a fiercely independent nature. This person could flourish alone, but he or she had a yearning for companionship, if only for the continuous exchange of ideas."

Arthur said, "You're describing John Hendrix very well. His temporary ownership of art and jewelry treasures stolen by the Nazis deprived him of normal connections with friends and family. He had to learn to be satisfied with his own company plus stimulation from art and books in his library. So long as he held onto that treasure, he had to keep it hidden and secret. He was wealthy, but couldn't reveal it to others. That treasure was both a blessing and a burden to him."

Peter stood and scanned the display of books. "Regardless of their history, we have to decide what to do with these books. I suggest that we should each retain a few of them, to maintain our individual connections to concepts and events that are historically important to us. We should price the remaining books in accordance with listings available from used book vendors that list their holdings online. I would feel much better about fulfilling Maria's instructions if we sold books to individuals than if we chose to clear them out quickly by means of an auction."

Arthur said, "That sounds fine to me, Dad, but we'd all have to commit to spending a substantial amount of time on pricing research, and you would end up seeking customers for these books over a long period of time. Even with use of the internet and specialized sites like eBay and Amazon, this project would require a lot of your time. Are you willing to make such a commitment?"

"I am, and I'll lay on you and Irma the burden of determining charities that will serve the interests of those groups of people who lost their treasures to the Nazis during the Second World War. Are you prepared to handle that effort?"

Irma said, "I'll speak for both of us with a hearty affirmation. I've known quite a few people along the way who lost both property and relatives to Nazi cruelty. If we can offset that in any small measure, we should and will."

"Fair enough ... spend the next couple of hours selecting books that you want for your private collections, and then we'll tabulate the remaining volumes and start researching their proper prices. Blake's Antiques is about to have an antiquarian bookstore section, in the building and online too."

CHAPTER 45 – JOANNA DIAZ

Jeremy had assumed that interviewing Joanna Diaz, the physical therapist who had left Parkville Rehabilitation Home shortly after the fourth patient's death, would be a simple matter. Unfortunately, when he called the telephone number listed in Martha's personnel file, he found the account to have been terminated and the phone disconnected. He searched the file for a cell phone number, but couldn't find one. He looked for an indication of her email address on her job application and other official papers without success. Jeremy was about to check whether she had a page on Facebook, when he spotted a printout of an email from Joanna in her personnel file. From this, he obtained her email address and sent off the following message.

The Sandley Agency works with various organizations to determine the views of past employees regarding their working conditions. We are currently performing a survey for Parkville Rehabilitation Home, your past employer. If you call the telephone number shown below and ask to speak with Jeremy Hadley, your views will be included in our survey on an anonymous basis. We will send you a cash incentive of fifty dollars if you participate in our survey.

Thirty-five minutes later, the telephone rang, and Debbie alerted Jeremy that he had a call from Joanna Diaz.

"Good morning Ms. Diaz; thank you for calling. I hope this means that you're agreeing to participate in our survey."

"It does if I'll get the fifty dollars."

"You certainly will. At the conclusion of our conversation, simply give me the address to which you want it mailed."

"I've already emailed it to you. Check your computer."

"That's fine. Getting on with the interview, was Parkville Rehabilitation Home the first place where you worked as a physical therapist?"

"No, I had previously worked at St. Therese Hospital in Waukegan, Illinois until 2006. That was when they sold the hospital to Community Health Systems. I decided that I didn't want to be part of the new organization and responded to an ad from the Parkville Rehabilitation Home."

"Did you enjoy working at the Rehabilitation Home?"

"It was an adequate place, but it wasn't anything special."

"Did you have much contact with management while you worked there?"

"No, I just did my job. Once, Martha Callahan complimented me in front of a patient, but she also would criticize you in front of patients if you screwed up on something."

"Was that why you left the Rehabilitation Home?"

"It was a factor, but the main reason I left was because I was bored there. Parkville isn't an exciting place for a single woman."

"They had several unexpected deaths among the patients. How did you react to them?"

"I didn't react, except to feel sorry that they died. I assumed it was just bad luck for them. We had deaths at St. Therese Hospital too."

"Occasional deaths are expected events at a hospital, but not nearly as usual in a rehabilitation facility. Did you personally work with any of the patients who died?"

"I did some preliminary work with Mrs. Cuspin, but she had undergone some tricky back surgery, and after her first week of rehab, they called in a chiropractor and a physical therapist who specialized in back treatments."

"Are you in a more exciting job and location now?"

"It's a definite improvement. I'm working in Las Vegas at a resort hotel with a rehab wing. The tips from the high rollers beat anything I ever saw in Parkville, and I'm engaged to one of the managers here. He's getting a divorce so that he can marry me."

Jeremy wrote this information into his notebook. "It sounds as though you are finding success both on the job and socially. Do you have anything further to say about your experiences while you worked at Parkville Rehabilitation Home?"

"If your report will be going to Martha Callahan, tell her she still owes me a final payment for special physical treatments I gave her cousin in her home. I won't go into details, but she'll remember the case. I have to go now. They're paging me. Send my payment to the address I sent you by email. I'll be watching for it."

"Thank you, Joanna; we'll send your payment today."

CHAPTER 46 – VALUATION

Arthur and Irma sat in Peter's office, surrounded by concentric circles of old books. Irma examined each volume and then wrote its title and a condition rating on her pad. Arthur would use that data in searching online for book dealer valuations.

After spending fifteen minutes checking various sites for prices for an 1885 edition of *Huckleberry Finn*, Arthur said, "This is absolutely crazy. I have prices for this relatively common book ranging from eight thousand to seven hundred and eighty dollars. How are we supposed to do a proper valuation of this library?"

"I'm sure you'll get even wilder numbers if you look at auction sites and listings by individuals instead of businesses. A book's value is what you're willing to accept for it. It takes agreement between a buyer and a seller to get a true worth, and even then, the next transaction for the same item will be substantially different."

"How do you even quantify the aspect of condition? Its importance varies with the person examining the book."

Peter entered his office, laughing. "I couldn't help overhearing your conversation. Now you understand the essence of the antiques business. Your comments don't apply only to books, but to anything that is old and rare."

Arthur said, "Dad, how have you managed over the years to arrive at pricing that is fair to both you and the customer?"

"It's an inexact science, but you have to negotiate, evaluate the level of desire of your opposite number, and suggest package deals so that you make something on more items when they won't accept your desired margin on a single piece."

"In other words, Irma and I shouldn't spend much time on valuation of the library, because each book will be sold at a negotiated price anyway."

"That's not exactly correct, son. If you prepare a nominal valuation table, it gives the potential customer and me a starting point for our negotiation. That's much better than pulling a starting price out of the air."

"Would you suggest that we average all the prices we find for a single book?"

"You can do that, but then take a long look at the book and ask yourself whether you feel that specific volume is worth more or less than your average price."

Irma said, "You're telling us that all valuations are subjective."

"That's a true statement, but the more data you have from other sources, the more enlightened is your subjective pricing of each specific item. Look at that Antiques Roadshow television program. Until the so-called expert comes up with his or her view that an item is extremely valuable, the owner of that item will be willing to accept a substantially lower price for it. Following that expert opinion, the price always rises."

Irma said, "Quite a few of those people with old treasures accept the inflated price as correct, but then decide to keep their item rather than even trying to sell it."

"That's the funny part of this business. If my piece or book is worth more to you, then it's worth more to me also."

Arthur walked over to his father. "If that's true, why are we going through this exercise?"

"It's just a matter of being able to state and document that we gave due diligence to the valuation process and didn't just guess at the proper sale prices. Our net

Richard Davidson

proceeds after expenses for the books will go to charity, so nobody will argue with us if we demonstrate good effort."

"Thanks, Dad; that's helpful. I think your comments about negotiations, reference values, and subjective determinations for these books will also apply to some of my church and investigative interactions. You reach your final price by evaluating people's qualities and motives just as I do in a crime case or when people ask me for special favors."

CHAPTER 47 – NOEL BURNSIDE

Debbie wanted to prove to Jeremy and Wally that she was as capable as anyone else was at handling a fieldwork assignment. She had found that Noel Burnside, the accountant who had left Parkville Rehabilitation Home, still lived in the village at the address shown in his personnel folder. Rather than simply making an appointment with him, she had monitored his activities for a week and had learned that each morning he stopped at Mandy's Coffee House for breakfast. Debbie decided to join him there *accidentally* on Monday morning.

At eight o'clock Monday, Noel entered Mandy's, picked up his coffee and sweet roll from the counter, and paused when he discovered his favorite booth already occupied. The trespasser was a young woman drinking a tall coffee and reading a book. Her body language indicated she planned to remain there for a lengthy period. Noel knew he couldn't simply wait until she left. He decided that a frontal assault might be his best tactic.

"Excuse me, Miss, but you're occupying the booth where I sit every morning."

"There are plenty of other seats, I've been here for a half hour, and I'd like to complete my book club reading assignment."

"It's a large booth. Would you mind if I joined you. You wouldn't have to stop reading. I won't disturb you."

She swept her right arm toward the other side of the table, and he sat down.

As he started to cut and butter his pastry, Noel's curiosity got the better of him.

"What is that book you're reading so intently?"

"Its title is *Impulses*. It's a mystery novel. Are you a reader? What types of books do you like?"

Noel thought for a moment. "Yes, I like to read, but I find it hard to label my reading by genre. I read a wide variety of things, both fiction and nonfiction. By the way, I'm Noel Burnside."

"I'm Debbie Danforth, and I guess I'm interested in reading habits because until recently, I worked for the University of Wisconsin Libraries. What nonfiction do you read?

"Hi, Debbie – pleased to meet you. I mostly get into business topics. I used to work as an accountant at the Parkville Rehabilitation Home. Right now, I'm brushing up on a number of commercial trends so that I'll sound up-to-date during job interviews."

"At that rehab place, did you calculate numbers all the time, or did you do managerial things? At interviews, you have to make your background sound as exciting as possible."

"I think I made a good decision in joining you. I like the way you think. Back at the Rehabilitation Home, I was the administrator's right-hand man. I took care of all the credit and legal paperwork, documentation exchanges between the patients and the insurance companies, plus the day-to-day accounting. They're probably learning how difficult that work is, now that I've moved on."

"With all that background, you shouldn't have trouble finding a new position, especially in the medical field. Would it be too personal to ask why you decided to leave that rehab place?"

"No, Debbie, I need to work through my thinking with someone, anyhow. I left because I had the feeling that they would be getting into trouble with the government soon. They had me processing some extra paperwork that was unusual, and I began to worry that they'd get into trouble and drag me along with them."

"I appreciate your outlook, Noel. Too many people just turn the other way when something unethical is happening in the workplace. You showed that you're willing to stand up for your convictions, even when it costs you something, like your job. Would you like to share what they were doing that bothered you so much?"

"We've just met, Debbie, so I don't feel right about that. You're about the same age as my daughter Sandra. My wife took her away from me after our divorce nine years ago. If you come here on a regular basis, we could talk at breakfast again. I'm just a lonely old guy, and I wouldn't be a threat to you if you would be willing to talk some more. If we get to the point where it's like talking with my daughter, I'll share more things with you, and perhaps you'll tell me more about what it takes to get along in a young crowd nowadays."

"That would be fine, Noel. I'm new to Parkville, and you could tell me whether there are dangerous parts of town that I should avoid. I won't be here tomorrow, but I could join you at the same time on Wednesday morning."

CHAPTER 48 – PARSONAGE

Irma sat at the head of the parsonage dining room table and called the meeting to order. "I thought I would add an air of formality to this meeting, because we're about to find out how well our two-stage investigative team and procedure works. With the advent of The Sandley Agency, Arthur and I can handle more cases or gain additional fieldwork capability, while the Sandley people have easy access to us. How does the arrangement sit with you, Arthur?

"We're about to find out. When we last talked, we agreed that the next step would be for the Sandley folks to learn what they could from and about the three Parkville Rehabilitation Home employees who left that institution within three months after the last patient death there. How did that work out? Wally, let's start with you."

"I located Patrick Hurley in town and shared a Guinness with him. He's the maintenance technician, and I enjoyed his company. He left Parkville Rehabilitation Home because he felt the equipment and the institution were going downhill and management didn't want to invest any money to improve things. He was also worried that they'd try to blame him for Janet Cuspin's death after that patient's electrocution by a faulty vital signs monitor. I don't see Patrick as being malicious in any way, and he certainly didn't benefit from what happened at the rehab place. He's broke and looking for any reasonable kind of job."

Arthur wrote a few lines on his pad. "Good summary, Wally; he obviously impressed you. Someday we may need

138

his technician talents on a case. Jeremy, how did your interview go?"

"I almost didn't have one. Joanna Diaz moved out of town without leaving any contact information with the rehab people or with her landlord. I finally found her email address and induced her to call me for a paid interview ostensibly as part of our consulting survey for Parkville Rehabilitation Home. She's now in Las Vegas. She gave me her address so that I could send her reward check following the interview."

"How much did you pay her?"

"I sent her fifty dollars, and it was money well spent. The offer got her to telephone me soon after receiving my email. I didn't have any idea where she was, so that saved me quite a bit of investigation time."

Arthur nodded. "That was an efficient and creative tactic, Jeremy. Did you learn that technique at the university, or was it an original idea?"

"I came up with that one on my own. When I worked for Bobby Andrews in the police department, they had me going door-to-door in old-fashioned evidence gathering projects, and I never liked it. The money was a worthwhile shortcut."

"Go on with what you learned from Joanna."

"I've recorded the details in my printed summary that I passed around, but I came away with three highlight points, if we believe her statements. First, Joanna is self-centered and left Parkville because it was boring for her. She was enthusiastic about the tips she gets for physical therapy in Vegas and about her engagement to one of the bosses there. Second, she disliked the way Martha Callahan would compliment and criticize staff members in front of patients and visitors. Joanna had been on the receiving end of arbitrary criticism on a number of occasions. Third, she said that she did private therapy work at the home of Martha's cousin and had never received the promised payment for it."

"Those comments start to raise questions about Martha Callahan's qualifications and behavior. Think about your opinions of her as we consider these interview results. We'll discuss her afterward. Does anyone think that the therapy work the cousin's house might refer to Joanna attacking Pastor Klingham? Keep that possibility in the back of your minds."

Several people murmured to each other before Jeremy continued his comments.

"After talking with Joanna, I have the impression that she'd be capable of doing any assigned task, whether criminal or not, without giving it much thought. She's materialistic and probably amoral, not too concerned about the ethics of what she does. Joanna practically bragged that the manager in Las Vegas was getting a divorce from his wife in order to marry her."

"That's an interesting picture of her. Debbie, I understand that you were to interview the accountant, Noel Burnside. How did that go?"

"Well, Arthur, I didn't attempt a straight interview, but instead found a way to meet Noel and learn things from him without an interrogation."

Irma said, "Well done, Debbie; that's the feminine way of handling it. A little subtlety goes a long way. Please continue with your report, and show these guys how well the indirect approach works."

"I researched Noel's daily activities and discovered he had some very strict habits. Yesterday, I made sure that I took my breakfast to the coffee shop booth that he always gets. When he saw me reading a book and not likely to leave soon, he asked whether he might join me in that booth. I agreed, and during the course of our conversation, he suggested that some of the paperwork at the Rehabilitation Home might end up getting them into trouble with the government."

"Did he get into any specifics about that?"

"Not yet, but we're meeting again for breakfast tomorrow, and I think he'll open up some more. He says I remind him of the daughter he lost in a bitter divorce. He wants to keep meeting with me."

Wally said, "That sounds like a pick-up line. Watch out for him, Debbie. He could be dangerous. I think I'll have breakfast in that same coffee shop tomorrow, just in case there's a problem."

"That's fine Wally. I'll be sure to avoid recognizing you when I see you."

Arthur said, "Let's take everything we've heard this morning and see whether we can form a new picture of Martha Callahan and the status of Parkville Rehabilitation Home during the period of time when the four female patients died there. Irma, you've taken quite a few notes. Please start the conversation."

"It appears that this institution was in trouble. They didn't have enough funds to keep the staff happy or the equipment up-to-date. Martha Callahan blamed others on the staff for the problems, but didn't accept blame herself. She lashed out at personnel publically, but asked them to do special jobs for her personally and didn't pay them as promised. Finally, she introduced something unusual and questionable into the facility's paperwork. We don't yet know what that was, but we have a good chance of learning details from Debbie's future conversations with Noel Burnside."

Wally said, "That's a great summary, and it points directly toward Martha Callahan as the central figure in all of the problems there. We don't have any evidence connecting her to the murders, but she must know a lot more than she's told us. We got along well at our last meeting. I think I should be the one who returns the personnel files to her. I'll try to spend more time with her one-on-one."

Debbie stood and raised her hand like a police officer stopping traffic. "Hold it, Wally. You saw possible danger in my continuing to meet with Noel Burnside for breakfast, but the interview reports paint Martha Callahan as being potentially much more dangerous than Noel. You'll have to be very careful in dealing with her."

"Thanks for your concern, Debbie. I see Noel as a possibly dangerous individual. The biggest danger with Martha will be a hidden accomplice or a mastermind who is manipulating her."

CHAPTER 49 – MEMORIES

Dr. Rosemary Swinton looked up from her desk when she heard the knock on the open office door. Facing her was Michelle Caspar looking energized.

"Rosemary, I hope you don't mind my barging in without an appointment, but I remembered something else about Kurt, and it's wild."

"What do you mean by wild?"

"I remembered that when I was Kurt, I went to prison."

"Do you know for sure whether you were an inmate or a visitor?"

"I was an inmate for sure. I could feel the dread as I remembered the bars and the stark cells."

Dr. Swinton had started her tape recorder as soon as she saw Michelle, knowing from past interviews how quickly this young woman covered multiple events and topics.

"That's very intriguing, Michelle. Before you had this memory, did you think of Kurt as being good or evil?"

"I didn't think of him as being either one. I remembered him as being normal."

"Do you have any memories about the prison that might help us identify it?"

"It had a weird entrance."

"What was weird about it?"

"The door was in a castle tower, the kind with notches in the stonework at the top for archers to hide behind."

"Are you sure you're not thinking of a different time in history?"

Michelle sat down with a thump. "Don't make fun of me. I didn't say I remembered archers. I just meant that the entrance looked like the kind of castle tower they show in books and movies about old England and King Arthur's days."

"Was there a moat in front of the prison?"

"Of course not – the prison walls extended outward from the sides of this castle tower, without having any water in front of it. Digging out these memories is hard enough without you teasing me about them."

"I'm sorry, Michelle, but sometimes we react skeptically to such memories in order to see whether the subject changes his or her story or defends it. Your response indicates that you are certain of the details you gave me. That's very good."

"Then you do believe me."

"I believe that you feel that these recollections are factual. Do you know why Kurt was in prison?"

"For me, it's a breakthrough to remember that he was there. I know nothing about the why of it."

"That's fine, and certainly a step forward in exploring this case. We may have enough from you to try to investigate the prison and the retirement home. If we can locate them, then we will have a fair chance of finding a real identity for Kurt."

"Do you still doubt my memories?"

"I'm sure that they're very real to you. We have to be scientific and objective. We can't just assume the truth of your story. You remember only fragments, and some of those may not stand the test of the discovery process. For instance, if the individual in your prior life memories had a name other than Kurt, your recollections would be more difficult to confirm. We have to examine every detail."

"Are you going to send someone to investigate my prior life memory fragments, Rosemary?"

144

"We'll have a meeting to determine whether we have a suitable investigator and whether we will be able to afford the process. Why did you ask?"

"I know someone who is well-known for investigating unusual cases, and his background, combining both engineering and religion, might be perfect for obtaining an objective study of a subjective phenomenon."

CHAPTER 50 – WALLY AND MARTHA

The autumn chill encouraged Wally Sanborn and Martha Callahan to walk rapidly as they advanced along the Mallard Lake path.

"If you don't mind my saying it, you walk pretty well for an old retired guy, Wally."

"I'm not that much older than you are, and I'm certainly not ready to become a fixture at your rehab place. I'm surprised that you can keep up, after all that sitting and paperwork that you do."

"You are right in saying that sitting hurts your physical performance, but I make sure I keep moving around our facility, checking up on everything and everyone."

"That sounds as though you're insecure about the performance of Parkville Rehabilitation Home."

"Well, shouldn't I be, now that we're looking at the deaths of those four patients as having been suspicious?"

"Is that the whole story?"

"What do you mean?"

"Let's sit on this rock and talk for a while. You know that in the Army, I was a logistics type. I can't walk through any kind of facility without checking out its equipment and condition. When we visited you at your rehab place, I saw some aged instruments and minimized maintenance. That suggests deferred spending because of a shortage of funds. I'm not being critical, but I hate to see you stressed out about what's going on over there."

"Wally, those comments suggest you're taking a personal interest in me. That's very flattering, and no,

146

you're not disturbingly older than I am." She reached over and patted his hand.

Wally returned the compliment by holding her hand. "An institution like that requires continuous attention. I know you have staff to work with the patients and to do routine maintenance, but are you handling the management all by yourself? Do you have the people and the inclination to delegate responsibilities, or do you feel you have to do all the administrative work by yourself?"

"I certainly have to handle more of it since Noel Burnside left. His responsibilities were accounting and the insurance company interfaces, but I could ask him to cover many additional matters that would normally go to an assistant director. We could never afford such a person."

"So, you haven't had assistants to cover negotiations and meetings for you?"

"I've always had the choice of informally assigning someone capable, like Noel, to do things beyond his pay grade or giving a fancy title to someone who doesn't deserve it in lieu of a higher salary."

"Did you try to get Noel to change his mind about leaving?"

"I did, but he said he was leaving for personal reasons, and it had nothing to do with the way we worked together." Martha withdrew her hand from Wally's, stood, and adjusted her jacket. "We should get back to walking before our muscles get stiff. Before I took over management of the Rehabilitation Home, I was a physical therapist at a similar place."

"Good, I'll look for your guidance on exercise routines, and I'll also look forward to one of your massages."

CHAPTER 51 – ROSEMARY SWINTON

As Arthur and Irma passed by Shirley Hadley's office on the way to the pastor's study, Shirley extended her arm through the open doorway and waved a piece of paper in front of them. Arthur took it from her.

"I take it that Bishop Chandler is after me again. Am I supposed to call or visit him?"

Shirley shook her head. "No, Arthur, you have a more interesting summons. You're to call a Doctor Rosemary Swinton at the University of Virginia. She sounded very authoritative on the telephone. Watch out, Irma, he's getting long distance female attention."

Irma said, "I've seen this phenomenon before, Shirley, and I've learned to cope with it. Seriously, though, didn't I hear you say that the University of Virginia was Michelle Caspar's destination and that Jeremy caught up with her there?"

"You're right. I didn't connect that college's name with Jeremy's adventure. I wonder if Dr. Swinton's call has something to do with Michelle." Arthur looked more closely at the paper in his hand. "Instead of speculating, I think I'll call the magic number on the message note." He left Irma and Shirley and proceeded to the study. Once there, he closed the door and placed a pen and a pad of paper on the desk. Then he keyed the number into the telephone.

"Is this Dr. Swinton? I'm Pastor Arthur Blake, and I'm returning your call. How may I assist you?"

"Hello, Pastor; I'm calling at the suggestion of Michelle Caspar, who indicated that you enjoy investigating unusual events and circumstances."

Rosemary summarized the nature of her department's studies and their occasional use of outside investigators to seek confirmation of statements made by subjects claiming prior life memories.

After she finished, Arthur said, "I assume that Michelle has been one of your subjects, and that her memories are the ones you would like me to check out."

"You're correct, Pastor ..."

"Please call me Arthur, and if you don't mind, I'll call you Rosemary. Formality gets in the way of clear communication."

"Fine, Arthur – Michelle has some interesting fragment memories of a prior life. Before I get into the details, I'll need to know whether your religious training prejudices you against the possibility of reincarnation or multiple lives."

"Rosemary, my personal outlook is quite open to all aspects of life possibilities. My religious belief is that the soul is immortal. There is nothing in my training or religious viewpoint that speaks to the issue of whether that immortal soul might occupy multiple bodies. Is that impartial enough for you?"

"It certainly is, Arthur. I understand from Michelle that you also have engineering training."

"That's correct. Before I entered the seminary, I served as a NASA engineer on space mission preparation and monitoring. I can be objective and logical about what I do or don't find during an investigation. My wife, Irma, frequently works with me. She's a forensic pathologist and an equally logical person."

"You two must have some interesting arguments and discussions."

Arthur laughed. "We work pretty well together, and we're usually both on the same side in attacking a problem. If we're not, she usually has the final word in the discussion. Tell me more about yourself, Rosemary. What got you interested in the possibility of prior lives?"

"It all started with my father. After he retired, he would read everything he could find about people's concepts of life after death. I think he was determined to catch the train that led to immortality. Then, a short time before he died, he discovered some of the work here in the Division of Perceptual Studies concerning children who remembered living a prior life. Most of those children had memories that could not have been the result of their very limited earlier experiences. They were too young to have learned the information from external sources. Anyway, my father latched onto the concept that you study life after death by looking for an earlier life before your current life, and he hooked me into traveling that road with him."

"He must have quite an impact on your thinking for you to have made this study your profession."

"I'm looking forward to the day when I interview someone who has the memory of my father's life. Wouldn't that be something special?"

"It certainly would be the capstone of your father's studies. ... Tell me about your reactions to Michelle's experiencing prior life recollections as an adult."

"You hit on a key point. Such memories are very unusual, but we do have some documented cases of adults remembering that they had been someone else in a prior life. The significant aspect of Michelle's story is that she has isolated memories from points in a different life that range from childhood, all the way until that other person's death."

"I assume that you'll send me a synopsis of her memories to check out."

"Yes, Arthur, I'll send you a summary of them by email today. I'll also include our standard contract for investigations of interview results. I'm flexible, but I suggest that you avoid coming to see Michelle or us until you have obtained at least preliminary results on this case. Maintaining an arm's length relationship with the involved parties might increase the objectivity of your work. We would, of course, recommend getting together once you have either positive or negative results to discuss."

"That sounds like a valid research approach to me, Rosemary. I'll look forward to receiving your email."

Arthur returned to the church office. As he entered, the animated conversation between Shirley and Irma ceased. "Ladies, don't let me interrupt you. I'll come back later, after you finish your discussion."

Irma said, "Not on your life ... it's finished now. We're much more interested in what someone at a university wants from you."

"We have a new case to investigate, and it has to do with life after death."

"That sounds appropriate for me, but I'm convinced that everyone I've autopsied is still dead."

CHAPTER 52 – NOEL AND DEBBIE

Debbie Danforth returned for breakfast at Mandy's Coffee House, picked up her coffee along with a toasted bagel, and sat in the booth she had shared with Noel Burnside during their last encounter. She noted that, per his earlier promise, Wally Sanborn sat in a booth on the other side of the room wearing a baseball cap and a heavy flannel shirt. Her guardian was in position. Five minutes later, Noel entered, waved, and joined her after getting his coffee.

"This is only the second time we've met, Debbie, but it feels as though we're old friends."

"That does sound like a pick-up line, Noel, but I agree that I've looked forward to seeing you again. Have you applied for any new positions since we last talked?"

"No, I've saved a fair amount along the way, so I don't have to rush things. I have a feeling that my best option is to wait and see what comes up. I'm kind of a passive person. I believe that I won't do any better by beating the bushes looking for something, than I will just keeping my eyes open for an opportunity that heads my way. What's your outlook for the future, Debbie?"

"I tried the passive approach in looking for a boyfriend, and no one even noticed me. Now I've taken a more aggressive approach with much better success. Some guys may not like the woman to take the lead in their relationship, but most like her to at least meet them halfway, so that they don't have to do all of the courting."

"Wow, you said courting. That's a very old-fashioned term. I didn't think young people had even heard of that one."

"I still call my mother twice each week, so I guess that some of her language has rubbed off on me. Anyway, you know what I mean. I didn't get anywhere with men until I became a little more aggressive."

"Are you talking about men in the plural sense, or is there one particular individual involved?"

"You are shrewd, Noel. Yes, I'm finally making progress with one particular man. He didn't take me seriously until I pulled him into a romance of sorts. I'm still not sure how long it will last, but I'm taking it one step at a time."

"That's smart, let things develop gradually."

"Well, I've confided in you, Noel. Last time we met, you started to talk about some problems you had with the way they did business at that rehab place, but you said you wouldn't talk about it until you knew me better. Are we friends instead of strangers now?"

"I think we have turned the corner on friendship. I need to share my thoughts with someone anyway. You have to realize that when you exchange thoughts with another individual, you may pick up a burden or two."

"That's fine. I'll expect you to treat my comments on my love life as confidential also."

"I'll accept that obligation. My problem at the Rehabilitation Home was that several patients died there, including three special ones. In the cases of those three women, management had me add extra papers to the usual ones that the patients had to sign. The extra papers were applications for life insurance policies with the majority shareholder of Parkville Rehabilitation Home as the beneficiary. After they died, I had to ask myself whether I had contributed to their deaths by putting them in a position where someone benefited from their not getting well."

"That's a terrible development. I can see why you felt you had to leave. Did any patients who are still alive sign life insurance policies?"

"There wasn't anyone that I processed. I don't know whether they continued the insurance practice after I left."

"I sure hope they didn't, if executing a policy application meant signing your life away."

CHAPTER 53 – STATUS INQUIRY

In response to his secretary's intercom message, Bishop Howard Chandler lifted the telephone handset. "Hello, Arthur, this is a pleasant surprise. You're calling to report progress to me, without any prodding from this end. What do you have for me?"

"This isn't exactly a status report, although I can say that we are making progress toward determining who killed Rebecca Klingham. I'm actually calling to determine whether you have selected a replacement for Rebecca. I'll be going out of town for a few days in the near future, but I'll be back in time to give the sermon on the following Sunday. It would be helpful for my scheduling on other matters to know how many more Sundays will be my responsibility before the permanent replacement pastor arrives."

"I wish I had a definite answer for you, Arthur, but we have not yet made our selection. We're considering three candidates, two of whom would be available on short notice. The third would require a two-month period to wrap things up at her current church before she could transfer to Parkville. I suspect that we'll make our decision within two weeks and that the transition period will be two to six weeks after that before we complete the process. You're looking at four to eight weeks before your responsibility to the Parkville church will end, possibly slightly less. I hope that you'll have the criminal case resolved within that same period. That's the best estimate I can give you."

"Thanks, Howard, I can live with that. At least it will guide my planning efforts. It's too soon to know how long the criminal investigation will take, but we are making progress. I'll keep you informed."

"Where will you be when you're out of town?"

"Initially, I'll be in New York, but I may have to travel to Europe and Virginia during the next few weeks."

"Good luck with your efforts on both the local and distant matters." Howard replaced the telephone on its cradle and wondered to himself how Arthur could have ever been content to remain full-time at a single church.

CHAPTER 54 – KURT

As Irma and Arthur reviewed the documents Rosemary Swinton had sent, she shook her head. "I feel left out. I never had feelings of having lived another life either when I was a child or later on. Maybe that means that my memory center was underdeveloped or something. How about you, Arthur; did you feel reincarnated?"

"I didn't have memories of a prior life, but I did repeatedly have feelings of déjà vu because it felt as though I had been in many situations before, when they should have been new and unique. It was a little creepy."

"Did those feelings disappear at an early age?"

"They lasted until I was at least seven years old, perhaps even older. It's possible that I had other unusual memories when I was very young, because I don't remember much before I was four years old."

"From what Rosemary Swinton says in her notes, it's very unusual for Michelle to recall these prior life highlights at such an advanced age."

"She told me that it's unusual, but not unheard of."

"How do you want to approach our confirmation investigation?"

"I suggest we summarize Michelle's memories. Then let's try to confirm or invalidate those that we can check on the internet, without traveling. Then we'll see if there are others that might be checked by email or telephone, and finally, we'll do whatever traveling is required."

"I agree, with the exception that if we fail to find something close to believability on the easy internet items, we may want to cancel the more complex parts of the investigation. In addition, if we're going to be objective, we can't go into this research hoping to find confirmations of Michelle's memories. The fact that we're receiving payment for our investigation shouldn't increase our willingness to accept a memory fragment as true."

"We will be objective. Having agreed to that principle, I summarize Michelle's fragments of memories from a prior life as:

- The individual had been a male youth named Kurt in Austria during the Second World War.
- He had been a student in a school occupying part of a castle in Austria. This castle had high ceilings and thick walls.
- Kurt had been tall for his age and felt awkward when he had to dance with girls from a different school.
- He and other male students had buried their Hitler Youth uniforms and insignias so that approaching allied troops would not find such items in their possession.
- The burial spot had been close to an abandoned autobahn construction site.
- As an adult, he had a wife. Michelle was uncertain whether Kurt had children.
- When he was older, Kurt had a bad heart and went to live in an assisted living retirement home in New York State.
- The retirement home was near a big lake. The home's name may have included the word Destiny.
- Kurt arrived at the retirement residence by ambulance from his home.
- Kurt died as the result of someone pushing his wheelchair down a flight of stairs.
- As an adult, Kurt went to prison.

- You entered the prison through a doorway cut into something resembling a castle tower with square notches at the top.

Irma said, "That's quite a lot of information about this Kurt."

"That's what bothered Rosemary the most. She said it was much more information than they normally receive from a subject, and it covered an unusually long period of time."

Richard Davidson

CHAPTER 55 – SANDLEY AGENCY

Debbie paced back and forth in the apartment while Jeremy and Wally watched their furious associate from a safe distance.

"I should have thought things through before I finessed my first casual meeting with Noel Burnside. I thought I was being so cool in keeping him from knowing I was an investigator. Now we're friends and he's sharing confidential information. I can't tell him I'm someone other than a friend, and I can't ask him for more details without revealing my purpose in meeting with him. I like Noel, and I feel terrible about building a false friendship on fraud."

Wally tried to calm her. "Debbie, it's the nature of our business. If you're going to be a private detective, you're going to have to do undercover work. Your only problem is that you've formed an emotional connection to Noel. We're supposed to avoid that in order to remain objective and not get too close to someone who might have committed criminal acts."

Jeremy said, "Careful, Wally; you may be in the midst of a *do as I say, not as I do* experience. I sense an emotional connection developing between you and Martha Callahan."

"Point taken; I'll try to be more careful about that."

Debbie continued her pacing, nervously shaking her head so that her hair flipped upward. "I wanted to be in on the field action, but I didn't have enough training for it. How do you get away with befriending someone while picking his pocket at the same time? I'm not being a detective. I'm a confidence swindler."

Jeremy grabbed her shoulders as she turned around. "Go easy on yourself, Debbie; you're just learning how believable you can be when you play a part. If Noel is as innocent as you think he is, and as good a friend, he'll accept your explanation when you tell him why you pumped him for information. Wally or I could even explain the situation for you. If Noel isn't innocent, you shouldn't care about his feelings."

Debbie broke away from Jeremy's grasp. "That's the problem. He's the kind of person I could see as a family member or close friend, but he isn't innocent. He followed his superior's instructions without objecting. He did get three women to sign applications for life insurance policies benefiting the owners of the Parkville Rehabilitation Home."

Wally said, "I missed that when you mentioned it before. Three of the women who died had those fraudulent life insurance policies, but the fourth woman didn't. They weren't all in the same circumstances. We have to find which woman didn't have one of those policies."

"Wally, I realized that right away. That's why I've been upset. The problem is that I can't ask Noel to clarify his remarks and give me more details, because he thinks he's shared confidential information with a friend, not responded to an interrogation."

"You're saying that whether you or I tell him we're detectives, you'll lose Noel as a friend, and you don't want that to happen."

"Yes, and I also know that if I keep dealing with him on a friend basis, I won't be able to ask for the information that will aid our investigation."

Jeremy said, "Debbie, I think I know a way to ease, if not solve, your problem. You might not be completely happy with it though."

"Go ahead; you can't make me feel any worse."

"We'll just backtrack to the point where you weren't one of our investigators. I'll contact Noel as an investigator who's also your boyfriend. I'll indicate that you inadvertently said a few things to me about your conversation that made me want to ask him a few questions. Then I'll press him for the missing specific information. It would mean that you would have to admit divulging a couple of confidential items, and you would have to stay in the background on this case for a while, but you should be able to continue meeting with him on a friends basis, so long as you didn't get too cozy with him."

"Now you're getting jealous. He's too old for me, Jeremy, and I like what I see right here." She gave him a hug. "I think I can live with your approach."

Jeremy asked, "Does it work for you, Wally?"

"It does on two levels. We'll get the data we need without too many ruffled feathers, and it buys us time to get Debbie properly licensed as a private investigator. We skipped that step before she started meeting with her friend, Noel."

CHAPTER 56 – IRMA AND ARTHUR

Irma studied Arthur's demeanor as they prepared to tackle the computer search portion of their assignment related to Michelle Caspar's prior life memories. He appeared to be calm and looking forward to this challenge, even enthusiastic about it. She hoped that their differences in outlook would not cause friction between them.

"Arthur, before we get started, I have to tell you that I'm not nearly as willing as you to accept the concept of someone having had a prior life. I think we go through life once and only once. I'm not even sure I accept the Christian concept of the immortality of the soul. Does it bother you that we're not thinking alike about this assignment?"

"I don't see anything to be bothered about. We have different backgrounds and outlooks; so what?" All we're going to do in this case is to check out Michelle's memories, in order to determine whether they are logical possibilities and to see whether they allow us to identify a particular person to whom they apply. Dr. Swinton and her associates at the University of Virginia will be the people charged with deciding whether these memories reflect a prior life rather than some other influence."

"Then you haven't declared that you accept the concept of someone having had a prior life?"

"Oh, I accept that concept. It would be compatible with immortality of the soul, and it would be a neat way to look at the question of life after death. What I don't yet accept is a statement that the University of Virginia

163

studies have proved that some people have definitely had prior lives. If some have prior lives, why don't all of us?"

"Yet, you appear to be enthusiastic about this project."

"I am, in the sense of undertaking an interesting scientific experiment. It's no different from my being enthusiastic when I worked for NASA, about sending a rocket with an unmanned scientific probe to check out an asteroid or another planet. You hope you'll find something interesting, but you can't prejudge the results."

"In other words, you'll learn something, whether we confirm Michelle's memories or completely invalidate them."

"Yup, as long as we learn something, the effort is worthwhile."

Irma sat down at her computer. "You've satisfied me that you're interest isn't making you less objective. Fire up your computer, and let's launch this mission."

Arthur logged on to the internet. "Let's start with the youthful memories during World War II. We need to look for the castle that housed Kurt's school. It would be in Upper Austria; it would be near a village or town where they had the girls' school that took part in the dance, and it would be near a section of autobahn on which construction had started before 1944 and shut down because of the war."

"You're saying that Kurt and his friends buried their uniforms near the autobahn site, and it wouldn't be far from their castle school."

They became silent except for keyboard clicks until Irma stopped searching and started to print something she had found.

"Here's something. We may be talking about the West Autobahn, the A1, between Salzburg on the west and Vienna on the east. Here's what Wikipedia says about its history:

The construction of the first two sections near Salzburg started a few weeks after the Austrian Anschluss in 1938, as the Nazi authorities had long before set up plans for an eastern continuation of the Reichsautobahn from Munich to Salzburg (the present-day Bundesautobahn 8) towards Linz and Vienna in what was to become the German Ostmark. An 8 km (5.0 mi) long segment was opened to traffic, when works discontinued in 1941 due to World War II."

"That matches Michelle's memory if we can find a castle near the road construction. Because the A1 Autobahn connected to the A8 Autobahn from Munich to Salzburg, construction would have started from the west end by Salzburg. Your excerpt says that they completed five miles of the road by 1941 and then stopped construction. Therefore, the castle and burial site had to be more than five miles east of Salzburg."

"We don't have to pin it down."

"What do you mean, Irma?"

"We're only charged with determining whether Michelle Caspar's prior life memories are believable. No one should expect them to be perfectly accurate. As far as this youthful period is concerned, we can believe them if there are castles in the area near the A1 Autobahn and if one or more of these castles used part of their buildings as schools during World War II."

"I've already looked at the school aspect of things. The Nazis used castles as euthanasia gas chambers for the weak and mentally incapable, as schools, and as detention centers for VIPs from conquered countries. The school-in-castle memory is feasible."

"That being the case, I think we've eliminated justification for us to take a romantic trip to Austria. Next, we'll have to move on to checking out some of Michelle's adult memories. Those will require more than a computer search."

CHAPTER 57 – NOEL AND JEREMY

Noel sat in the booth at Mandy's, looking forward to eating and chatting with Debbie. She had become a habit for him after just a few of their morning sessions. She would have to be a platonic habit because of the significant difference between their ages, but he looked forward to an occasional fantasy involving her. Noel didn't see himself as a lover, but he craved closeness, a feeling that had been rare in his past.

As time passed, he could sense his stress level building. *Where is she? Has she turned her back on me and our morning get-togethers?* His eyes scanned the room and the doorway relentlessly. People entering on a regular basis, but she wasn't among them. Finally, he noticed someone approaching *their* booth, a tall, muscular young man he had never seen before.

"Are you Noel Burnside? Would you mind if I joined you?"

"I don't know you, and I'm expecting someone to join me any minute now. What do you want?"

"I'm Jeremy Hadley. Debbie Danforth won't be coming today, but I'd like to talk with you if I may. Debbie is my girlfriend."

Noel's voice reflected a rising sense of alarm. "I haven't been a threat to Debbie. We enjoy talking during breakfast, that's all."

"Please relax; I'm not a threat to you either. Debbie told me about your enjoyable mornings, and I wanted to meet you too. May I sit down?"

Noel gestured for Jeremy to sit. "Why didn't you bring Debbie with you?"

"She thought it would be better if she didn't come today. I think she was afraid you'd be angry with her."

"Why would I change my attitude toward her? I enjoy her company."

Jeremy tried to look relaxed, but he wasn't sure how his comments would affect Noel. "As I said, Debbie is my girlfriend. We're very open with each other, and she shared a few items from your conversation. She was a little worried that you would resent her doing so."

Noel's posture stiffened slightly. "What exactly did she share with you?"

"Before I get into that, let me tell you that I'm a private detective at the Sandley Agency. We're assisting the Parkville Police Department on a number of matters, one of which involves the deaths of four women at Parkville Rehabilitation Home while you worked there."

"Is Debbie a detective too? Did she meet with me to ask me questions?"

"Debbie was a library researcher at the University of Wisconsin in Madison when I met her, and I brought her to Parkville to be with me. She is not a detective, although she may become one in the future. According to Debbie's remarks to me, you accidently met here, and you shared some information with her in the course of conversation. She didn't ask you any questions."

Noel thought back to his sessions with Debbie. "I guess you're right. Debbie was just being a good listener. They're rare nowadays."

"May I tell her you're not angry with her, and that you'd like the breakfast meetings to continue?"

"I would appreciate your encouraging her to join me here again. We're still friends. Now, what did she tell you that led to your coming here this morning, and how may I assist your efforts? I always try to cooperate with the police and their agents."

Jeremy knew the critical moment had arrived. "Most of it was idle chit chat, but she did mention management asking you to have three of the deceased women sign life insurance applications along with their other legal papers. Without any question about the propriety of that process, I'd like you to tell me which three of the four deceased women were involved."

Noel thought for a few moments. "The three women who signed insurance applications were Janet Cuspin, Mary Welker, and Beverly Mandow. The insurance was probably meant to cover the patients' bills in case they died before making payment."

"Why didn't management ask Phyllis Landholm to sign a life insurance application?"

"She had already died before they put the insurance procedure into effect."

"And who was the beneficiary?"

"The payoff would go to the majority stockholder in the Rehabilitation Home."

"Who is that?"

"I don't know. It's a trust. Many wealthy people making investments use a trust arrangement so that they don't have to reveal their names and holdings."

"One final question, Noel: once they started the life insurance application procedure, did it apply to all patients? Did everyone have to sign applications?"

"No, I only remember getting signed applications from those three women, but I don't know what the practice has been since I left their employment."

"Jeremy stood. Thanks, Noel; I enjoyed meeting you. You've been very helpful."

"Will Debbie join me for breakfast tomorrow?"

"I'm sure she will."

CHAPTER 58 – COMPARING NOTES

They gathered in the conference room of the Parkville Police Department, Chief Bobby Andrews having called for a meeting to determine whether his unofficial associates had anything new to contribute to the current related investigations. Facing the Chief from seats around the table were Arthur, Irma, Wally, Jeremy, and Debbie.

Bobby thanked them all for coming and proceeded to the focus of the meeting. "We've had enough time pass since the parsonage meeting for you folks to give me feedback on whether this three-sided investigation plan is working. I'm accustomed to working informally with Arthur and Irma, but what have we gained by introducing the Sandley Agency? Have our private detectives discovered anything? Jeremy, you look enthusiastic and ready to burst with news. Why don't you speak for your group?"

"Chief, I think we have something that will demonstrate our worth. Your people researched the four patients who died at Parkville Rehabilitation Home. We looked at the staff members who had access to those patients, and especially the administrator plus three people who left the Rehabilitation Home shortly after the final death. We've come up with a motive for three of the killings plus evidence that one death differed from the others."

"So, Arthur, you may have scored again by suggesting we look for a killing that didn't match the others. Give us some details, Jeremy."

"The first death, that of Phyllis Landholm was unique. We don't yet have a motive or suspect for that one, but we think Rehabilitation Home management or ownership might be responsible for the other three killings."

Irma asked, "Why would they want to kill their own patients? That would reduce their income and taint their reputation."

Debbie tapped Jeremy on his hand, and he nodded for her to take over the narrative. "I became friends with Noel Burnside, who handled all the legal and other paperwork that the patients had to sign. He was one of the three staff members who left shortly after the last victim died. I learned from Noel that for the last three women who died, management had him include life insurance applications with the standard forms requiring signatures. The beneficiary on all of these policies was the trust that constitutes the majority shareholder of the Rehabilitation Home. We don't know what person or persons are hidden by that trust."

Wally said, "The general theme that came out of our interviews with the three employees who quit was that Parkville Rehabilitation Home was in financial trouble. They skimped on maintenance and new equipment and needed an injection of cash. The insurance payoffs on three women's deaths would have been very welcome."

Arthur tilted his chair back while he spoke. "So, you're suggesting that management or ownership at the Rehabilitation Home killed three patients to save the business. I wonder who killed the first victim, Phyllis Landholm. Management had no motive to kill her, in the absence of a beneficial life insurance policy. Do we have two different killers here?"

Bobby looked up from his notes. "Every time you speak, Arthur, the case gets more complex. Police like motives. My hat's off to the Sandley Agency. You've made significant progress in a short time. What do you have on the murder of Pastor Rebecca Klingham?"

Jeremy said, "We didn't specifically investigate that crime, Chief, but Joanna Diaz, a physical therapist who quit following the four Rehabilitation Home deaths, indicated that she had done physical therapy at the home of her former boss' cousin, and hadn't received payment for it. This could be a euphemism for attacking Pastor Klingham, but we have no proof of that. It might be worth a police follow-up."

"Is Diaz still in town?"

"I'm afraid not ... she went to Las Vegas."

"Let's skip that thought for now. We have budget problems. If and when she looks like a serious suspect, I'll have LVPD check her out."

Wally stood to get attention. "Martha Callahan, the Administrator at Parkville Rehabilitation Home, remains a puzzle for us. She has been very cooperative with our investigation, furnishing personnel files of the three employees who quit at the key time. She has also openly discussed skills and weaknesses of employees and the degree of access they had to the patients who died. Martha has virtually been an ad hoc member of our investigative team; yet we have to consider her the chief suspect.

"Martha has the intelligence and capabilities to create a scheme to have patients accidentally die. She would have been the one who instructed Noel Burnside to have patients sign life insurance applications. Her motive would be to save the facility from financial ruin. Yet, she acts as though she wants to focus on the dual goals of finding the killer and rescuing the institution's reputation. I don't know whether she's the devil or an angel."

Arthur said, "She may be both."

Everyone stared at Arthur, expecting him to continue speaking. After a long pause, Bobby Andrews smiled and said, "Would you like to explain that comment for the benefit of those of us who think conventionally?"

"My point is that the thing Martha loves most in life is the Parkville Rehabilitation Home. She may be the devil in that she would be willing to kill to save the institution, and she may be an angel because she would be equally willing to take the blame for someone else's treachery in order to protect the facility's reputation and keep it in business."

"How do we find out what she has actually done, rather than what she would be willing to do? I need evidence before I can make an arrest."

"Bobby, we're a long way from understanding these crimes and arresting anyone. I suggest that Wally should continue to befriend Martha Callahan and learn more about her relationships with others. We also need to focus on the murder of Phyllis Landholm, the one that doesn't fit the pattern, and look more closely at the murder of Pastor Rebecca Klingham."

"Fine, my police will concentrate on the Klingham murder. Let the Sandley Agency folks continue to work on Martha and the three similar killings at the Rehabilitation Home. Arthur and Irma should examine the details of Phyllis Landholm's death, because it was unique. Hopefully, we'll learn enough to make some sense out of these crimes and gather some real evidence."

CHAPTER 59 – PHYLLIS LANDHOLM

Arthur and Rex re-entered the parsonage after a long walk by Mallard Lake. Irma sat waiting for them at the dining room table. "Did you boys have a good walk?"

"I think Rex enjoyed it almost as much as I did. He kept pace with me while I jogged for a while, and he didn't drag me back or pull me forward. Fortunately, the ground was dry, so he's not muddy. You look satisfied with yourself; you must have accomplished something interesting while we were gone."

"I did. I called the Indiana Secretary of State's office. That's where Phyllis Landholm worked until she retired last year prior to having hip replacement surgery. That surgery landed her in the Parkville Rehabilitation Home after she moved here to live near her younger brother. I picked up some interesting information."

Arthur let Rex off his leash and rubbed the dog's belly after the golden retriever rolled onto his back.

"Are you going to share your findings with me?"

"I might, if you cook supper tonight."

"It's a deal, but you'll have to agree to mock seafood casserole, using those imitation crab legs we have in the refrigerator."

"That will work for me. I learned that Phyllis Landholm had been the lead attorney in the Business Services Division of the Indiana Secretary of State's office. Her specialty was tracking down cases of fraud and prosecuting them. That background would make her dangerous to anyone around her who had done something illegal. The people in Indiana said Phyllis had a reputation for being able to detect even a slight hint of fraud. That suggests a motive for someone wanting to kill her."

"I agree. To some people she would have been a threat. That reminds me of one other thing I saw in her file that bothered me."

"What's that?"

"Her expected stay in the rehab facility after hip replacement surgery was five to fourteen days. Why would someone want to kill her there instead of waiting until she left and went home, where there wouldn't be any witnesses?"

"That's a great question, Arthur. I have three possible answers."

"Show your brilliance, Irma. What are they?"

"First, Phyllis represented an immediate threat, so she had to be eliminated before she could alert someone else to a problem or crime."

"That's a logical possibility."

"Second, she was a threat to someone on the staff of the Rehabilitation Home, so that they had to kill her before she left the facility and got out of reach."

"That's reasonable."

"Third, she was a threat to another patient, who couldn't let her get away from him or her."

"That's the most interesting possibility, because the police would not be likely to suspect another patient. It would have to be a patient who would remain at the Rehabilitation Home for longer-term care, rather than one who would be free to leave around the same time as Phyllis Landholm."

"Now, all we have to do is figure out which was the real reason for killing her there."

Richard Davidson

CHAPTER 60 – NEW YORK STATE

Irma delivered a mug of coffee to her seated husband and then began to massage his back and the nape of his neck.

"Keep that up, Irma; I'm enjoying the rub and the delivery of coffee. Does this mean you want a favor or something?"

"No, I'm just softening you up for the realization that you're working on multiple cases again. You were unhappy about people expecting too much from you a while ago. Now that you're committed to personally working on the Rehabilitation Home killings, the Pastor Klingham murder, and examination of Michelle Caspar's prior life memories all at the same time. Are you upset or energized?"

"I hadn't given it much thought, but I'd have to come down on the *energized* side of the coin. I'll attribute my earlier nightmares to formless fears that arose when there was nothing concrete to occupy my mind. Now that we have specific mysteries to tackle and approaches we plan to take, I feel much better."

"I'm glad you kept saying *we* during that response. We are a team. This part of said team suggests that we need to turn our focus back to Michelle's enigma. We either confirmed or failed to invalidate Michelle's prior life memories of youthful events in Upper Austria. Now I think it's time for us to look at some of her adult memories. Do you agree?"

"I do, and I find those recollections particularly intriguing, especially the memory of having been in prison."

"We don't have enough information for a time line. The prison sentence must fall somewhere between the end of World War II as a youth and death in a New York State nursing home. The war ended in 1945, when Kurt might have been twelve or fourteen years old. Let's split those numbers and say he was thirteen then. If we guess that he went into the nursing home with his heart condition at the typical retirement age of sixty-five, that would have been fifty-two years after the end of the war, or 1997."

"He may have been a little older, but that's fine for brainstorming purposes. The point that I have trouble wrapping my mind around is that Kurt was still alive during Michelle's lifetime. She's now twenty-seven years old, which means that she was at least nine years old when Kurt went into that nursing home. I'm assuming his age to have been sixty-five at that time. He wasn't exactly a prior life for her. His life essence could enter her consciousness only recently because Kurt and Michelle were both alive when she was a child, or perhaps even a teenager."

"Are you suggesting that Kurt's memories come from his ghost?"

"I don't believe in ghosts, but we would have to conclude that two different immortal souls are currently communicating within Michelle Caspar's body."

"Now that's a spooky concept!"

"Getting back to Michelle's memory of Kurt having spent time in prison, I suggest that if Kurt lived in New York State and the nursing home was there also, he probably went to a prison in that state."

"It would be very easy to argue with your logic on that one, but I'll go along with it because it gives us an easy place to start. I'll dredge up pictures of the entrances of all the New York prisons to see whether any of them resemble the one that Michelle remembered."

"That's a good approach."

"Your job will be to figure out how we proceed after I locate the prison. The name Kurt may be inaccurate or an alias. How do we find out his identity and the data on when and why he went to prison?"

CHAPTER 61 – MARTHA CALLAHAN

Martha exited the cafeteria kitchen and continued her daily informal inspection of all the Parkville Rehabilitation Home departments. She watched several patients in the midst of their three hours of physical therapy. Then she toured the private patient rooms, and headed for the common areas, where patients chatted, watched television, and played cards. She was always cheerful and called every patient by name. This was her institution, and it would long survive those four women's deaths. She was confident that the investigations would show her administrative staff to be free of guilt in those events. As long as she maintained an efficient staff and proper operational procedures, she would have nothing to fear.

Martha had enjoyed exchanging opinions and data with the people from that Sandley Agency. Those folks wouldn't taint patient attitudes toward her and the other staff members the way uniformed police would. She especially enjoyed spending time with Wally Sanborn, although he had seemed less open to revealing his thoughts during their last meeting. She hoped Wally didn't consider her a suspect. That development would decrease her chances of building a romantic relationship with him. The next time they talked or met, she would discuss her theory that visitors, or persons pretending to be visitors, had murdered those four women. If finances ever improved, she would hire a full-time security guard to screen visitors as they arrived and left.

As she continued her inspection, Martha signaled three therapy aides to join her in one of the empty patient rooms. There, she gently chided them for standing in a corner gossiping and laughing at each other's jokes. She told them that appearances have an effect on patient morale, and suggested that they take a coffee break in the cafeteria or replenish supplies between assignments.

The final stop on her tour was the maintenance area. She knew that Ben Hendry, the new technician was a disorganized person, but she hadn't expected to find such a mess. All of his tools lay in a jumbled pile on the workbench, except for one saw that was in its proper position on the pegboard above the bench. Ben had left the doors of the steel broom cabinet door open, and all the brooms and mops lay on the floor in front of it looking like a game of Pick-Up Sticks. Even the shop vacuum sat in a corner with its power cord extended where someone could trip on it. She wondered when Ben had last used the vacuum. Its suction hose was missing, rendering it useless. Martha made a note to schedule a work evaluation meeting with Ben on a high priority basis. Then she returned to her office.

CHAPTER 62 – BREAKFAST WITH NOEL

Debbie wasn't at all convinced that Noel Burnside would enjoy her presence at Mandy's for breakfast. After all, Jeremy had used his detective persona to extract key bits of information from Noel. Jeremy had said that Noel wanted to continue to breakfast with her, but she feared that there wouldn't be the same atmosphere as in past meetings.

As she entered the shop and ordered her sweet roll and coffee, Debbie eyed *their* booth. It was empty. Perhaps Noel had decided to eat elsewhere, despite his comments to Jeremy. She took her breakfast to the booth and sat back to ponder the day's schedule. As she did, she saw Noel emerge from the restroom. He actually looked happy to see her. He approached, smiled at her, and sat down.

"I'm so glad you decided to come. Jeremy said that you would, but I wasn't sure."

"I wasn't convinced you'd be here either, after your questioning session with him."

"Actually, I felt better, not worse, after that meeting. My guilty thoughts about forcing insurance applications on patients disappeared after I told Jeremy about that procedure. Once something's out in the open, it can't cause as much trouble. Now someone with authority will be able to examine the facts about the insurance. May I get you something else to eat; you don't have very much."

"This will be enough for me, Noel. I have to leave soon for an appointment, but I wanted to be sure we were still friends who would continue to meet for occasional breakfasts."

"We are definitely friends, and I appreciate the fact that you have a life beyond breakfasting here with me. Jeremy appears to be a good match for you."

"Thanks, I think so too. Now that we can speak openly with each other, I'd like to know your opinion of Martha Callahan."

"She's a puzzle, isn't she? The problem is that there are, in effect, two Marthas."

"What do you mean?"

"One Martha is completely dedicated to Parkville Rehabilitation Home, and she'll do whatever it takes to keep it running and successful. The other Martha, when she manages to relax and be an individual instead of an institutional manager, is sweet and creative. It's almost as though that career that's so important to her, is likely to end up destroying her individuality and potential. She needs love. It's the only development that might save her."

"Are you volunteering for that job?"

"Martha would never look at me for love. She craves more charisma than I could offer. I'm thinking of exchanging this town for a warm place and becoming a schoolteacher. It's time for me to reinvent myself and become less boring."

"I don't find you boring."

"You would if we kept this routine going for a long time. You've kindled a spark in me, and I know it will only flare up if I move on to something new. I'll stick around until I'm free of suspicion that I did something bad at the Rehabilitation Home, but then I'll head for greener pastures. My life needs a new outlook, and I think I'll succeed at achieving that."

"Are you saying that our breakfast meetings are ending?"

"They are, and they should. I have my new hopes for the future, and you have Jeremy. Don't let him get away; I think he'll be good for you. If you have a specific reason

Impulses

for our doing the breakfast thing again, of course I'll be here for you, but we're both strong enough to move ahead to other challenges."

Noel half rose, leaned across the table, and kissed Debbie on the cheek. Then he winked at her and left Mandy's for the last time.

CHAPTER 63 – POLICE WORK

Detectives Gene Murphy and Hank Robbins sat facing Bobby across his desk. He had called them in because he knew it was time for a pep talk.

"We did some sloppy work when we accepted Pastor Klingham's death as being a suicide instead of checking out the details. You two did much better when you collected all of the data on the four women patients who died at Parkville Rehabilitation Home. We have to be sure to check for details in every aspect of our investigation, because successful solutions and court convictions depend on seeing things that other folks miss."

Gene said, "That's how Arthur and Irma Blake sometimes outsleuth us on some cases. They see things that we miss, Chief."

"Part of that is their approaching each investigation from a different direction than we do. They're less constrained by formal procedures. Nevertheless, you're receiving my message, Gene. We need to look at the fine points of each situation and crime scene. How about you, Hank? Do you have any comments about gathering evidence?"

"I completely endorse what you're saying, Bobby. That's why the last time I visited that rehab place, I acted as though I was a visitor and stayed in the background, listening in on other people's conversations. Nobody thought I was anyone official. Surprisingly, you don't have to sign in and declare that you're seeing a particular patient at that place. You can just walk in, and if you look like you know what you're doing, no one bothers you. It turns out that they have a chapel there on the other side of a wide arch in the corner of the main lobby sitting room."

"What's interesting about the chapel?"

"For one thing, both visitors and staff members are free to visit it. For another, they have a basket, where they invite you to leave a written prayer in an envelope."

Gene said, "That's a little different, but creative."

"What's even more creative is the fact that while I was standing in the background, I saw several visitors put envelopes into the basket. Two deposited green envelopes in there, and two contributed white ones."

Bobby said, "That's not unusual, so far."

"How about the fact that a staff member – I think she was a physical therapist – visited the chapel after a while and removed the two green envelopes? Twenty minutes later, she returned and put two pink envelopes into the basket."

Bobby stood up. "Arthur likes to amaze us with his breakthroughs that appear to be magic. I'll do one of my own. I'll read your mind, Hank. You're about to say that after another interval, the two visitors who left the green envelopes returned and took the pink envelopes out of the chapel basket and then left the rehab facility. Am I correct?"

"That you are, Bobby. I followed their car to the corner of Tilsby and Magnus Streets, where they stopped and passed something out the car window to a man who walked away with it."

"Were you able to see where he went?"

"I'm afraid not, Bobby; he cut down a narrow alley between two stores. I couldn't drive into it, and I knew that if I found a place to park and then followed him, it would be too late. I did get the license number of the car driven by the couriers."

"Don't worry about losing the walker, Hank. You've clarified a major aspect of this case by noting the details of what was going on. I'm beginning to understand now."

Gene said, "Would anyone like to enlighten me? You two are just confusing me. How about it, Chief?"

"Hank has done some good police work. It appears that, instead of prayer requests, those visitors deposited money in those green envelopes. The staff member exchanged the green envelopes for pink ones that probably contained drugs. The so-called visitors then acted as couriers, delivering the drugs to a street dealer. This throws a whole new perspective on the case."

"What's that?"

"Remember that Pastor Rebecca Klingham had overcome a drug habit in her past. If she had visited the chapel and examined the prayer request envelopes, she would have realized their significance. Rebecca wasn't the consulting chaplain that the Rehabilitation Home called in to perform religious services, but during patient visits she probably became curious about the prayers that people requested there."

Gene asked, "How does that change the case?"

"We had expected to find that someone killed Pastor Klingham to make it look as though she had been responsible for the four patient deaths. We now have a second possibility. Someone may have killed her because she knew about drug dealing at Parkville Rehabilitation Home."

CHAPTER 64 – BISHOP CHANDLER

Irma Blake had spent most of the morning playing with Rex in the parsonage back yard. Upon coming back inside, she gave Rex fresh water and a couple of dog treats. The telephone rang. Irma wiped her face and hands with a towel and then lifted the portable phone from its cradle.

"You've reached the parsonage; Irma Blake speaking."

"Hello, Irma, it's Howard Chandler. Is Arthur there?"

"Good morning, Howard ... I'm afraid Arthur is out visiting church members. May I take a message for him?"

"It's good to hear that he's actually taking care of pastoral duties for a change, instead of playing detective."

"If you'll check with Shirley at the Church, Howard, I think you'll find that many of our members are happier to have counseling sessions with Arthur than they were with Rebecca Klingham. It's a question of their willingness to share personal information with someone they trust."

"Well, those individuals are going to have another transition to make. I called to inform Arthur that he's off the hook for tending to the Parkville church. We've appointed a new full-time pastor. Her name is Marianne Rendley, and she comes to us from Detroit. She has a background in missionary work and is about five years from retirement."

"Marianne sounds very interesting, Howard. Arthur will give her whatever assistance he can."

"Then you won't be leaving the area right away? I had the impression that you might be traveling in connection with a case."

"We may have to make brief trips, but we'll stay local until we clear up the matters of Pastor Klingham's death and the murders of the four church members at Parkville Rehabilitation Home."

"Then, those definitely were murders?"

"I'm afraid so, Howard. All five of those deaths were murders."

"I hope you and the police solve them soon. It's time for our members to get away from thoughts of death."

"Amen to that thought, but we have to play the hand that God deals us."

"I wish you had phrased that differently, Irma. You know our church has taken a strong position against gambling."

"If it appeals to you more, I'll use that other saying; we have to bloom where we're planted."

"That's much better. Pastor Rendley will be arriving in a few days. I'm sure Arthur and you will want to meet with her and help her get settled."

"We'll do that, Howard. Thank you for calling."

After she disconnected, Irma mentally shook her head at the way Bishop Chandler needed to make the real world sound like the version he would prefer."

CHAPTER 65 – PRISONS

When Arthur returned to the parsonage after his counseling visits, Irma informed him about the call from Bishop Chandler and the pending arrival of Pastor Marianne Rendley.

"The new pastor's appointment means that we'll have to go back home to Amboy and commute for the balance of the investigations in Parkville."

"That shouldn't be a problem, Irma. We selected our Amboy house with the idea of being close enough to visit our friends here. It also means that I'll be free to visit New York State and check on that prison that Michelle remembered as associated with her Austrian persona."

"I knew there was something I forgot to tell you, Arthur. I did some online research to check on a prison in New York State with a castle-like entrance."

"Did you find one?"

"Not exactly – I found three. Apparently, New York prison architects in past centuries liked to design prisons that looked like castles. They're both old and old looking. One of them actually dates back to 1816."

"What prisons are they, and where are they located?"

"I came up with Attica Correctional Facility in Attica, New York; Auburn State Prison in Auburn, New York; and Ulster Correctional Facility in Napanoch, New York. I saw a second reference to the Auburn institution listed as the Auburn Correctional Facility. Apparently, correctional facility is the modern euphemism for a state prison. The old term must have fallen out of favor."

"Isn't Attica the place where they had a prisoner rebellion some years back?"

"It is. My notes say that it happened in 1971, with thirty-three inmates and ten staffers killed before the state police regained control of the place."

"If Attica is the prison Michelle remembers, would Kurt have been there that long ago?"

"It's possible. We guessed that Kurt would have been thirteen years old at the end of World War II in 1945. That means that he would have been thirty-nine years old when the Attica Prison riot occurred. That would put him there at an age when he was in good physical condition."

"That would also put him there before Michelle's birth. I'm still bothered about her remembering someone who was alive during part of her life. I'm new to paranormal things, so I don't know the ground rules."

"Arthur, there are no ground rules. That's why we call all these strange happenings paranormal. All the academics can do is study memories and testimonies using scientific techniques, and then try to confirm and interpret their data."

"We still don't know which prison is the one in her memory, assuming that Kurt is real and these things actually happened. I'll arrange a meeting with the New York State Correctional Services people and fly out there to check their records. We have only Kurt's first name, his approximate age, and his unusual height as factors that might lead to his identification. I'm not overly confident that we'll find him, but I'm cautiously optimistic, as they say."

CHAPTER 66 – NEW VIEWPOINTS

Debbie answered the phone with her sophisticated voice. "Good morning; you've reached the Sandley Agency. Miss Danforth speaking; how may I assist you?"

Wally responded, "That sounded great, Debbie, and you may indeed assist me. I have a job that begs for the use of your skill set. Take notes as I outline your mission."

When Jeremy returned from the police department after meeting with Bobby Andrews, he found Debbie working with two laptop computers and a large pad of paper. As he watched, she held straightedges up against information on the two display screens and then wrote something on the pad.

"You appear to have a project working."

"It's not just a project; it's a mission assigned by Wally, and I'm hoping it will reveal something that will change the way we look at this case."

"It's funny that you used that phrase. Bobby Andrews said the same words when I met with him a short while ago to learn what the police have learned recently. He was right too. They've come up with something to change our perspective."

"What is it?"

"If you don't mind, I'll save the details for our meeting this afternoon with Wally. What's he pursuing ... do you know?"

"Wally is having a brunch meeting with Martha Callahan to make her feel included in our inquiry and to clarify his own thinking as to whether Martha is on the side of the angels or the demons."

"She is in the center of our puzzle, but doesn't fit into an obvious gap in our picture of what happened. I wish him luck at coming to a conclusion about her. What exactly are you studying?"

"You'll receive details at our meeting, assuming I have some results by then. For now, I'll just say that I'm online with Google Search and tapped into the database at the University of Wisconsin libraries at the same time." Debbie stood and kissed Jeremy, but then she sat again and returned to her research work."

Jeremy took the hint. He went out into the kitchen to get coffee and left Debbie to do her work undisturbed.

Martha Callahan touched Wally Sanborn's arm as he prepared to sit in the restaurant booth. "Sit next to me instead of taking the other bench. We won't have to talk as loudly if we're on the same side."

Wally wondered whether Martha was thinking confidentiality or romance. "That's fine, Martha, but I'll expect you to be completely candid in what we discuss."

Once they had given the server their orders, Martha said, "Your request for me to be frank is more than acceptable, Wally. I need someone to be my friend and let me share some of my stressful thoughts. Can that someone be you?"

"I want to be your friend, but you know that our group is investigating the deaths at the Rehabilitation Home. You'll have to realize that I may have to tell my colleagues things you reveal to me."

"I can live with that. I honestly don't believe that I have done anything improper. I want the Rehabilitation Home to survive and prosper, but not at the expense of constant rumors and innuendos. I'll answer all of your questions, and I'll share my thoughts on unrelated topics too."

They halted their conversation while the server placed their food and drinks on the table.

"I need to know one thing, Martha, before I'll be able to fully trust and share with you."

"Go ahead. I'll answer any question."

"Who is your boss, the person who was the beneficiary of those life insurance policies?"

"I don't know the answer to that question. The lawyer who hired me, Quentin Edwards, represents a trust that owns the majority of the stock in Parkville Rehabilitation Home. On several occasions, I've asked him who is behind the trust, but he tells me that he can't give me that information because of the attorney/client relationship."

"Who sets policies and gives you your working instructions?"

"Everything comes in writing or by telephone from Quentin Edwards, acting for the trust. To save you questions, I'll tell you that my instructions about the life insurance application forms came as text messages from him, and no, I didn't check whether the messages came from his phone. I've even changed my cell phone since then so I have no record of them. I assumed that the insurance was a precaution against patients failing to pay their bills. Banks do that when people take out mortgages."

"There's a difference here from the bank procedure. Banks pay the premiums out of the loan payments. The Rehabilitation Home would have to commit to pay the premiums for former patients, although they might find some way to include the insurance costs in bills for current patients and for those paying off their balances through monthly payments. Weren't you surprised that they applied the insurance requirement to only three people?"

"I was surprised, but I suspected that the trust had determined that those were the patients with the greatest financial risk for us. The lawyer, Edwards, and the trust process all of the credit paperwork. My administration job involves operations, not finance."

"Don't take this the wrong way, Martha, but either you are part of the problem, or you're very lacking in curiosity about things going on around you."

"Wally, you were a career Army man. Did you know or even want to know everything about how the Army operates? I had more responsibility than my salary justified, and no spare time beyond that required for my regular duties. I was willing to let others in a large organization assume their own shares of responsibility, so that I wouldn't get in over my head. There was and continues to be a limit to my capabilities. That's why I need to share some of my stress with you."

He patted her hand. "I understand, and I'll support your position so long as I don't run into any facts that contradict what you tell me. We have to build trust. It doesn't happen in an instant."

She slid closer to him while they finished their brunch.

CHAPTER 67 – SANDLEY MEETING

When Wally arrived at Jeremy and Debbie's apartment for the Sandley Agency meeting, he found Arthur chatting with the others.

"Hi, Arthur, I didn't expect to see you here, but I'm glad you could make it. We'll bring you up to date on everything we've discovered so far."

"That's why I came. I'll be flying out to New York on a different case, and I wanted to see whether I could contribute anything helpful before I left."

"That's the theory behind using our agency to assist you – handling more than one case at a time."

"There may end up being a difference between theory and practice, Wally. I think that you three are working so well together that you'll find yourselves pursuing some investigations without any input from Irma or me."

Jeremy said, "Thanks for the compliment, Arthur. We'll use it as our cue to start the meeting. Everyone gather up your papers and refreshments, and head for our new dining room table. As host, I'll kick things off once we're settled."

Arthur grabbed a mug of coffee and sat down with it, watching the others assemble their notes and materials for the meeting. *So far, they appear to work well together. I'll guess that Debbie and Jeremy's relationship will benefit from joint efforts on these projects. The ongoing question will be whether Wally will eventually lose interest in continuing this arrangement.*

Once they had all settled at the table, Jeremy said, "This will be a special meeting because we have each worked on a different area of information gathering, and we'll now present our individual findings and try to improve our overall picture of the crimes we are studying. Debbie, please report on your research which, I understand, was an assignment from Wally."

Wally interrupted. "Before she does that, and in deference to our guest, I'll have to state that I made that assignment at Arthur's request."

They all looked at Arthur. "Yes, I instigated the request for additional research on the backgrounds of the four women who died at Parkville Rehabilitation Home. I did so because I'm sure that we are looking for more than one killer. In terms that they used on the Sesame Street children's television show, 'One of these killings was not like the others.' That also makes me wonder whether the murder of Pastor Rebecca Klingham was really an attempt to convince people that she had confessed her guilt in the killings of the four patients and committed suicide. That theory becomes questionable if we believe that more than one person was responsible for the four patient deaths."

Jeremy stared at Arthur. "In the past, I've heard Chief Andrews talk about the magic tricks you play during investigations. You've just done another one of them. I'm getting away from my planned presentation sequence, but I was going to startle you all by reporting that the Parkville Police have suggested that Pastor Klingham's murder may have had nothing to do with the four dead patients. They think someone may have murdered Rebecca Klingham because she had detected a drug ring operating out of the Rehabilitation Home." He summarized the story of drug transactions in the chapel and the passing of those drugs to street dealers.

Arthur said, "I won't take a bow. I suspected a different person killed Rebecca, but I didn't have any theory as to his or her motive or identity. The Parkville Police deserve all the credit. Detective Hank Robbins observed and tracked the drug purchases, and Chief

Andrews reasoned that Rebecca Klingham died because, as a past user, she knew how to spot drug deals. Just remember that the drug-related motive is only an alternate theory. We have not yet disposed of the theory that someone killed Pastor Klingham to make her death look like a confession to murdering the women from her church."

Wally said, "The police tracked the couriers to the street dealers, but we have to look at the other end of this drug chain. Who on the staff of the Rehabilitation Home is behind it?"

Arthur refilled his coffee mug. "We may have to go undercover to figure that one out. Hank Robbins may be able to identify the staff member who exchanged the colored envelopes in the prayer basket, but someone is going to have to get her to tell us how she received her drug supplies, and we'll have to get that information before the police arrest the couriers and street dealers, putting the operation out of business. If Hank identifies the inside person as a physical therapist, one of us may have to show up as a therapy outpatient to talk with her. That sounds like a job for Wally."

"My shoulder has been a little stiff lately. My news is that Martha Callahan, the administrator, and I have become friends, so I'm sure I'll be able to have her set me up as an outpatient. I see her as a staff person who's too busy to look around and see the bad things that are happening in the Rehabilitation Home. I'm watching for signs that she is one of the bad people, but so far, her explanations ring true. Martha told me more about the trust that hides the ownership of the organization. She gets her instructions from the lawyer who is the front man for that trust. He won't identify the trust principal. Maybe someone official, like the police, could discover the identity of the trust person or people. Would you request that, Jeremy?"

"I'll do that. I'm becoming our liaison with the Parkville Police anyway. I also agree that we should identify the Rehabilitation Home people in the drug ring before we go after the street dealers."

Debbie slapped the top of the table. "I've been very patient so far, but it's time for me to demand some attention. In case you forgot, Jeremy started this meeting by saying that I'd present my research results first. Since that moment, I haven't been able to get one word into this conversation. It's been useful and interesting up to now, but tangential to the original agenda. May I please speak, as previously announced?"

Jeremy said, "Sure, Debbie, the floor is yours. We apologize for getting carried away by new developments."

"Your apology is accepted. My assignment from Arthur via Wally was to examine the backgrounds of the four women who died at Parkville Rehabilitation Home."

Jeremy asked, "When you tackled this research, did you know that Arthur had originated the request?"

"No, I didn't, but that wouldn't have affected my results. If you'll stop interrupting, I'll tell you what I found."

"Go ahead."

"Thank you. Now, I'm going to summarize my findings for each woman in the sequence in which they died. You may ask questions or make comments following each summary. Pay attention, because I believe we're trying to identify the profile of a potential killer, maybe more than one."

Arthur nodded his agreement.

"Phyllis Landholm was the first to be killed. Landholm's killer tried to make her death appear to be an accident by entangling her in the bedclothes. My guess is that the killer smothered Phyllis with a pillow, and then staged the tangled bedding scene. Phyllis was retired, but had worked for the Indiana Secretary of State in the

Business Services Division, where she investigated business fraud cases. She never married, but had several multi-year live-in relationships with men who all worked in some phase of law enforcement. She had a younger brother who lived in Parkville until one month before her death, when he moved to Omaha to start a retirement project as a railroad historian. She was at Parkville Rehabilitation Home to regain her strength and flexibility after hip replacement surgery at Parkville Care Center. She was seventy-seven years old and had been a member of Parkville United Methodist Church for six months."

Arthur said, "Phyllis joined our church after I went to work investigating Conference problems for Bishop Chandler. Because of that timing, I didn't know her, but she sounds like a straight shooter, even though she didn't conform to church teachings about marriage and cohabitation. You would have known her at the church, Wally. What's your impression?"

"I did know Phyllis, and she made an impression when she entered a crowded room. She was tall, thin, and walked ramrod straight. I don't think there were many at church who knew her work background. Despite her age, no one thought of her as being old. She could hold her own in any debate and had a contagious laugh."

"Phyllis obviously made a strong impression on you, Wally."

"She did, and she would have appeared to be a threat to anyone at the Rehabilitation Home who had something to hide. Phyllis probably died because her killer was afraid of her."

Debbie resumed her research report. "The second female patient to die the Rehabilitation Home was Janet Cuspin. She was recuperating from back surgery at Parkville Care Center. Janet had been an office worker in the old Illinois Bell Telephone Company. Her highest position had been manager of a small department. Janet

was a widow with no children. Her deceased husband had
been a history professor at Northern Illinois University.
She, like Phyllis Landholm, was in the Rehabilitation
Hospital section of the Rehabilitation Home, meaning that
she would have a short stay there."

Jeremy said, "That means that Janet Cuspin could
not have killed Phyllis Landholm, because they were both
in for a short period and were not up to full strength or
body movement capability."

Debbie stared at him. "That's interesting. You're
saying that it's likely that one of the other patients killed
Phyllis Landholm. Why assume a patient instead of a staff
member did it?"

"I didn't think I said that; I just eliminated one
person."

Arthur said, "You may not have looked consciously at
the other patients as potential killers, but it's a good
insight to include them as suspects." He winked at Irma
because of their similar previous conversation. "What else
can we say about Janet Cuspin? Was she a threat to
anyone?"

Wally said, "She certainly wasn't an obvious one. If
Janet attended a meeting with a bunch of other people,
very few would remember that she had been there. She
was extremely quiet and faded into the woodwork in
people's memories. I knew her for three years at church,
but the bulk of Debbie's summary is news to me."

Debbie continued. "I failed to add that Janet died from
an electrical shock received from a faulty vital signs
monitor."

Arthur said, "Janet was the second woman to die at
the Rehabilitation Home. Again, it appeared to be an
accident, but her death was different from Landholm's,
because Janet had signed the life insurance papers. The
beneficiary had a motive to kill her, even if no one else
did."

Wally said, "Right; Phyllis Landholm's death was the unique one. As such, we should examine it closely."

Debbie hastened to keep the discussion from again heading off-course. She picked up a new sheet of notes. "The third woman to die there was Mary Welker. She was younger than the first two victims, at sixty-eight years old. Despite her relative youth, she had been a member of the Parkville church for the longest time, twenty-eight years. Mary had been a performer on Broadway, appearing in *This Was Burlesque* in 1970 and *The Pajama Game* in 1973. In 1980, Mary was divorced from her husband who was a jazz musician. I'll keep searching, but so far, I haven't discovered his name. Mary was in the Sub-Acute Program at the Rehabilitation Home, meaning that she would receive longer-term treatment after suffering a minor heart attack. Her emergency treatment following that attack took place at Rochelle Community Hospital. Mary died from drinking grapefruit juice with or shortly after her heart medications. Grapefruit juice causes the body to absorb some drugs more rapidly, effectively increasing their dosage beyond safe limits. It's also possible that her killer assured the juice reaction by giving her a higher dose than normal of the medication. We'll never know for sure."

Wally said, "I liked Mary. A Broadway dancing career ends when you get a few years behind you, but she moved to Parkville and helped with our church plays and musicals for many years. She kept herself in shape and could make moves that most younger people couldn't."

Debbie gestured for attention and continued her summary. "The last of the four victims was Beverly Mandow. For twenty-three years, she had been a salesperson and department manager at Halls Department Store in Kansas City, Missouri. Halls, owned by Hallmark Cards and named after its founder, Joyce C. Hall, has been in business since World War I. Beverly was the youngest of the four Rehabilitation Home victims at sixty-seven years old. She had been a member of Parkville United Methodist Church for sixteen years. She was divorced, her retired ex-husband having had a career in banking at an Indianapolis branch of Old National Bank. Beverly Mandow was a Sub-Acute Program patient at the Rehabilitation Home due to complications from diabetes. She died when someone combined her anti-anxiety agent, alprazolam, with two drugs that are highly incompatible with it. Those mismatched medications came from her roommate's prescribed supply.

"Before I let Wally comment on his church memories of Beverly, I'll mention that none of the four women who died had children. I consider that an unusual statistic. I suggest that whoever made them sign insurance papers selected them because they didn't have close family members to complain about that procedure. Wally, do you have any comments about Beverly Mandow?"

"I knew Beverly, but not well. She was active in the Women's Circle, but didn't attend church on a regular basis. I think she may have visited her sister in Florida during most winters. Arthur, do you know more about her?"

"When I was pastor at the Parkville church, I met with Beverly occasionally to discuss family matters and medical conditions. I came away with the impression that she was highly talented, but had fragile health. I also thought she was a bit of a hypochondriac. She kept talking about articles she had read about new medications and how she had tried some that had performed well in effectiveness tests."

Wally said, "That would fit with her being willing to take several pills together if someone told her they would be beneficial. That also says that her murderer knew about drug interactions and Beverly's tendencies."

Jeremy said, "If we assume that Phyllis Landholm's killer was different from the person who murdered the three women who signed up for insurance policies, we'll need a separate analysis of her case. Aside from that investigation, we're saying that the killer of the last three victims electrocuted one, got the second one to take grapefruit juice with her medications, and conned the third into taking a bad combination of drugs. Who would be a candidate for using those three murder methods?"

CHAPTER 68 – DEPARTMENT OF

CORRECTIONS

Following the meeting with the Sandley Agency team, Arthur telephoned the New York State Department of Corrections and Community Supervision to set up an appointment at their headquarters in Albany. That turned out to be the easy part. The problem came when the person who took the call asked why Arthur couldn't use the online search program to find the inmate he was seeking. When Arthur said that he knew only the party's first name and had no information on the years of incarceration or the prison involved, the public relations person transferred the call to her supervisor. That individual wanted to learn much more about Arthur's identity and motivation before tackling what would be a difficult and probably fruitless search.

"Sir, my name is Alfreda Jensen, and I'll need more information from you before we'll be able to justify the expense of a manual search and to arrange for you to visit here."

"I'm pleased to discuss my project with you, Ms. Jensen. I completely understand your wondering whether my quest is frivolous, because I question its probability of success myself. My name is Pastor Arthur Blake. I'm with the United Methodist Church, but I'm contacting you in connection with a project I'm pursuing for the University of Virginia. We're trying to determine whether you had a particular inmate in your system during the past few decades. We can't use your online search application due to the fact that we have only fragmentary identification information on this individual."

"How much information do you have?"

"We know that his first name was Kurt, that he was quite tall, and that he was originally from Austria. We also know that he was born within a year either way of 1935, and that he's currently deceased."

"That's not much input data for a search, and if he's deceased, why do you need this information?"

Arthur silently prayed for forgiveness in advance of his creative response. "The university has asked my investigative group to determine the details of this individual's time in your system as part of its study of previously undocumented important historic events. One of the people interviewed about those events gave the university this information, and we are charged with checking the facts in order to determine whether the interviewed person's story is reliable and accurate."

"I understand. You're saying that if this inmate did not exist, you can't trust that testimony about key historic events. Now that you've given me that background information, I have no problem with setting up a meeting. I have an opening in my schedule the day after tomorrow at three o'clock. Will you be able to arrive here at that time?"

"Your timing sounds perfect. I'll look forward to meeting you then."

After disconnecting, Arthur made a few notes and relaxed. *I didn't bend the truth too much. Remembered events are historical, even if not importantly historic.*

Shortly before three o'clock on the specified day, Arthur emerged from a taxi in front of the Albany headquarters building of the Department of Corrections and Community Supervision. He entered and told the receptionist he had a scheduled appointment with Alfreda

Jensen. Five minutes later a secretary came to the lobby, and guided Arthur to Alfreda Jensen's conference room, overlooking the building's enclosed courtyard. Alfreda rose as Arthur entered, shook hands with him, and motioned for him to join her in one of two chairs facing a computer terminal.

Arthur said, "Thank you again for meeting with me. I have one piece of additional information that may assist us in confirming the story of Kurt. The interviewed person said that Kurt had been in a prison or correctional facility with architecture that resembled a castle tower with notches at the top. Our group's preliminary research of your system suggests a match of that description with the Auburn, Attica, or Ulster Correctional Facilities."

"I'm glad to see that you've done some homework before dropping this puzzle in my lap. Those three would match the building description, although we now call Ulster the Eastern Correctional Facility. Let's get started. I have the information you gave me over the telephone, and based on that, I'll search first for all inmates having a date of birth in 1934, 1935, or 1936."

She keyed the search parameters into the computer and then examined the results. "Well, we're making progress, but not much so far. I started looking for inmates from 1955 onward, so that people born in the key years would be approximately twenty-one-year-old adults. Coincidentally, 1955 was the starting year of nationwide efforts to remove mentally ill inmates from the prison system. I'm assuming that your Kurt would not have been one of those removed for that reason."

Arthur nodded his agreement.

Alfreda continued, "The removal of prisoners with mental problems was not a complete success, because a study in 1987 showed that of 3332 of our New York State inmates interviewed, eight percent had identifiable mental difficulties. Getting back to looking for Kurt, you said he was deceased. Do you know when he died?"

"I'm afraid I don't, but he was supposed to have been in a nursing home when he died, so he wouldn't have been extremely old when he left the Correctional System."

"Let's say that he wouldn't have been in prison beyond the age of fifty-five. That gives us a search range from 1955 to 1990. If I insert that timing into my population of prisoners born in 1934, 1935, and 1936, I get 2310 possible candidates."

"That's almost, but not quite, a small enough number to manually check. Can you see how many of those individuals were named Kurt?"

She entered that additional sort parameter and then pushed her chair backward. "Arthur, I'm afraid I have bad news for you. I show only two people named Kurt, but neither one indicates an Austrian birthplace. I have Kurt O'Malley, who was born in Providence, Rhode Island, and Kurt Burton, who was born in England."

"It is possible that his name should start with the letter C."

Alfreda made another computer entry. "That adds Curt Roundtree, born in Toronto, Canada and Curt Wallace, born in Buffalo, New York. We're still striking out."

"If the interviewed person got his first name wrong, we're stuck because we don't have any way to figure it out. I'm afraid we've both wasted our time on this effort."

"Before we give up, Arthur, I'm going to try one more thing. I have the inkling of a hunch."

Arthur watched as Alfreda Jensen inserted some new data. She saw the results of that step and then made a few additional changes. The tension revealed by the tightness of her facial muscles eased.

"I've found him. He's real, but he wasn't an inmate. Kurt Linser was a corrections officer at Auburn Correctional Facility from 1975 to 1988."

Arthur wrote that information on his pad. "Does it say anything additional about him?"

Alfreda returned to her computer. "He must have done an adequate job, because he received a promotion to Sergeant after six years."

Arthur stood up and extended his hand toward Alfreda. "Thank you so much. Your findings will have great implications for the University of Virginia project. What made you think of looking through the staff records after you couldn't find him as an inmate?"

"It was partly stubbornness about checking every possibility and partly a vague recollection, from when I first started working here, of inmate complaints about harsh treatment from a corrections officer with a German accent."

CHAPTER 69 – FEEDBACK

Arthur waited through several rings for someone to answer the telephone. Finally, he heard a familiar voice.

"Good morning, Rosemary. I visited the New York State Department of Corrections and Community Supervision yesterday, and I have news for you."

"Good morning yourself, Arthur; is it good news or bad news?"

"I'll have to say that it may be some of each, but it's mostly good. We've determined that the Austrian individual in Michelle Caspar's memories actually existed, and his name was Kurt Linser. The interesting part of our findings is that Kurt didn't commit a crime. He was one of the prison guards."

"That's surprisingly good news. What's the bad part?"

"It turns out that Kurt Linser treated the inmates roughly. They hated him and complained about him to the Department of Corrections administration. The person remembered by Michelle mistreated those around him and went out of his way to be difficult. I don't know what this information will do to Michelle's self-image."

"I understand, Arthur. We'll have to be diplomatic in relaying these findings to Michelle. We don't want to adversely affect her feelings or her willingness to talk about her memories."

"How will you manipulate the information you tell her while keeping this an objective study?"

"That's a good point. We'll need some serious discussions among our department members before proceeding. Anyway, thank you for your efforts. You've done everything we requested. Send us your invoice, and we'll pay it promptly."

"We'll do that, but there are a few more related matters I think we should study, whether we're paid for the work or not."

"What kind of matters?"

"Now that we have a name for this individual and a few behavioral qualities, it should be much easier to learn what he was really like, how he lived, and how he died. I feel we should go beyond merely proving that he existed."

"You're probably right, but we have budget limitations. How about sending us your additional findings, and we'll pay for those that are valuable to our study?"

Arthur hesitated. "We'll continue our investigations, and then we'll tell you the general areas in which we learned something. You can then decide whether to pay for the results in any aspect of the study, in order to receive the details. I can't abruptly drop this investigation. If someone murdered Kurt Linser, we need to try to solve that crime.

CHAPTER 70 – TRANSITIONS

Irma sensed that something was bothering Arthur. She watched him for ten minutes as he sat on the couch, staring at some distant point beyond the walls of the parsonage. It was time to intervene.

"Are you ready to tell me what has you so pensive?"

"I'm back to questioning whether we should treat our investigations as a business. Whenever I discuss cases with Bobby Andrews, he complains that by showing him the complexities of an investigation I'm using up too much of the Police Department's budget. When I talked to Rosemary Swinton at the University of Virginia, she said pretty much the same thing. She thanked me for my initial information and then talked about budget constraints when I told her there was more that we had to check in connection with Kurt Linser. Everything in a business or other organization is about budgets. When I investigate something, I want to pursue it to its logical conclusion."

"We'll do that, Arthur. We just have to get creative about our fee structure and reward system. I'll handle the administration part that bothers you. The trick is to make enough on cases that have economic value to our clients, to give us a surplus for use in cases where clients can't pay or where we want to delve further into mysteries than they do. It's the same principle that doctors use in receiving different amounts for the same service, depending on the wealth of the patient and whether he or she has insurance coverage."

"There are ethical aspects of that approach that bother me, but I see what you're suggesting for us. It's a touch of the Robin Hood philosophy of investigations. Take more from the rich in order to do more for the poor. In the real world that lacks church support as a pastor, we'll have to live with entrepreneurship."

"Do you feel better now?"

"Sure, you always improve things with your alternate point of view."

"Good; now that you're stable again, we have to pack and clean this place for its next resident, Pastor Marianne Rendley. We'll head home to Amboy and commute when we have meetings to attend or church business in Parkville. I know that Rex will be happy to go home to familiar surroundings."

As they prepared to transfer locations, Arthur realized that Irma was using the physical effort of these transition tasks to free his mind from focusing on business concerns. He wondered how he would get along with the new pastor, Marianne Rendley. She would be older than him. Bishop Chandler had said that she was only five years away from retirement. Howard had also said that she had a missionary background. Missionary work had never appealed to Arthur, although he had been more than willing to let his investigations take him away from the conventional church scene. In any event, once she settled in at the Parkville church, he would be back on his leave of absence and would be free to go anywhere.

Once Irma declared the parsonage ready for its new occupant, they loaded their car and drove toward their home in Amboy. As he drove, Arthur's thoughts returned to the case of Michelle Caspar's prior life memories.

"Irma, now that we have a name for Michelle's remembered person, Kurt Linser, do you think we'll be able to find where he lived and the location of the nursing home where he died?"

"That shouldn't be difficult. We can follow the paper trail of legal documents. He probably purchased a home and sold it when he went into the nursing home. After he died, there may have been legally filed property distributions."

"That sounds like a good plan of attack, but first, we'd better check the status of the Parkville Rehabilitation Home and Pastor Klingham inquiries.

CHAPTER 71 – WALLY AND MARTHA

Wally Sanborn knocked on the half-open door of Martha Callahan's office. She looked up from her paperwork with a slightly irritable expression on her face. It morphed into a smile when she saw who had interrupted her.

"May I come in, Martha?"

"You're always welcome, Wally. Why are you here? Are you looking for a lunch date? If so, I'm available."

"That's a distinct possibility, but I'm actually here to ask a favor." He closed her office door for privacy.

Martha took the closed door as a signal. She walked over to Wally and kissed him. "I was hoping you felt the same way I do. Name your favor, and it's yours."

Wally returned the kiss. "The favor I need relates to our investigation. During the next week, I'd like you to set me up as an outpatient with one of the physical therapy people to have her work on some stiffness I have in my shoulder. Within the next two days, I'll identify the therapist who should work on me."

"Come over to my place, and I'll work on your shoulder. I have physical therapy training."

"That's tempting, but I have to interview one of your therapist employees in a context where she won't get suspicious."

Martha pouted. "I'll set up an appointment for you with any staff member you want, if you come over to my house this evening for dinner and whatever."

"That sounds as though you're a lot more interested in the whatever than the dinner, but it's a deal. I'll bring the wine."

She wrote the address and time on a business card, kissed him once more, and then wiped the extra color off his lips with a tissue. After Wally left, she started to plan the event, including leaving a little early to do some shopping on the way home. It had been too long since she had last seriously pursued a man, and Wally definitely deserved special preparations.

CHAPTER 72 – BOBBY ANDREWS

Parkville Police Chief Bobby Andrews smiled as he looked across the McNoonan's Steakhouse table at Arthur Blake. For this lunch, he had worn civilian clothes, allowing the host to seat them in a prime location booth instead of the rear corner to which he relegated uniformed police officers. "You decided to make good on the second lunch I said you owed me. At least you pay off your debts, Thanks for the treat, Arthur. I do enjoy this place."

"You do realize that this will be a working lunch? Since I've moved home to Amboy, I have to be very efficient with my time allocations during my short trips to Parkville."

"You'll have my full attention when I'm not engaged in enjoying their barbecued ribs. They are something special. Now, what's our agenda for this meal?"

"I've reviewed all the case notes from the four deaths at the Parkville Rehabilitation Home, and I'm wondering whether we'll be able to get enough evidence against the probable two killers to get convictions in court."

"I had wondered the same thing about the murder of Pastor Rebecca Klingham, but once we linked her killing to drug ring transactions, the potential for a conviction increased. I think we have to take the patient killings further down the road before we'll know how to proceed toward a conviction."

"That's a conservative approach, but how do you even prove the murder methods? The deaths occurred over a nine month period, and only the final two victims received autopsies."

216

"We have a problem with the killer of the first victim, Phyllis Landholm, because we decided that we have a different perpetrator of that crime, and we're just assuming that the suffocation was due to smothering with a pillow, because there was no autopsy. The other three killings were almost certainly the work of a single killer, because of the fraudulent life insurance angle. The second killing, that of Janet Cuspin, by electrocution was obvious, and they didn't discard the life signs monitor, so we have it in our evidence locker. The final two victims did receive autopsies, so we have forensic evidence there. As I said, the hardest problem will be to determine the killer of the first victim and get a conviction. We can only hope that a future development clarifies that portion of the case. We got lucky on the pastor's murder by detecting the drug transactions at the Rehabilitation Home. A similar development could arise with regard to Phyllis Landholm's death."

"That's an optimistic and passive approach to solving a murder."

"That's the approach I'm going to take. I see good potential for solving the murders of the last three patients and Pastor Rebecca. That will satisfy me. ... Right now, I see my ribs coming, so if you don't mind, I'll consider this discussion closed until after I've enjoyed my feast.

CHAPTER 73 – RESEARCH

Irma began her search for Kurt Linser information, and the computer rewarded her with some good news. *This shouldn't take long at all. It says that there are only 168 Linsers in the United States. Looking down the list of names and addresses, I see that a surprising majority of the individuals are female. It also indicates that there is no Linser named Kurt. I'll try a different website. I might get different results. ... I thought it would make a difference. This site says there are 196 people with the last name of Linser. They show one Kurt Linser plus eight more with variations in spelling of the last name. The Kurt they show is too young to have been the Kurt we are seeking. I see my problem. This database only includes living people. I'll have to try something else to get data on people who have died.*

She found a death records search site and typed in the key name. *That's better ... they have fifty-six death records for a Kurt Linser. Most sites are generous with their numbers to make them appear more valuable. As on the last listing, I'll bet I'll find a bunch of different spellings. ... You're right again, Irma. They show only seventeen death listings for a Kurt Linser with the correct spelling. We know that he died in New York State. What does that do to our results?*

I came up with three New York locations, Poughkeepsie, Bronx, and Geneseo. Michelle told Rosemary Swinton that the home was near a big lake. That eliminates Bronx, which is part of the New York City complex, and Poughkeepsie, which is on the Hudson River. Is Geneseo near a lake? – Yes, it's near one of the Finger Lakes, Conesus Lake. Now, we'll have to look for the nursing home in that area.

Impulses

That was unexpected. There are a large number of nursing homes scattered across the Finger Lakes region. It may take me a while to figure out the correct one. If I look at online photos of local establishments, it will be one with more than one level, because Michelle had a memory of someone pushing Kurt's wheelchair down the stairs. ...

CHAPTER 74 – MARTHA'S HOUSE

When Wally arrived at Martha's house for that promised evening of *dinner and whatever*, he carried a small boutique-style shopping bag with two bottles of wine in it. He parked in the driveway of the neat little New England flavored brown house, approached the front door, and was about to ring the doorbell, when he saw the sign. Next to the bell, Martha had tacked up a five by seven inch index card marked *Wally, please use the kitchen entrance in back, and take this sign with you.* He took the sign as directed, walked down the driveway, and passed through a white picket fence gate on his way to the kitchen door. Once there, he knocked three times on the door. As he waited, he saw the main kitchen light turn off. Then, Martha opened the door while standing behind it.

"Come on in, Wally."

He saw that she had set the kitchen table for their meal and had reduced the room's light to that emitted by the two table candles. As he walked in, he turned toward Martha as she closed the door. "I brought both red and white wine, because I forgot to ask about tonight's menu."

Martha took his bag, and as she did, she let her green silk robe fall to the floor, revealing her wearing a red and white candy-striped bib apron and nothing else. After closing the door, she pulled Wally into an alcove away from the candle light. "I decided it would be more fun to have our *whatever* before we have our dinner. Is that acceptable to you?"

"In case you didn't notice, we're not a couple of kids anymore."

"There's nothing to keep us from acting younger. Just take my hand and I'll lead the way to the fountain of youth."

Wally mentally shrugged his shoulders, took her hand, and blew out the candles as they passed the table. As she led the way into the illuminated hallway, he noticed a tattoo of a bird on her derrière.

"I have to ask. Why do you have a red cardinal tattoo in that particular location?"

"I'm a Chicago Cubs fan, and I take my baseball seriously."

"I guess you're the fanatic type of fan. I don't do tattoos, but yours is impressive."

When they reached the bedroom, Martha said, "I hope you won't treat me as a suspect anymore." She removed her apron. "I have nothing to hide."

"I guess this will be another Army training exercise – maneuvers and infiltration."

By the time they had progressed to the dinner phase of the evening, Martha and Wally had discovered they were quite compatible in most aspects of outlook and intimacy. She returned to the kitchen in a more normal outfit than before, blue jeans and a western style blouse. He relaxed with increased confidence that he could trust her. He would test that confidence during the salad course.

"Martha, that was quite an appeteaser, to coin a term for it. You're not the all-business person you appear to be when you're in the office. I do have to ask you about your reactions when those four women patients died. In our past discussions about them, you hardly showed any emotion. I've learned how sensitive and passionate you can be. Why didn't those four deaths affect you on an emotional level?"

Richard Davidson

"My first response is that before you and your friends argued that those women's deaths had most likely been murders, I took them in stride because I had accepted them as unconnected accidents. People in the healthcare field receive training to have a clinical and objective demeanor when faced with death or the possibility of death. Even on a routine basis, we have intimate contact with our patients in ways that they would never tolerate from individuals outside of the healthcare process. You have to truncate your emotions and be objective if you want to succeed in this field. It doesn't mean that I don't have emotions. I'll be far more distant if I see you at the Rehabilitation Home tomorrow. There's also the aspect of not getting personally attached to your patients and not letting patient deaths be like deaths in your family."

"I agree that you have to show different faces to professional and personal contacts. I'm glad to have discovered your emotional side and to have at least visited your personal side of life. I'll plan on making additional visits there."

She smiled and nodded her affirmation.

Wally continued. "What I can't understand is how you can continue wearing your impartial, unemotional outlook in the face of the Rehabilitation Home disintegrating around you. Don't you realize that people may blame you for everything that has gone wrong there?"

"My secret is that since I met you and your agency partners, I've reflected and reordered my priorities. Parkville Rehabilitation Home was my *raison d'être* in the past. Now, I'd have no qualms about leaving it for something better."

Wally stared at Martha and began to have qualms of his own.

CHAPTER 75 – UNEXPECTED STARDOM

Jeremy Hadley was not an early riser, but Debbie Danforth thoroughly enjoyed getting outside for a brisk walk before six o'clock, when nature and a few commuters had only recently started to stir. Her typical walking route took her around four blocks lining Maine Street plus a side trip to look for wildlife along the Mallard Lake paths. By the time Jeremy forced himself awake and stumbled toward the kitchen, she would have made coffee and laid out pastry or other breakfast items for him, following which she would have settled in to work at her computer in the apartment's back room research area and den.

This morning was different. When Jeremy reached the kitchen, he looked in vain for coffee and food. The only thing awaiting him on the table was a note. He did his best to focus his barely open eyes to read it. *Help yourself to breakfast. I've gone to meet Bobby Andrews at Mandy's Coffee House. I'll fill you in on my latest discoveries later. Love, Debbie*

That jerked him to full awareness. Jeremy dashed back into the bedroom, pulled on jeans and a sweatshirt, briefly brushed his hair, dropping the hairbrush on the lamp table near the front door as he inserted his feet into loafers without socks and rushed out toward Mandy's. He did not want to be the last to learn of Debbie's news.

When Jeremy arrived at Mandy's Coffee House, he spotted Bobby and Debbie in a back booth. He ordered coffee and a well-done English muffin, and then carried those trophies to the booth.

"May I join you two? I hear there are new developments."

Debbie laughed. "You've never moved so fast on any morning since I've known you. You're afraid we won't keep you informed."

Bobby said, "I have to plead guilty to having thought earlier that Debbie was the junior partner in the Sandley Agency. After receiving this morning's information from her, I've decided that she qualifies as a full partner and talented researcher. Make sure she gets full credit for her discoveries, Jeremy."

"Debbie, you are an equal partner with Wally and me. Now, please tell me what you've discovered."

Debbie winked at Bobby. "He really hates being left out. Here's the scoop. I've learned a lot more about Mary Welker; she was the third woman to die at Parkville Rehabilitation Home. We already knew that she had been a performer on Broadway when she was younger, appearing in *This Was Burlesque* in 1970 and in *The Pajama Game* in 1973. We also knew that she had been married to a jazz musician, but that they had divorced."

"So much for old news; what's the new scoop?"

"Impatient, isn't he, Bobby? The scoop is that I've identified Mary's ex-husband. He's Larry Jakes, who plays the alto saxophone. He's still active in jazz, but the key discovery is that Mary and Larry never lost contact during all the years since their divorce. They were in business together in a long series of enterprises, with Mary providing financing as needed, while Larry took care of operations."

Jeremy said, "That's all fine, but hardly earth-shattering. So, what's special about their having been in several businesses together?"

Bobby smiled and shook his head at Jeremy's impatience. "What your girlfriend and associate discovered was that these were all fraudulent businesses. Larry took the risks by running them, while Mary stayed in the background as the innocent but talented woman who ran church shows. The pair would monitor public records for a business that had voluntarily ceased operations. They would apply to reinstate the selected firm. They'd then conduct business based on the credit of the original management and run up bills that they never intended to pay. Once they reached a key level of debt, they would disappear, leaving the creditors to seek payments from the original owners who may have closed the business years earlier and thought they'd have no further obligations."

Debbie added, "Secretaries of State may be forbidden by their state laws to transfer company records across their borders because states try to steal businesses from each other. That makes it easy for criminals to register and reestablish a closed business as an out-of-state firm in a different state from the original."

"How do they detect these frauds?"

Bobby said, "States have investigators in their Secretary of State offices. Phyllis Landholm had been one of those investigators until she retired. Do you see the pattern, Jeremy?"

"Uh-huh; either Phyllis suspected Mary Welker, or Mary feared that Phyllis would get the authorities to come after her and Larry. Either way, it's a good bet that Mary killed Phyllis Landholm to keep her from blowing the whistle on their operations. How do we prove that?"

"Debbie found the reinstatement application for Larry's latest business, which is, appropriately, in Indiana. I've emailed the information to the Indiana State Police, indicating that in addition to operating a fraudulent business there, Larry may have been an accomplice to the murder of Phyllis Landholm in Parkville. I cited Landholm's Indiana credentials, so they'll make Larry's arrest a high priority matter."

Debbie's pride in her achievement was obvious. "We have solved the murder that was not like the others, except for pinning down the final details; right, Bobby?"

"That's correct; and I'm pleasantly surprised, because I thought that would be our most difficult homicide to solve. We don't have to worry about taking Mary to court. She was a killer who later became a victim. Next, we'll go after the person who killed her and the other two women."

Jeremy said, "Before you get too optimistic, Chief, we'll have to actually arrest Larry Jakes and get him to admit his part in all of this."

CHAPTER 76 – ROSEMARY AND MICHELLE

Rosemary Swinton sat across from Michelle Caspar in one of the University of Virginia interview rooms. This follow-up session would allow her to gauge the impact of the investigation results on Michelle's memories.

"I have good news for you, Michelle. Our investigators, Arthur and Irma Blake have confirmed most aspects of your memories. Thank you for recommending them."

"What do you mean by most aspects? I assume you're saying that Kurt really existed."

"They identified a man named Kurt Linser, who was compatible with your memories from Austria during World War II and who lived and worked in New York State later. Does the name Linser have any significance for you?"

"That name sounds somewhat familiar, but I can't identify with it."

"They also found that Kurt Linser didn't go to prison as an inmate. He worked as a correctional officer, a prison guard."

"I welcome that bit of news. It bothered me that I might have been a criminal in a past life. It was bad enough to think that I had once been male. When did this Kurt Linser die?"

"We don't know that yet. We do know that he worked for the New York State Department of Corrections at the Auburn Correctional facility from 1975 to 1988. Why do you ask?"

"Rosemary, I was born in 1988. Unless Kurt Linser died right after he left his prison job, he was alive during my lifetime. He wasn't a prior life at all."

"As I said earlier, Michelle, your memories are unusual, coming as an adult. While I don't yet know exactly when Kurt died, I'm fairly certain that he died before you started experiencing his memories."

"Are Arthur and Irma trying to determine when he died?"

"Arthur did indicate that they were going to take the investigation further."

"You didn't insist that they pin down the final events of Kurt Linser's life?"

"I thought that it was sufficient for our purposes to have confirmation that he existed."

"That may be sufficient in childhood cases, when the subject is quite young, but I'm an adult who was probably alive while Kurt was still living. That's not a prior life. His memories or soul or whatever you want to call it, entered my consciousness only recently. I've experienced two different lives at the same time, and it scares me. Have you ever studied such a phenomenon before?"

"Not exactly, but we have questioned whether all experienced and remembered events are linear in time."

"What does that mean?"

"In your case, it would suggest that the overlap of Kurt's life with your life does not cause conflict because you didn't experience his memories until after he had died. He may have lived those memories while you both were alive, but you had only your own consciousness when those events actually occurred."

"It almost hurts my head to work through that convoluted logic, but I think I understand what you mean. Would you continue to consider my memories an experience of a prior life?"

"That's the crux of the matter. Your experience is a variation that we'll have to study further. If one can share memories with another individual who died while the study subject was alive, would it be possible for two

individuals who were both still alive to share their
memories?"

CHAPTER 77 – LARRY JAKES

Larry hadn't been himself since Mary Welker had died at that rehab place. They had blamed her death on a problem with her heart medication, but he didn't really understand it. He had arranged for burial of her body in her home town of Bennington, Vermont, but he hadn't accompanied it or attended the ceremony. It was all part of their agreement at the time of their divorce many years ago. They had learned that they couldn't stand living with each other, but they gave each other loving support from a distance.

Their problems had stemmed from Mary's inability to keep her dancing and singing talents on a par with those of younger competitors. Mary and Jake had married when they both were part of *This Was Burlesque*, she in the chorus and he in the orchestra. They'd continued working together as one of Broadway's favorite couples through the run of *The Pajama Game*, but then reality struck. Mary's talents turned out to be ephemeral. She was a two-show wonder who couldn't keep up with her younger castmates. He, on the other hand, was a jazz musician who could play his sax forever, either in a show orchestra or in a dingy nightclub. Once they couldn't continue to entertain together, their magic and their marriage disappeared. She settled for running church and community shows, while he reflected his disappointment by playing the blues.

For many years, they had lost touch with each other, but then Mary found him at a New Orleans club and hit him with a proposition that changed both of their lives. She had thought up a way for them to be in business as partners without living together on a regular basis. They could share both continuing revenues and occasional sex. It had turned out to be great for both of them, coming as it did with the spice of slight illegality.

Mary had worked out a scheme for reinstating abandoned businesses with good credit ratings. She would select the enterprise and handle the reinstitution paperwork, hiding behind an alias. He would run the business, placing large orders for inventory and equipment. Then they would close the business after transferring salable items to a warehouse. Over time, they had developed a network of fences, black market outlets, and online auction sites for disposal of the warehouse stash. They discovered that they could operate almost continuously by frequently changing the locations and the categories of their recycled businesses.

Once Mary had died, Larry abandoned their latest business and returned to playing the blues, touring small towns with some of his old buddies. The money wasn't much, but the lifestyle matched his depressed mood. Someday, he would learn whether Mary's death had been an accident or if someone had deliberately caused it.

CHAPTER 78 – THERAPY

Detective Hank Robbins on several occasions had loitered for an hour or more in the lobby of Parkville Rehabilitation Home. The receptionist had smiled at him enough during one of these visits to stimulate a blooming casual friendship between them. He seasoned their trivial conversation with his cover story of evaluating the Rehabilitation Home as a suitable place to send his mother after her pending hip replacement surgery. Margie, the receptionist, did everything she could to convince him of the facility's merits, including proclaiming the virtues of their physical therapists and assigning names to them as they walked through the lobby and into the chapel area. Margie congratulated herself on doing a good sales job when she saw Hank smiling as he departed after their conversation.

Thirty minutes later, Wally Sanborn telephoned Martha Callahan. "Martha, I need to collect on that favor you promised. Please set me up for outpatient physical therapy on my right shoulder with Esther Ramirez."

"Hello to you too, Wally – I'll arrange your session for 1:30 this afternoon, but you owe me a beer later for being abrupt and not giving me a proper greeting."

"Sorry about that; I do have to work on my manners, even when I'm preparing for a mission."

"Am I one of your missions, soldier?"

"You're a very positive addition to my small circle of friends, and I hope to spend an increasing amount of time with you. You'll have to bear with my occasional social flaws."

"I can handle that, especially after that 'increasing amount of time' comment. Just remember when you're with Esther, that she's supposed to massage your shoulder, not the other way around."

"I'll save that version for you. Thanks for arranging the session. I'll let you know how it goes."

Wally disconnected after their conversation and mused that Martha needed to relax and let their relationship develop casually if she wanted it to continue and grow.

At 1:20 that afternoon, Wally entered the Rehabilitation Home wearing a bright red plaid flannel shirt hanging loosely outside his jeans and told the receptionist he had an appointment with Esther Ramirez. She told him the room number and gave him directions for going there. As he walked toward the indicated hallway, Wally scanned the people in the lobby and received a barely perceptible nod in return from Hank.

Esther's therapy area turned out to consist of an examination table in a corner of a gymnasium. Looking around, he saw that some therapists were assisting postoperative patients to bend and stretch their limbs, while additional patients performed daily routines on their own. Esther shook hands with Wally, and asked him to take off his shirt while she set up an L-shaped portable screen for a measure of privacy. Wally noted that Esther was about his height and had shoulders at least as large as his. Apparently, she took her therapy work seriously, even if she had become involved in drug distribution.

Once Wally had removed his shirt, Esther probed his sore right shoulder with fingers that felt like steel rods. Then she repeated the process on his left shoulder for comparison purposes.

"You're right-handed, and you over-rely on your right arm and shoulder when doing physical work. We can do a program of exercises to improve the function of your right shoulder, but I'll have you apply the same exercises to your left shoulder in the hope that you will improve the balance of physical effort between both sides of your body. You should make it a habit to do more with your left arm and shoulder, or both sides combined."

Wally decided to start doing his own probing. "I'll work on both sides, as you ask, but my left shoulder is pain-free. My right shoulder is quite painful most of the time. Over-the-counter painkiller medications haven't been enough to alleviate the soreness and sharp pains as I work. Can you give me anything for the pain?"

Esther showed no reaction to his question. "Only a doctor can give you a painkiller prescription. The pain should abate as we proceed through our exercise program. We'll see how well you respond to the exercises. Then I'll decide whether you should see a doctor for a prescription."

Wally saw that Esther was handling his case by the book. Had Hank Robbins reached a wrong conclusion about her being involved? "If I continue to have pain after we go through your exercise program, is there anything you can do for me to ease it?"

"I don't do acupuncture, if that's what you mean, but I might be able to find someone who does that kind of therapy."

Wally felt that he was getting nowhere. He'd have to try a more direct approach. "I'd be more interested in some kind of drug. I hear there are things you can take that make you feel happy and oblivious to your pain. Would you be able to find a source for therapy of that nature?"

Esther looked uncomfortable, as though she were having an internal debate with herself. "Are you a religious man, Mr. Sanborn?"

"I had a Christian upbringing, but I don't get to church much anymore."

"We have a chapel next to our lobby. I've heard that a written prayer accompanied by a donation sometimes can alleviate pain like yours. I'll give you some special green envelopes. If you seal your written prayer and donation in one of these envelopes and place it in the chapel prayer basket, you may receive a pink envelope with your name on it later in the day. That envelope may contain the answer to your prayers."

"Thank you; I'll do that."

"Fine, Wally, if I may call you by your first name; now it's time for therapy. We'll start with some stretches, and then move on to a series of strengthening exercises, standing, kneeling, and lying down. Once I teach you these procedures, you'll have to repeat them at home, three to six times each day, for three to seven days each week. I'll give you written details for each exercise. You'll have to keep up this routine and come to me for weekly evaluations. If you respond well to the program, it will take four weeks, but we may have to continue it for as long as six weeks."

"That will be an ordeal, but I'll see it through. Make sure you give me those green envelopes when I leave today. I'll need the prayer support to get through this."

One hour later, Wally deposited a green envelope in the chapel prayer basket and as he left, winked at Hank Robbins, who sat studying a Parkville Rehabilitation Home brochure.

After another hour, Esther Ramirez walked into the chapel and approached the prayer basket. She reached into the basket, removed a green envelope and replaced it with a pink envelope marked with Wally's name. As she started to walk away, she noticed the man sitting in the corner with his camera aimed at her. He approached her, and after a brief introduction, escorted her outside to his unmarked police car.

CHAPTER 79 – JEREMY AND DEBBIE

Jeremy Hadley stretched his long frame well beyond the confines of the bed and realized that Debbie was not in the room. He pulled on his jeans and walked into the living room, where he found Debbie exercising on a yoga mat. He watched her shift into a bridge pose, facing upward, shoulders and arms flat on the floor, torso arched off the ground, knees bent, and feet flat on the floor.

"That's an interesting position. It looks awkward as hell, but I assume you're doing it because it's good for you."

As she lowered her body slowly to the floor, Debbie said, "It's good for both of us. I have to keep my body in good shape to please you, especially while we're in this mutual approval period."

"Debbie, are you still worried about Michelle reentering the scene? You've defeated your competition. As soon as we started to work together on investigations, we became a couple. You don't have to worry about some kind of approval period."

"I said *mutual* approval period. You still have to worry."

"What did I do wrong now?"

"You're too tall, and you keep shifting positions while you sleep. I'm going to have to get a shorter boyfriend or a larger bed."

"One king size bed coming up; we'll go shopping this afternoon. In the meantime, we could get some extra activity on the one that will be departing. Any interest in that?"

"It's tempting, but I'd rather talk about us and about Michelle too. You never did tell me what happened to cause you to break up. If we're officially past the approval stage, I'll feel safe about discussing her."

Jeremy sat down cross-legged next to her yoga mat and held her hand while he spoke. "I can't tell you the full story of why Michelle and I broke up, because I don't know it. She was very mysterious when she told me that she had changed and was no longer interested in a relationship. I do know that she visited the people at the University of Virginia that study people who think they've had other lives prior to their births. I also heard through Wally that Arthur and Irma have been working for that group at the university, checking out some of the things that Michelle told them in an interview. I feel strongly enough about our future that I didn't check with Arthur and Irma for details. If I quizzed them, it would be like spying on Michelle, and I no longer want to know her business."

Debbie pivoted forward and hugged him. "That was a sweet statement of how you feel about me. Thank you. One of these days, I'll fill you in on my deep, dark secrets."

"I'll look forward to that. I was afraid you didn't have any."

Debbie pushed Jeremy onto his back and jumped on top of him.

CHAPTER 80 – NURSING HOME

Irma looked just a little smug as she entered Arthur's office and study at Parkville United Methodist Church. "How's your final sermon coming?"

"I'm working it into a changing of the guard piece to be appropriate for the arrival of Pastor Marianne Rendley. I'll use Deuteronomy 34:4 as my text, when God allowed Moses to see the promised land of Canaan, but kept him from entering it because of his earlier disobedience in the way he brought water out of a rock in Numbers 20:12. Joshua had the honor of leading the people to their destination."

"Are you comparing yourself to Moses and saying you were disobedient?"

"I suppose I am. I haven't exactly been a toe-the-line pastor whose only interest is to shepherd the flock in his assigned church."

"I'll differ with you on that one, Arthur. You've been a great pastor, but your flock hasn't been limited to this single church. You started with your assignment, but took on the shepherding of connected individuals and flocks, wherever they led you. That's what Jesus meant when he talked about the shepherd with a hundred sheep. That shepherd left the main flock of ninety-nine to find and rescue the one that had strayed into danger. Being that kind of pastor makes you special, not deficient, even if Bishop Chandler can't appreciate it."

"Wow! You're a better preacher than I am. Thanks, Irma, I needed that different way of looking at things." He gave her a warm and lengthy kiss.

"I should give you more endorsements based on all you do, but I don't want your head to get too big."

"I always thought that big head thing was a strange saying, but I did note an upbeat expression on your face when you walked in. Is your head getting big because you're the bearer of good news?"

"I'll settle for calling it a bit of accomplishment. I've convinced myself that the nursing home where Michelle's Kurt Linser died is in the Finger Lakes region of New York State, possibly in or near the town of Geneseo. I'd like you to review the logic that led me to that point, and to work with me to deduce a specific nursing home to visit."

"That's a great progress report. I'll quit now and continue with my sermon preparation later. I may even use the lost sheep parable you referenced to explain the different strengths and weaknesses of pastors, and how the congregation always benefits from exposure to new approaches."

"That's a good thought. Be sure to point out that Rebecca Klingham had the strength of communicating with people who faced personal problems, because she had overcome so many."

When they arrived home, they had a light lunch. Then Irma brought her computer and papers to the big old-fashioned kitchen table, where Arthur joined her.

"I came up with the Finger Lakes region for the nursing home by searching for death records for a person named Kurt Linser within New York State. Our list of Michelle's memories indicates that Kurt had lived in New York and that he had arrived at the nursing home via an ambulance from his residence. He had a weak heart, so I assumed that they wouldn't have driven him to a facility in a different state."

"That's a reasonable assumption."

"Then I looked at entries on the list of deceased people named Kurt Linser within New York State, and I came up with one each in Poughkeepsie, Bronx, and Geneseo. Michelle remembered that the nursing home was on a big lake. Bronx is part of Metropolitan New York City and is on the ocean. Poughkeepsie is on the Hudson River. Only Geneseo is near a lake, namely Conesus Lake, which is the westernmost of the Finger Lakes."

"Everything is logical so far."

"It turns out that the whole Finger Lakes Region is peppered with nursing homes, many of which are near those long, thin lakes. Apparently, older people find that region an attractive place to spend their senior years."

"So, how do we pinpoint the nursing home where Kurt lived and died?"

"We have two clues, one of which may not be reliable. The weaker clue is that Michelle thought the facility might have the word *destiny* in its name. Rosemary Swinton indicated that Michelle expressed uncertainty about that memory."

"What's the stronger clue?"

"Michelle was definite about her memory of how Kurt died. She remembered that someone pushed him down the stairs in his wheelchair. This means that the place we are seeking has to have at least two floors. Many nursing home designs feature a single floor to avoid the need for stairs and elevators for people with limited mobility. That will eliminate a fair percentage of homes in the Finger Lakes area."

"We can also disregard any built after Kurt died. My notes say that he worked at Auburn Correctional Facility until 1988. He would have had some healthy retirement time prior to moving to the nursing home and then some more time prior to his death in the institution. I'd guess that he died around the year 2000."

"That's not a bad guess. If the Kurt Linser I have on the death list for Geneseo is correct, he died in 1999. However, you just added another clue, Arthur."

"I'm always spouting words of wisdom. What great insight did I make?"

"Kurt retired from the Auburn Correctional Facility, and that is in the Finger Lakes region near the north end of Owasco Lake."

"So, for completeness, we should look at nursing homes from Auburn westward to Geneseo."

"That includes facilities on or near Owasco Lake, Cayuga Lake, Seneca Lake, Canandaigua Lake, Honeoye Lake, Hemlock Lake, and Conesus Lake. I've omitted the slingshot-shaped lake that lies south of the others. We'll have many nursing homes to check."

"Did you search for one with *destiny* in the name?"

"I already tried that shortcut, Arthur. That's why I called it a weak clue. There is no facility with that word in its name."

"Try *destination*."

Irma squinted at Arthur, then shrugged her shoulders, and entered the new search word into her computer. Then she examined her results and keyed in a variation or two. Then she said, "How do you always manage to make it look easy? I came up with Carefree Destination Nursing Home in Geneva, New York. It's at the north end of Seneca Lake, and it has three resident floors plus a basement. It fits the *need for stairs* criterion."

"The word *destiny* has the connotation of finality. That sounded too close to death. If one is selecting a retirement or nursing home, the name should be more welcoming and assuring. Carefree Destination Nursing Home is a rather pleasant name that might actually comfort a potential client. Let's give it a visit and interview some staff there."

CHAPTER 81 – ESTHER RAMIREZ

Chief Bobby Andrews faced Esther Ramirez across a stainless steel table. Hank Robbins sat in a dark corner of the room, ready to contribute information when asked, but yielding the primary questioning to his boss. When Bobby had first taken over in Parkville, the interview table had been a prestigious walnut antique. He preferred to have a stark and foreboding interview room; hence, the stainless steel centerpiece. Hank triggered the video recording for documentation purposes upon detecting Bobby's cue.

"Ms. Ramirez, I hope you realize that you are facing serious charges. Drug dealing is a serious crime, and judges will tend to be extra harsh on people who deal drugs in a healthcare setting. What do you have to say for yourself?"

"I'm no drug dealer. I'm a physical therapist. I didn't do anything wrong."

"Hank Robbins, over here, witnessed you exchanging green money envelopes for pink envelopes containing controlled and illegal substances on multiple occasions, and he even recorded your transactions on video. We have the pink envelopes you placed in the prayer basket; he recorded your doing so to document the fact that they contained illegal narcotic painkillers."

"I was only delivering medications to clients."

"Those medications are tightly controlled and can only be distributed by a doctor who has examined the patient and issued a limited quantity prescription. You had no right to fill those envelopes. Further, we have checked with the administrator of Parkville Rehabilitation Home, and she has certified that the facility did not purchase the specific drugs you distributed, and that those items did not come from the institution's medication inventories."

"She lies. She doesn't know half the things that go on over there."

"Perhaps you would like to tell me where you obtained these painkillers. You may cover some of the other things you mentioned as going on if you wish."

"All that Callahan woman cares about is neatness and respect for her when she visits. We laugh at her behind her back. She doesn't even know about extra short-term patients who are friends of staff and who pay reduced rates informally and without record keeping."

"Where do you get the painkillers and other substances you deliver to the prayer basket?"

"I don't know. A girl who worked here but then quit used to supply them to us. Since she left, they've still been in the usual special place, but I don't know who puts them there."

"What is the name of the girl who left and earlier supplied the painkillers?"

"Joanna Diaz; she was a physical therapist also. As I said, Diaz is gone, but the goods are still there, so maybe I was wrong about her. Who knows?"

Bobby's frustration over her changing story was evident. "Wait a minute, Ms. Ramirez. You said that you witnessed Joanna Diaz supplying drugs before she left the Rehabilitation Home. Was your statement correct or not?"

"Yes, I saw her then, but I can't figure out how the supply continues to happen now, with Diaz gone."

"You leave that for us to discover."

"She said we weren't the only ones."

"Please explain what you mean by that. I'm confused."

"When Joanna Diaz worked here, she said many places like ours had special painkillers for special clients.

She called it the premium rehab service. She always laughed when she said that."

"Did she mention any other facilities by name?"

"I don't think she did, and I didn't want to know. I try to mind my own business so that I don't get into trouble."

Bobby stared at Esther, wondering whether she was naïve or trying to manipulate him. "You do realize that you are in trouble right now. Your drug dealing is a serious crime."

"No, I was just doing what has always been done, since Joanna's time, and maybe even before. Joanna trained me to do that when I first arrived."

"We'll end this interview now." Bobby nodded to Hank, who turned off the recorder. "You had better get a lawyer to represent your interests before you say anything more."

CHAPTER 82 – THE TRUST

Jeremy Hadley and Debbie Danforth had assigned themselves the task of figuring out the identity of the person or persons masked by the trust that was the majority owner of Parkville Rehabilitation Home. This would be a critical and potentially dangerous project, because they believed their target or targets to be responsible for the murders of the three fraudulently insured patients. The insurance payoff money would be a prime motive for those murders.

The usual computer search had yielded no results. Apparently, the lawyer who had created the trust had avoided any sloppiness that might have generated peripheral paperwork containing names. They would have to confront the trust's legal representative, Quentin Edwards.

From Martha Callahan, they learned that Edwards had local offices on the second floor of the Mallard Bank & Trust building. Because he had other offices outside of Parkville, they decided to phone for a local appointment, rather than waiting for him to show up at his office. Martha Callahan supplied the telephone number, and Jeremy left a message requesting an appointment before the end of the week.

Thirty minutes later, Jeremy received a callback offering a Parkville meeting at three o'clock that afternoon. Jeremy indicated that he and his associate would be there.

When Jeremy and Debbie arrived at Mallard Bank, they discovered that there were only two active offices on the second floor, that of Quentin Edwards and Associates, and that of a small CPA firm. They also found that Edwards' office was quite plain, having only a secretary's desk area, immediately inside the front door, and an unmarked door leading to an inner office. In the absence of a secretary at the front desk, Jeremy knocked on the blank door. The door opened to reveal a man wearing designer blue jeans and a green sweatshirt over a blue dress shirt.

"Hi, I'm Quentin Edwards. You must be Jeremy Hadley. Introduce me to your charming associate."

"Mr. Edwards, this is Debbie Danforth. We work together at the Sandley Agency."

"Cut the formality. Please call me Quentin, or Q, and if you don't mind I'll use your first names to keep things casual. Now, what may I do for you? My secretary indicated that your tone on the telephone suggested a weighty discussion matter."

Debbie said, "Jeremy does have a tendency to sound serious, but in this case, it's appropriate. We're hoping that you'll share with us some details about the trust that controls the Parkville Rehabilitation Home."

"What details would you like from me?"

Jeremy gestured to Debbie that he would reply. "We would like to learn the identity of the person or persons represented by that trust arrangement."

"Come into my office and sit down. There's a pitcher of ice water and glasses on the bookcase. I'm afraid I don't have any coffee or soft drinks. ... Now, with regard to your question, I can't reveal names because of the attorney/client relationship. The whole purpose of a trust arrangement is to mask the ownership of it. I'm able to relay any messages you may have, but I can't reveal any applicable identities. Why do you want to know?"

Jeremy didn't want to be too open with this attorney for fear his client or clients would disappear. "We're investigating some aspects of the management of the

Rehabilitation Home for the Parkville Police Department, and our report will be incomplete without the ownership information."

"You may insert the term, Rehabilitation Home Trust, wherever you need to refer to the ownership, and you may insert a footnote that I speak on behalf of that trust. Will that be satisfactory?"

Debbie stepped into the discussion. "How would you respond if the Parkville Police obtained a court order requiring you to supply the ownership details?"

"I would be more than happy to present my counter-arguments before the judge who issued that order. The attorney/client relationship has a long and well-established history, both in America and in England, going back to Common Law days. I doubt that I would have trouble convincing a judge of the merits of my refusal to supply the information you request."

Jeremy said, "We'll table this discussion at this point until we get that legal order. Then we'll let the judge contribute to our debate."

CHAPTER 83 – FOREBODINGS

Irma studied Arthur as they packed for their visit to the nursing home they had identified as possibly matching Michelle's memories.

"Arthur, are you still having those recurring dreams?"

"Now that you mention it, I haven't had one for a while."

"Does that mean you think the new support from the Sandley Agency will help you cope with your multiple investigation demands?"

"*Help* is a slippery term. Sure, the people in the Sandley group will be useful. They're already gathering valuable information regarding the deaths of the four women at the Rehabilitation Home and Pastor Rebecca Klingham. The problem is that they and Bobby Andrews' troops are doing conventional police work. I have the disturbing feeling that they'll make good progress, but they won't get all the way to a solution ... I may be wrong."

"Well, nobody said they had to relieve your load by leaving you or us out of the picture. We're getting close to the end of the trail for the mystery of Michelle Caspar's alter ego memories. As soon as we feel we've accomplished all that can be expected on that case, we can return to Parkville and help solve the case there."

"I'll look forward to that. They have a nest of vipers. I see at least three separate cases there, and we may find there are more."

"What do you think about Jeremy's latest feedback about their not being able to unmask the person or people behind the ownership trust?"

"That's one of the misgivings I mentioned before. They're going after that information the conventional way. They'll have to overcome too many obstacles."

"Would you do it differently?"

"I already have."

CHAPTER 84 – CAREFREE DESTINATION

When they arrived at Carefree Destination nursing home in their rental car, Irma asked Arthur to drive around the outside of the facility before they parked and entered. They noted that the facility had a large grassy area surrounding it, crisscrossed by paved paths, a central gazebo, and several picnic tables. The latter had benches on one side only, apparently to make convenient the use of wheelchairs on the other side. A few hardy patients and their caretaker companions were outside, well bundled against the fall chill. The building had three floors in the living areas, but only one floor behind the main entrance and in the rear, where a large dining room encased in large windows faced a wide lawn with trees and garden beds. The exterior of the institution showed careful maintenance.

They parked and passed through the main entrance. A woman seated at a desk greeted them and buzzed them through a second set of security doors after giving them directions to the director's office.

Director Millicent Gilbert turned out to be a tall dark-haired woman who had to be less than thirty-five years old. She wore a conservative navy blue suit and a severe tightly gathered hairstyle, probably designed to make her look older. The walls of her office displayed photographs of a carnival for patients and caregivers that had been the highlight of the recent summer.

Irma and Arthur introduced themselves, and told Director Gilbert that they were looking for details about the death of a patient named Kurt Linser some years earlier.

Arthur said, "You appear to be too young to have personal knowledge of that period, but perhaps you have a few long-term staff members who might."

Millicent laughed. "It's never safe to discuss age with a woman. Oddly enough, I do remember the incident you describe, even though I was quite young at the time. You see, my parents founded this nursing home, and served as its co-directors for twenty-five years. I grew up in this place. The word *destination* in its name comes from my always asking 'Are we there yet?' when we went on driving trips."

Irma said, "I did the same thing as a child. If you were here when Kurt Linser died, would you be able to tell us when it happened."

"I'd have to go through some tedious computer and paper files to be exact, but he died in 1993, when I was ten years old. I remember because it was a traumatic experience for me."

"Surely, if you grew up in this facility, you would have witnessed death before."

"Yes, Irma, but my parents and their staff always handled old-age illness deaths as natural and serene events. Everything was low key, and very few people talked about what had happened, except to express sympathy. Kurt Linser's death was violent. To this day, I can't remember another death that was a deliberate killing."

"Did you witness the violence yourself?"

"No, because one of the nurses made me go into the dining room to distance me from the commotion and the arrival of the police and paramedics afterward. However, I can introduce you to someone who saw everything and assisted with subsequent events."

Arthur said, "That would be very helpful to our inquiry."

Millicent lifted the telephone, keyed in an extension, and requested that someone named Robert Shanza come to her office."

That individual joined them within five minutes of Millicent's call. After exchanging introductions and explaining their mission without going into the question of prior life memories, Arthur asked Robert what he knew about the incident in which Kurt Linser had died.

"Before we get into that specific event, let me give you a little background that will be useful to you. At the time of Kurt's death, I worked here as an orderly, assisting the patients and nurses. Kurt and I became good friends, even though I had served time in the Auburn Correctional facility where Kurt had been a guard."

"Before you continue, Robert, I had heard from the people in the New York State Department of Corrections that many of the inmates complained about the treatment they received from Kurt when he was a guard. You say you were friends. Does that mean that Kurt had been a popular guard?"

"No, Arthur, there's no inconsistency here. The complaints about Kurt came from those hardened prisoners who were aggressive and bullies, the ones who wanted the rest of us to bow down to them and do errands for them. Kurt defended the more passive inmates, such as me. We were the ones who wanted to serve our sentences and then get back to as normal a life as possible. The rough guys wanted us to join gangs and head for a lifetime of crime. Basically, Kurt saved me from all that."

"I understand. Please continue with your story. You said that you and Kurt were friends here."

"We were, and inadvertently, our friendship may have contributed to his death. I've felt guilty about it for a long time, but I realize now that I couldn't have done anything differently. Let me start by saying that Kurt had been born in Germany or Austria ..."

"It was Austria."

"Good; now I know for sure. Anyway, he still had a German accent, even though he had been in the United States for many years.

"The original design of this building had a decorative open stairway from the common area on the second floor, leading down into the back end of the lobby. It was a graceful design. On the day of Kurt's death, he and I had shared coffee near the top of that staircase. While I cleared our cups and snack dishes, one of the patients, an old man, came up to me and asked me what I knew about Kurt's background. I didn't think there was anything unusual in his question. People in a nursing home have lots of time on their hands, so they tend to fill it with trivial conversations. I told that man that Kurt had been a prison guard, and his reaction was immediate and vicious. He ran over to Kurt's wheelchair, grabbed its pushing handles, and aimed it at the top of the stairs before I grasped his intentions. I still see Kurt's face appealing for help in many of my dreams. The old man pushed Kurt's chair down the stairs and shouted 'That's for my wife and my daughter!' It was only after I saw the chair bouncing down the stairs and off the wall, that I noticed the serial number tattooed on the old man's forearm."

Millicent put a reassuring hand on Robert's shoulder and continued the story. "That old man had combined Kurt's accent with the prison guard information and had concluded that he had been a Nazi guard in a World War II death camp. He saw a way to avenge his family members, and he took it."

Irma asked, "What did the police do afterward? Was that man convicted of murder?"

Millicent shook her head. "The authorities decided that it had been a case of temporary insanity due to extenuating circumstances, and the man never stood trial. He died of a heart attack the following year. We converted the ornamental staircase to a safer one, enclosed and guarded by alarm-fitted fire doors. We also agreed that no one in our nursing home would ever identify by name the man who pushed Kurt to his death. You'll notice that Robert never mentioned a name during his summary, and he won't even if you question him further. Kurt died because of a tragic mistake, and his assailant's family should not have to bear any more suffering growing out of that death."

Arthur and Irma nodded to each other. Arthur said, "We came here feeling that Kurt deserved to have his death investigated and his murderer identified and charged. We now agree with you that there has been enough tragedy for everyone concerned. Robert, your part in that event was innocent and well meant. Don't feel guilty. You should feel blessed for having tried to be a friend to someone in need."

Irma said, "When we exchanged introductions, we forgot to mention that Arthur is a pastor. Forgiveness and blessings are the order of the day. Guilt shall be banished from this place."

Arthur looked intently at Irma. "Well said; you are getting the hang of pastoring."

CHAPTER 85 – STATUS CHECK

While Arthur drove their rental car back toward the Rochester airport, he contemplated how the life story of Kurt Linser had stemmed from those out-of-context memory fragments experienced by Michelle Caspar.

"We now have a good picture of Kurt Linser's life, Irma, except for those years that didn't enter into Michelle's consciousness. The process of assembling that biography from fragments reminds me of the way biblical scholars attempt to derive the life stories of people mentioned in the Bible from their statements and what others are quoted as saying about them."

"That's an interesting observation, but now that we know the story, I'd better call Rosemary Swinton and fill her in on our discoveries. That information may help her when she next works with Michelle."

Irma took her phone out of her purse and contacted Rosemary while Arthur continued to drive toward the Rochester airport. Irma and Rosemary talked for about ten minutes before their call ended.

Arthur said, "That was an animated conversation. I heard your half. Did Rosemary come up with anything new or unusual?"

"The most intriguing thing she said was that the key to why Kurt's memories attached themselves to Michelle was his traumatic death. Many of the memories of prior lives they receive at the University involve a violent or sudden death."

"That suggests that souls or spirits that are at peace at the time of death don't want to come back tied to someone else. I don't know how far I want to take the question of reincarnation, or souls that don't want to allow their lives and deaths to be without some form of record, but speculation stimulates some interesting possibilities."

"Do you want to share any wild thoughts with me?"

"Maybe later – we're at the rental car return kiosk. We'll have to hustle to catch that bus that's about to leave for the terminal. Last time I checked, our flight's listing showed it as departing on time."

After arriving at Chicago's O'Hare Airport, they ransomed their car from the parking garage and drove back to their home in Amboy, Illinois. Once home, they would spend their evening reviewing their notes on the Parkville mysteries so that they would be ready to depart early for a morning meeting at the Sandley Agency apartment.

Bobby Andrews was in one of his better moods when he joined them at Jeremy and Debbie's apartment. He waited until Arthur and Irma arrived before saying anything about the underlying reason for his upbeat attitude. He wanted a larger audience for his narrative. Once everyone had arrived and settled onto chairs and couches in the living room, he revealed his development.

"We hauled in the drug dealers and a bunch of their customers last night, with the assistance of the Sheriff's Department and the State Police. We cordoned off four blocks around the spot where Hank Robbins witnessed the transfer of drugs from the Rehabilitation Home couriers to a street dealer. We included the network of back alleys they used that were too narrow for cars to follow them. We blocked all exits from the neighborhood and then sent in foot patrols to corral everyone. I made sure that our operation had complete secrecy, and it paid off because one of the drug customers we caught turned out to be an attorney in Mayor Finch's office. If I had alerted the mayor in advance, the crooks would have known we were coming."

Wally applauded. "Do you think this will rid Parkville of drug dealers for a while?"

"The operative phrase in your question is 'for a while,' which is probably correct. We haven't had large amounts of heroin and cocaine getting in here because we're too small a market for them. With elimination of the illegal painkillers that came out of Parkville Rehabilitation Home, Parkville street drug sales should dry up for a significant time."

Arthur said, "Congratulations, Bobby ... who has something to contribute regarding the supplier of the painkillers?"

Bobby gestured his willingness to speak to that point. "Wally did a good job of going undercover and getting Esther Ramirez, a physical therapist, to supply him with illicit painkillers so that we could catch her delivering them. When I interviewed her, she said that Joanna Diaz, the therapist who quit following the four patient deaths, had delivered these drugs to the Rehabilitation Home in the past, but that someone else must be handling deliveries now. Ramirez also said that Joanna Diaz claimed that many other rehabilitation facilities were also included in this drug supply network."

Wally said, "That says that we have the chance to cut out the whole network if we can discover how the supplier works with our local Rehabilitation Home."

Irma completed a note on her pad before speaking. "I think we can go after the source from both ends of the supply chain. Esther Ramirez is the most junior of the therapists at the Parkville facility. I'll wager that one of her more senior colleagues, someone close to Joanna Diaz, handles the final placement of the drugs within the building. Someone might identify Joanna's close friends. We might be able to track the network source by using forensic techniques. You have a sample of the painkiller that Esther delivered. I'll have a lab analysis prepared for that one, and we'll run similar analyses on samples from different pharmaceutical companies. Once we learn who made the painkiller, we'll be able to check for leaks in that company's distribution system."

Arthur said, "That analysis and tracking sounds as though it would take a long time to accomplish, but would be rigorous and would lead to reliable evidence. Can we shortcut the process in some way, Irma?"

"I didn't mention it before, because drug dealers might crush and re-press pills, but if they keep the painkillers in their original configuration, we could compare the color, shape, and markings of the pills with those shown in *The Physician's Desk Reference* to see whether they are a standard prescription item. If they are, we would be able to identify the manufacturer directly from that book. If an underground compounder presses the pills, we would have to take the longer comparative analysis route that I suggested earlier. Either way, I'll work on tracing the painkillers."

Wally said, "I'll identify the close friends of Joanna Diaz. Martha Callahan should have that information."

Jeremy asked, "Are you two becoming an item? You appear to be together quite frequently."

"Almost all of our time together is spent on business."

"Almost all?"

Debbie said, "Leave Wally alone, Jeremy. He's blushing like a teenager."

Everyone laughed, and then Arthur waved for attention.

"We didn't plan it this way, but we're focusing on the drug connections. Continuing with that aspect of the several cases that involve the Rehabilitation Home, we earlier suggested that Pastor Rebecca Klingham might have died because she spotted the drug trafficking there.

Who was her killer? Wally, do you have a suspect or evidence?"

"The obvious suggestion is Joanna Diaz. Esther said she had seen Joanna placing drugs in the container from which therapists removed small quantities for clients. Joanna had the physical capability to inflict Pastor Klingham's injuries. However, shy of her confessing, I don't know how we could get enough evidence to convict her."

Arthur said, "I suspect that Joanna headed for Las Vegas because that was the location of her drug supplier. She had connections there. She also told Jeremy by telephone that she is doing quite well in Las Vegas. I suggest that an inquiry by the police out there or a federal agency might lead to convictions for Joanna and others out there for drug distribution through the network of rehabilitation facilities. It may or may not reveal where they get their painkiller drugs. As to your question about getting enough evidence to convict Joanna for Pastor Klingham's murder, I doubt you'll succeed, because I don't think Joanna murdered anyone."

CHAPTER 86 – ARTHUR AND BOBBY

A hush fell over the meeting group as Bobby stared at Arthur in disbelief. "Are you going to shoot down my theory that the person who murdered Pastor Rebecca Klingham did so because Rebecca had discovered the drug dealings at Parkville Rehabilitation Home?"

"Not necessarily; I don't have enough information about the drug aspects of this case to do that. I'm simply convinced that Joanna Diaz wasn't Rebecca's murderer."

"And what convinced you that she didn't do it?"

"You did."

Bobby gave Arthur another piercing stare. "What do you mean? I think she did it."

"You told me that the Rebecca Klingham's killer was inexpert at applying a carotid sleeper hold. You told me that the killer compressed and cracked some of Rebecca's vertebrae."

"I did say that."

"Joanna Diaz is a highly trained and experienced physical therapist. She would be extremely careful to avoid fracturing bones if she wanted a murder to look like a suicide."

"If Diaz didn't do it, who did?"

"I'll need to learn more the other people involved in the drug trafficking and other aspects of this case before I'll be ready to name the killer."

"Then you definitely believe Rebecca's murderer was someone in the drug ring."

"Not necessarily; I have to look at all the possibilities."

"That statement takes us back to the beginning of this case."

"I didn't say that either. Let's change the subject and consider the trust that was the majority owner of the Rehabilitation Home. Has anyone information to present on that one?"

Irma said, "Thanks for changing the subject, Arthur. I thought you and Bobby were about to have a fight."

Bobby shook his head negatively. "I value Arthur's friendship enough to avoid an actual fight. He frustrates me with his unusual ways of looking at things, but he's been right enough times to make me test his theories. Besides, he based his opinion on what I told him. There's no better source than that."

They all laughed. Then Jeremy stood to speak.

"I'll summarize where we are on the topic of the ownership trust. We tried a direct confrontation with the lawyer who represents the trust, and he stonewalled our inquiry by standing behind the attorney/client relationship barrier. We're hoping to find that this attorney has something in his past that we can use as leverage to make him volunteer some information."

Debbie said, "What Jeremy means is that we've failed. That lawyer is not likely to have anything to hide. He was too smooth in handling our questions. We're not sure how to proceed."

Jeremy appeared agitated at Debbie's comment, but then he shrugged his shoulders and said, "She's right, Arthur. Do you have any suggestions?"

"I don't have any suggestions except that you relax and not worry about it. I already know who is hiding behind that trust."

CHAPTER 87 – HIDE AND SEEK

This time, Jeremy stared at Arthur as the room fell silent. "How can you know who is hiding behind the ownership trust when you haven't even been in town to investigate it?"

"You said that the attorney stonewalled you when you questioned him about the trust. There are two ways to get to the other side of a high blocking wall. You took the conventional approach and tried to climb over it. I chose to go around it instead. Rather than ask who is behind the trust, I asked which of the people who might be behind the trust has had frequent and large transactions in his or her bank account."

Bobby asked, "How did you access bank account information? You didn't go through our department."

"I called Penny Gonzalez and asked her to use the powers of her federal agency to get the account information. I suspected that someone who was hiding financial activities would not do so through a local bank. The feds can query banks all over the world."

"What did you learn?"

"Bobby, I learned that someone local has a record of moving substantial amounts of cash through several accounts in a bank in the Cayman Islands. One of those accounts carries the label, Rehabilitation Home Trust."

Jeremy said, "I'll bet that account had disbursements to a drug network."

"I didn't ask Penny to check into drug aspects of our case because she and Joe are currently assigned to work on a terrorism undercover sting, and that takes priority. I was lucky to get a small slice of her time for the banking inquiry. Penny promised to get in touch with us if they finish their current assignment ahead of schedule."

"Arthur, enough talk; are you going to tell us who is behind that ownership trust?"

"Not quite yet, Bobby; I don't want any of us to treat a suspect differently than we have before. It would be automatic for us to vary our interactions if I identified the suspect before we knew about the drug aspects of our case and before we were ready to seek an arrest warrant."

"Will you at least tell us that you have complete confidence in your information, so that we no longer have to try to outwit that attorney?"

"Jeremy, I have complete confidence that I know who is behind the trust. However, I'll also say that you and Debbie should continue to pester the attorney, so that he doesn't realize how much we know."

"That makes sense Arthur, and since I really can't yet identify the trust person, Debbie and I will be pleased to keep bugging that pompous shyster. I for one will enjoy it."

Debbie nodded her agreement. "That Quentin Edwards was about to make a play for me and to try to move Jeremy out of the picture. He deserves an unexpected rejection."

CHAPTER 88 – MARIANNE RENDLEY

After the meeting, Arthur stopped at Parkville United Methodist Church to check for emergencies that might have developed while he and Irma were in New York. He received an unexpected greeting when he entered Shirley Hadley's office.

"Hello, visitor, you're always welcome here."

"What did I do to earn the change in my designation, Shirley?"

"Your temporary pastor card has expired. Permanent Pastor Marianne Rendley has arrived and set herself up in your former study space. If you would like to stop in to see her, I'll equip you with a mug of coffee to take along. She never touches the stuff and won't have any to offer you."

Arthur had always thought that people who didn't drink coffee were introverts, but he accepted the mug of steaming brew from Shirley, mouthed his thanks, and headed for the pastor's study to meet his latest replacement. Surprised by the closed door, he knocked, seeking permission to enter.

A resounding voice responded to his knock. "This is the day the Lord hath made; come on in and rejoice in it."

Arthur opened the door slowly, uncertain what to expect. Looking through the open doorway, he saw a tall woman holding a Bible in her left hand as she stood up from the comfort of her reclining chair. He glanced around the room and saw no other furniture except for a light pole with three swiveling lamp heads on it. He wondered what had happened to his desk.

"Greetings, sir; I'm Pastor Rendley. How may I assist you?"

Richard Davidson

Arthur shifted his coffee mug to his left hand and shook hands with her. "You already have assisted me by removing my temporary status. I'm Arthur Blake, and I've been keeping this place going in preparation for your arrival."

"Pastor Blake, I've looked forward to meeting you. I hope you don't mind my having changed this room before you returned."

"This is your bailiwick now, so by all means put your personal stamp on it. May I call you Marianne? Please call me Arthur."

"Of course, as colleagues, we should be informal with each other, Arthur. I usually maintain a degree of formality with the flock though. I find that a little distance between people facilitates respect."

Arthur thought she would have problems with that attitude in Parkville, but he simply said, "Bishop Chandler told me of your appointment and your missionary background. Where did you serve as a missionary?"

"I spent the last five years in India, trying to bring as many Hindus as possible into Christianity."

"And were you successful at that mission?"

"We had varying results, until we were asked to leave the country."

"What was your problem there?"

"The authorities told us that we had to be tolerant of other religions and not preach that Christianity was the only valid way to salvation. They also took offense at some of our people calling Hinduism a primitive religion."

"Were you one of those people?"

"I was, but not the loudest voice taking that attitude. I just wanted to open their eyes to the truth."

"The Hindu religion and Indian civilization are much older than the teachings of Jesus. It's no wonder that they resisted missionaries looking down on their ways."

266

"You talk as though you aren't speaking for Christ in your work."

"There's a difference between forcing yourself on someone else and accepting questioners into your flock. I've never done missionary service because I find it hard to preach that ours is the only way. In any case, I wish you success here. Let me know if you have any matters where my assistance would be of value. I served here for five years before my recent temporary return."

Marianne Rendley debated between two versions of a closing remark. Finally, she said, "The word among clergy I met was that you half-served here while you spent most of your time on outside interests."

Arthur did not reply, but simply left her office and the building.

When Bishop Chandler returned to his office that afternoon, he found a message from Arthur indicating that he had met with Pastor Rendley and that the police had made good progress toward determining who had killed Pastor Rebecca Klingham. Bishop Chandler smiled in recognition of Arthur's ability to have matters always under control.

CHAPTER 89 – ARTHUR AND IRMA

Arthur drove to Bobby Andrews' house, where Irma had spent the day visiting Bobby's wife, Renee. When he arrived, he was pleasant and unusually calm, so much so that Irma knew that they would soon be discussing problems. After fifteen minutes of Arthur's conversations with Renee and her young daughter, Thelma Lou, Irma told Renee that they would have to leave because of a scheduled appointment.

As soon as they had left the Andrews' driveway, Irma asked, "Do you want to tell me what has you so upset, Arthur?"

"It's just that I wonder sometimes how the church has survived so long. This new pastor, Marianne Rendley, is going to do her best to destroy our peaceful congregation in Parkville."

"How bad is she?"

"She's a former missionary who thinks she has all the answers and that everyone should have her point of view. She's intolerant of other religions. She wants all members of her flock to agree with her, but she wants to maintain formalities and distance herself from them. She won't even let church members call her by her first name. Further, if she gets any resistance from the congregation, she's going to bad-mouth me and say that I didn't give the Parkville Church sufficient attention while I was in charge."

"Wow ... she is a winner. Do you have anything good that you can say about her?"

"She's going to make it easier for me to decide to make my leave of absence a long-term thing."

"Howard Chandler won't like that."

"What do you mean? The bishop will be happy to have me out of his hair. He thinks I'm irresponsible and that I tend to embarrass the church when I investigate cases."

"True, but he also knows that you've saved him from much larger embarrassments on several occasions."

"Like when?"

"Like when you kept him from retiring and pushing the election of a murderer to take his place as bishop."

"But, as you said, I did keep him from retiring."

"What do you think Bishop Chandler wants to do when he retires?"

"I don't know; do you have inside information?"

"He wants to learn how you solve problems and investigate cases."

"Not him too! My nightmare is becoming reality. Instead of it being about my investigating too many cases at the same time, it's about being a clone master who has to train and supervise an army of investigators.

Richard Davidson

CHAPTER 90 – ROSEMARY AND MICHELLE

Once more, Dr. Rosemary Swinton sat across from Michelle Caspar in the interview suite of the Division of Perceptual Studies. Michelle had just completed and signed a form authorizing the group to publish or verbally report on her case study. She looked up as Rosemary spoke.

"This will be our last formal session, Michelle, but you are welcome to visit us at any time, and we may call on you to attend a scientific conference where people may want to meet you and ask questions. If that happens, we will make arrangements to cover your travel costs and give you an honorarium."

"That would be fine, Rosemary, but I wouldn't want to be treated like a specimen to be dissected."

"We would be sure to avoid that. You are much more of a breakthrough for us. We rarely encounter someone your age with currently active prior life memories, especially ones that correspond to a documented individual as your memories have."

"I was rather astounded by the amount of information Arthur and Irma Blake were able to find."

Rosemary leaned forward to study Michelle's reaction to her next question. "We now have a detailed summary of Kurt Linser's life and death. Do you feel any different for having learned so much about him?"

Michelle joined Rosemary in leaning forward. "I wondered earlier how this knowledge would affect me. The odd thing is that I feel quite comfortable with it. When I first experienced Kurt's memories, I felt disturbed by the remembrance of an additional individual's life within me.

It was even more challenging because that person was male. I wondered whether I would approach my future as someone who was half female and half male. Now that I know Kurt's entire story, he has become a separate person, and I am back to being my original female self."

"Does that mean that you'll try to get back together with the boyfriend you dropped because of your gender confusion?"

"No, he's probably moved on to someone else, and I would have trouble relating my experience to him."

"Are you sure you mean that last comment, Michelle? It suggests that you would have trouble talking about this to anyone, even though you agreed to let us publish it and said you would answer the questions of researchers and other interested parties."

"You're right; I withdraw that comment. It's probably too early for me to think about discussing what has happened to me. I'll have to take some time and ease into it."

"Since you already know them, why don't you consider discussing the entire process with Irma and Arthur Blake? They were the ones who, so to speak, added the flesh to the skeleton of your fragmentary memories and found Kurt Linser. They know him as well as you do. A discussion with them should be no more difficult than the ones you've had with me."

"That's a good idea, Rosemary. I'd like to see them again and thank them for helping rid me of my confusion. I also want to thank you for all of our sessions and informal discussions."

CHAPTER 91 – ENTERTAINMENT

Wally Sanborn glanced at the screen of his ringing telephone and added a smile to his voice as he answered it. "Hello, Martha; how's everything going for you today?"

"I think it's going to be a great day, Wally. A musical ensemble contacted me. They do concerts and sing-alongs at nursing homes and rehab facilities. I've booked them for an afternoon of entertainment next Friday. We've had enough sadness and other difficulties around here. It's time for something upbeat."

"That's a good idea. Even though we're still straightening out some problems that have occurred over there, you should turn the page and aim for a brighter future. Will you need any help with the setup for this program?"

"I have it under control. I convinced Patrick Hurley to return to our staff as the Physical Plant Manager. He'll take care of the sound system for this special event; on a regular basis, he'll also handle capital equipment planning and he'll supervise Ben Hendry, the person I hired to take Patrick's old technician job. That Ben certainly needs some supervision. His shop area is a mess. He doesn't take care of his tools or put things away. Ben even has a shop vacuum without a hose on it, so I have no idea how or if he uses it. His room certainly doesn't look as though he has ever taken time to clean up."

Wally made a mental note to discuss that missing hose with Arthur and Bobby. "This entertainment program will be a good thing for you, Martha, but if Patrick is going to handle the logistics of preparing for it, why did you call me?"

"I called because I like the sound of your voice and because I want to be sure that you'll be there for this event."

"Are you asking me out on a date?"

"I guess I am. What's your answer?"

"Sure, I'll be happy to be there. Just don't expect me to pick you up and buy you a corsage."

"No pick-up is required; I'll be working at the Rehabilitation Home anyway. As for the corsage, I'll settle for a glass of punch – that's what we're serving, and it won't even be spiked with booze."

"I'd better take you to church some Sunday. Your unspiked punch would be appreciated by the Methodist powers-that-be."

"Just remember that alcohol is appreciated when we go to a tavern or the like. My name is Callahan, after all."

"I'll take that as an invitation to another date. You certainly are a forward woman, Martha. Your male companion never gets to ask you out."

"I'm glad you appointed yourself my male companion. I'll look forward to seeing you soon, Wally."

CHAPTER 92 – QUENTIN EDWARDS

In keeping with their agreement to treat the trust attorney as though they were still trying to identify the person or persons he represented, Debbie Danforth arranged for a second appointment with Quentin Edwards. This time, she would go alone, on the theory that he might be more willing to talk without Jeremy present. When she arrived, Debbie wore a businesslike navy blue tweed suit. She was somewhat surprised that Edwards, the upscale fashion model, wore an old plaid flannel shirt and had his shirtsleeves rolled up.

Quentin greeted Debbie and asked whether she would like to sit on his couch while she presented her prepared information.

Debbie said, "No, Quentin, I want to get on with our business, and I have a tight schedule. I'll sit opposite you at your desk."

She took the visitor's chair and waited for him to sit in his desk chair.

"Before I sit, I'll pour us a couple of glasses of white wine so that our meeting won't be completely formal. By the way, in that suit you could pass for a trial lawyer. Have you had any legal training?"

"Just one contract law course ... the wine isn't necessary. We should get down to business." Debbie watched Quentin carefully, using the mirror behind his desk, while she appeared to be reviewing the papers in her briefcase. He had added something from a small bottle into one of the glasses of wine."

Quentin returned to his desk with the two glasses, placed one in front of her, and then sat in his swivel chair with the other glass in his hand. He raised it and said, "Here's to a good meeting and a continuing friendship."

Debbie raised her glass, mirroring his motion, but she returned it to the desktop without drinking from it. "The good meeting is all I need right now." She withdrew three sheets of paper from her briefcase and laid them on the desk.

"Here are copies of three applications for life insurance, signed by the three patients who later died at the Parkville Rehabilitation Center, specifying that your ownership trust would be the beneficiary in all three instances."

"Confidential patient documents aren't supposed to have copies."

"Noel Burnside is very efficient; he makes copies of every paper he handles, regardless of instructions to the contrary. He has a self-preservation instinct that makes him want to distance himself from anything that might be or appear to be unethical. What happened to the insurance company payoffs on these policies?"

"If you won't join me in a drink, I won't respond to your questions."

Reluctantly, Debbie raised the glass to her lips.

"Now, Mr. Edwards, please tell me about the handling of these insurance policies. Did the benefits from the insurance company go into the Parkville Rehabilitation Home account or into somebody's pocket?" Debbie stumbled on the pronunciation of rehabilitation and her words slowed noticeably as she approached the end of that sentence. Then her head nodded a few times before it came to rest on her chest, her eyes closed.

Quentin Edwards stood and walked around to Debbie's side of the desk. He pushed her shoulder twice to see whether she was awake enough to react to his touch. She did not respond.

He pulled her chair away from the desk and picked her up, cradling her unresponsive body in his arms. Then he carried her over to the couch and lowered her onto its surface.

Quentin felt the tingle of excitement as he unbuttoned Debbie's jacket and blouse. "You're mine now and I'm going to enjoy this, but very slowly, to prolong the pleasure." He slipped his hand inside Debbie's bra and felt her breast and nipple. Then he unfastened the bra's hooks and moved the loose fabric out of the way so that he could study her breasts. She surprised him by moaning and slipping sideways. He didn't realize that she had pushed a button on a device hidden under her skirt.

The door to the office crashed open, and Detectives Hank Robbins and Gene Murphy rushed in, followed by Jeremy Hadley, Noel Burnside, and Irma Blake.

Hank announced, "Quentin Edwards, you are under arrest for the attempted rape of Debbie Danforth." He proceeded to read the attorney his rights, while that individual nodded continuously in recognition of the litany.

Edwards said, "She passed out while we were talking. I was just unbuttoning her outer garments so that she could breathe better."

Irma asked, "Are you OK, Debbie?"

"I'm fine, but I'm glad you hurried in after I pressed that button. A few minutes more and I would have had to smash him myself."

Edwards asked, "You weren't unconscious from the wine?"

Irma said, "That's both perceptive and self-incriminating. I'll take the wine glass from the visitor side of the desk for analysis." She poured the wine from that glass into a small bottle and then placed the small bottle plus the wine glass into an evidence container.

Debbie sat down after finishing the repairs to her wardrobe. "Edwards is someone who always has had everything he wanted. He thinks he can take anything or anyone. I saw him add something to my wine, so I only pretended to drink from my glass. I was sure I knew how to act afterward."

Jeremy put his hands on her shoulders and kissed her lightly on the cheek. "You're a hero, Debbie. You've put Mr. Fancypants where he belongs."

"Actually, Noel is the hero. You'll hear my audio recording of this meeting, but you should have seen the look on Quentin's face when I showed him that we had copies of the signed insurance applications."

Noel Burnside smiled. "Having copies of critical documents almost always pays off. I'm sorry you had to go through this trauma, Debbie."

"Thanks, Noel; you're a good friend. We'll have to meet again for breakfast sometime, when Jeremy isn't wearing his jealous hat."

"Don't worry, you two can meet any time. I know that I don't own you, Debbie."

CHAPTER 93 – BOBBY AND ARTHUR

Once more, Pastor Arthur Blake and Chief Bobby Andrews sat in a booth at McNoonan's Steakhouse for lunch, this time with Bobby having promised to pay the bill. He had again worn casual clothing to avoid his uniform's causing the host tension during the busy lunch hour.

"Arthur, with you living in Amboy and no longer on temporary duty at Parkville United Methodist Church, we're going to have to find a new spot for our private meetings. Using McNoonan's as a conference room gets expensive."

"For larger group meetings, we can use The Sandley office at Jeremy and Debbie's apartment, but for one-on-one sessions our only choices are a restaurant or a room at Parkville Police Headquarters. You could set up a consultant's office there."

"That's a possibility, but there are times when my officers shouldn't know about confidential meetings. I guess we'll have to settle for restaurant space after all. Anyway, I wanted to discuss Quentin Edwards and the mysterious person behind the ownership trust at Parkville Rehabilitation Home. You had wanted to keep the hidden individual's identity secret for a while. I suspect that you'll have to reveal that information now, and I'm quite curious about it."

"Why do you think it's time for that revelation, Bobby?"

"For one thing, Martha Callahan has always received her administration instructions for the Rehabilitation

Home from Quentin Edwards as the Trust's attorney. Now that Edwards is locked up for attempted rape, Martha will have to learn where to turn for guidance."

"I suspect that the person behind the trust will find a way to communicate with her, or she'll manage quite well, flying solo for a while."

"You're enjoying my unsatisfied curiosity, Arthur. Give me one good reason for continuing to keep that identity secret."

"My main argument is that the individual behind the trust has not simply been a passive witness to events at the Rehabilitation Home, but has taken an active part in them. If he or she becomes aware that his or her identity is known, we lose our ability to learn how all the events and all the involved people tie together."

"There you go again with your secrecy; 'he or she' and 'his or her' – you're nitpicking again and teasing me. I have an argument for you to tell me so that I can share your secret."

"What's your reasoning?"

"You need to share that identity with one other person, so that it doesn't get lost if something happens to you."

"There's a delightful thought. It is logical, though. I'll tell you, but you'll have to use your considerable training and skills to avoid revealing our knowledge when you deal with others involved in the case."

"You mean that you don't want an 'I know that you know that I know' situation."

"That's it exactly."

"Good, then tell me who it is."

"Fair enough, Bobby; the person hiding behind the ownership trust at Parkville Rehabilitation Home is ..."

CHAPTER 94 – PARTY PREPARATIONS

Patrick Hurley was glad to have his long period of inactivity behind him. He had stayed in shape by interspersing his afternoons at the tavern with long walks and calisthenics, but now he would be able to get back to creative efforts and socializing with old friends. Already, several of the physical therapists had greeted him. One had even asked him to repair her massage vibrator. It was almost as though he had never left the rehabilitation building.

The Classical Jazz party that Martha Callahan had scheduled would be a good change-of-pace for this outfit. A few people on the staff had been oblivious to the investigations in progress, but most were concerned that a murderer might be working alongside them. Some of the long-term patients vacillated between being nervous about their futures and being excited to be in the midst of a murder mystery. The jazz party would be only the first step toward the resurrection of morale, but he hoped it would be an important one.

Patrick had rented a complete sound system for the occasion, which he would set up that afternoon in the dining room, with the assistance of someone named Belle Simmons from the rental company. He had been surprised that the technician would be female; the salesperson on the telephone had corrected him when he repeated the name as Bill instead of Belle. She undoubtedly knew more about sound systems than he did.

He had rigged a stage platform in the center of the room and had rearranged all of the tables in a semicircle surrounding it, leaving space between the arc of tables and the stage for non-ambulatory patients in wheelchairs. An opening at the stage side of the semicircle would serve as the entryway for the musicians and as a safe corridor for cables and equipment. At the extreme end of this walkway, he had set up a small desk where he would sit to monitor the audio levels and control the lighting during the performance.

As Patrick left the dining room, he encountered Wally Sanborn, on his way out of the building after leaving Martha Callahan's office.

Patrick said, "How's the retired Army officer today? Are you still working on the job for that agency?"

"Hello, Patrick; it's good to see you back at work. I'm sure all that time sitting idle did you little good. Yes, I'm still working for the Sandley Agency. Hopefully, we're making some progress on our assignment."

"I came back to work here in the hope that all the scandals were a thing of the past. I hope it turns out that way. By the way, Wally, you don't sound nearly as Irish as you did when we last met."

Wally laughed. "I'll plead guilty to emulating those around me. On that earlier occasion, I spoke with one of your Irish neighbors and then met with you in that Irish pub. I just couldn't resist adding some green to my speech patterns."

"I would have thought you'd still be talking that way. Scuttlebutt has it that you and Martha Callahan have been spending time together."

Wally flinched. "I didn't realize we had attracted that much attention. We meet in connection with my assignment, but occasionally for other things."

"Don't worry, Wally; I don't gossip. Take my words as a caution that some of those who do like to spread rumors have noticed your relationship with Martha."

"We're only friends; there's no relationship."

"Right; and I can't stand the taste of Guinness."

Wally laughed and gave Patrick an overly hard pat on his shoulder. Then he headed for the front door exit at top speed. He would soon have to decide on the degree to which that relationship existed.

CHAPTER 95 – BOBBY AND ARTHUR

At Bobby's request, Arthur had joined him in the parking lot by Mallard Lake, based on the spycraft theory that conversations in outdoor spaces had the lowest susceptibility to eavesdropping. Arthur parked and walked over to the rock upon which Bobby sat.

"I suspect that you selected this spot for privacy. What are our topics for discussion today?"

"You are astute, Arthur. Yes, I wanted to talk about more than one confidential subject. The first is the new pastor at our church, Marianne Rendley. I met her yesterday, and I found her a little difficult to take. I think she's going to irritate some of the members, beginning with me."

"She does have some strong opinions."

"How did you react to her?"

"As I said, she does have some strong opinions."

Bobby chuckled. "I know that you have to be diplomatic, but don't expect me and a bunch of others to take that course. If she doesn't ease up and accept people the way they are, the church will definitely lose members."

"The same thought had crossed my mind, but we both know that in the United Methodist Church, the Bishop and the District Superintendent present their candidate, and it is rare for the local church to be able to reject that selection."

"I just thought I'd better draw your attention to the problem, in case you had any influence in such matters."

"Actually, Bobby, I doubt that I'll continue to have much influence with the church officials on any matters. Now that there's an official replacement here, I'm back on extended leave of absence status, and I expect that my future relationship with the church won't go beyond a consultancy. Even your new Pastor Rendley brought up the fact that some church officials think my ministry suffers from the time I spend on investigative pursuits."

"That's just another reason for us to give her a very difficult time in her new assignment. Don't say any more on the subject. We'll handle her."

Arthur shrugged his shoulders in lieu of any further comment. "I assume you had something official you wanted to discuss as well."

"I do indeed. You've shared with me the name of the person behind that ownership trust, but we'll need a plan for linking that individual to the murders. The beneficial insurance policies constitute a major motive, but a good lawyer could argue that they were simply economic self-protection against people dying without paying their bills."

"I'm sure that would be the defense approach. You have the legal front man under arrest for attempted rape. If you try to get a warrant to search his files, he'll claim attorney/client privilege, and you'll have a problem. However, if you hint that you're planning to start disbarment proceedings against him because of the sexual attack, he might want to offer access to his files in exchange for a delay in the disbarment process."

"He'll know that disbarment will happen anyway if he's convicted of the attempted rape felony, but he might go for the delay bargain in the hope that he'll be able to avoid a conviction in court. I'll see what I can do. That's a reasonable approach."

"Even if you do get access to Quentin Edwards' files, we don't know what they contain. It's quite likely that they won't include anything that will incriminate the person behind the trust. We've just assumed there's something there to find. This case may not be that simple."

"In other words, Arthur, you're saying that we have to cover all the bases, but that after all that work, we're as likely to strike out as to get evidence that will lead to a murder conviction."

"I think you just summarized the definition of good police work, Bobby."

CHAPTER 96 – THE BOYS IN THE BAND

Larry Jakes had felt a tingle of excitement when the business manager for their band told him that he had a signed contract for one performance in Illinois at the Parkville Rehabilitation Home. The manager had executed that contract with one slight modification from their usual routine, per Larry's request. Larry had insisted that for this particular engagement, they should change their group's name from the Larry Jakes Band to the Jake Lawrence Band. Given the frequent legal difficulties encountered by traveling musical groups, this minor alias assumption felt entirely reasonable.

For this one-shot appearance, they would simplify the band structure to sax, string base, piano, and drums, eliminating trumpet and guitar. The Rehabilitation Home had promised they would have a well-tuned piano in the hall. The abbreviated band configuration freed up their youngest two members for other things. Trumpeter Dez Gentry would handle advance preparations at their next booking site, while guitarist Jack Milgrim would cover a special assignment for Larry. This division of assignments was normal, because Gentry and Milgrim had military backgrounds and could handle special tasks better than their older colleagues could.

Larry looked forward to the appearance in Parkville, Illinois with mixed emotions. He wanted to see the facility where Mary Welker – his Mary – had died, but he didn't know how he would react to meeting the person directly or indirectly responsible for her death. Had someone murdered Mary, or had she been a victim of staff carelessness?

CHAPTER 97 – IRMA AND ARTHUR

As Irma and Arthur walked through the Rehabilitation Home lobby on their way to Martha Callahan's office, they looked into the dining room to view the preparations for the pending party. As they did so, Irma nudged Arthur.

"Are you sure you know what you're doing? By withholding the name of the person behind the ownership trust, you're taking a chance that someone will be hurt or killed. People know that there's a killer in their midst, but they don't know who that person is."

"You're making an unwarranted assumption. You usually require facts before you reach a conclusion."

"I think you enjoy teasing me."

"No, I'm simply justifying my withholding that person's identity because it might be dangerous and confusing to release it. Anyway, I've passed that information to Bobby, so I'm not the only one who knows it."

"Why didn't you tell me, Arthur? We usually don't keep secrets from each other."

"This is a special case. I trust your thinking, and I want to see how you approach the solution of this case without that key piece of information. I will tell you that I'm trying to keep people from jumping to premature conclusions."

"In other words, you think that because of the insurance policies forced on the last three women who died, everyone assumes that the person behind the trust killed them."

"I told you I like the way you think and apply logic."

"That's why you said I reached a conclusion without sufficient facts to justify it. You're questioning whether those insurance policies benefitting the ownership trust were the only motive for the deaths of those three women."

"Bingo – I'm not saying that the policies weren't the true motive, but I want to look for alternate motives before I grab the obvious one."

"I know you well enough to understand what you're saying. You absolutely resent an easy solution. Just be prepared to accept it if you can't find a viable alternative."

"I will, but I have to prove to myself that I didn't overlook something in favor of the easy path."

"We understand each other. Now let's have our talk with Martha Callahan."

When they entered Martha's office, they found her talking with someone on the telephone. She gestured for them to take seats and held up one finger to indicate that she would be through with her conversation shortly. A minute later, Martha put down the telephone and turned to them.

"Welcome, you two. I rarely get to see both Blakes at the same time. What may I do for you?"

Arthur nodded to Irma, and she took the lead. "Martha, we're still trying to get a feeling for the way Parkville Rehabilitation Home functions, in order to better understand how the three patients' murders might have occurred. I don't want to appear disrespectful, but I've had the feeling that your employees work on their own, with varying degrees of efficiency, and with very little guidance from this office. Is that a fair statement, or would you like to correct my impression?"

"You're not being unfair, except when you refer to 'guidance from this office.' Please name me in your indictment. I take full responsibility for what goes on here. The facts are that I look at the staff and consulting medical people as being professionals who are capable of functioning on their own. I also feel that the greatest contribution we make to the rehabilitation of our patients is time away from their everyday pressures, so I don't want to give them new stress by putting rigorous demands on them during their stays here."

Arthur said, "That all sounds like a reasonable and practical strategy, Martha, but from what we've personally observed and learned from the Sandley Agency folks and the police, is that many on your staff don't qualify as self-sufficient professionals. Are you comfortable with the fact that some of your healthcare people treat their friends in your facilities and with your medications without charge or with personal pocketing of the proceeds?"

"I know that some of that goes on, Arthur, but I treat it as a minor inefficiency in the system. If I were to set up a task force to eliminate personally beneficial side jobs, it would cost our institution more than our losses if we just overlook such actions. Besides, we get increased staff loyalty and improved morale when staff members augment their salaries through personal transactions."

"You have a very tolerant and unusual attitude toward inefficiencies in the system. Don't you have to worry about denial of benefits by insurance companies or Medicare?"

"That's a sensitive topic, so let's keep this conversation confidential, but so long as entrepreneurial side jobs are not recorded in the books, they have no effect on institutional reimbursements. Because you've touched on such delicate matters, I would like to end this chat now. Please forgive me if you feel it's abrupt, but I can't see any good coming out of continuing this discussion."

Irma waited until they were in the hallway, out of range of Martha's hearing. Then she said, "You avoided any mention of drug transactions."

"That was deliberate. As a police matter, Bobby should initiate that conversation. We don't know enough details about who might be involved."

CHAPTER 98 – SELF-IMAGE

During a country drive outing with Martha the next day, Wally Sanborn pulled off the road into a state park and stopped his car near a stream.

Martha looked across from the passenger's seat. "Are you stopping for early-morning necking as in high school days, or do you have something else on your mind?"

"I stopped because it's time for us to have an in-depth talk. I don't know enough about you and your outlook. We've shared some preliminary attraction, but I need to understand someone before I open myself up to the possibility of a more serious relationship."

"I'd say that we've shared some experiences that are more than just preliminary, but I know what you mean. What would you like to know?"

"Tell me how you see yourself, Martha. Who are you?"

"I'm a product of an Irish background neighborhood in a tough part of Boston. In high school and beyond, I got into a few fights, mostly with girls, but occasionally with boys. I slugged a boy during a torchlight parade once, just for the hell of it. I stopped my formal education after two years of junior college, but I picked up a lot more during on-the-job training in more than a dozen assorted jobs prior to landing in Parkville at the Rehabilitation Home. I never got married, but I've had four live-in boyfriend relationships, including one who's in prison for trying to defraud an older woman after he left me. Needless to say, he didn't try any of that scamming with me."

"I hear you telling me you're as tough as nails. What do you want out of life that you haven't already achieved?"

"What is this, Wally, a job interview? I'll tell you up front that I don't want kids, and I don't want to get involved in a big family. I never asked, but do you have a bunch of brothers and sisters?"

"Now you're turning the questioning back on me. I have a couple of half-siblings who in turn have some more relatives that I've only met a few times. Why don't you like family?"

"I've always been my own person, and I don't like obligations to others."

Wally stared at her. "Martha, isn't that a strange statement for someone who runs a rehabilitation facility? Your whole job is concerned with obligations to others."

"My job is centered on providing temporary care to people who come into my life for a short while and then go home or to a more permanent treatment institution. I never consider them to be like family, and I don't get emotionally attached to them."

"I guess you won't want an emotional attachment with me either."

"You're a special case, Wally. You intrigue me and make me want to find out whether we're that mythical matched pair. This conversation is starting to get too mushy. Start the car, and let's get out of here."

CHAPTER 99 – PARTY TIME

Debbie and Jeremy arrived one hour early for the Rehabilitation Home jazz party because they, at Wally's request, had volunteered to help Martha Callahan with last-minute details and ushering for the event. They welcomed the assignment because it would give them the opportunity to access sections of the facility they had not yet visited. It felt unusual that Martha had scheduled a party in the midst of drug and murder investigations, but perhaps the merriment would cause one or more suspects to be more open to conversation, revealing their involvement and guilt. The event would be open to the public for a small fee, so the investigators mingling with the crowd would not appear out of place. Jeremy knew that Bobby Andrews would be there with his family, and his detectives, Hank and Gene, would haunt the background. Arthur and Irma Blake had already arrived and were talking with the musicians during a break in their rehearsal.

Patrick Hurley had enlarged the dining area by removing food handling equipment and a few large pieces of furniture. He had also left all of the double doors open so that people beyond the room could look in and hear the music. This last arrangement had engendered complaints from a few patients who didn't like music and didn't want to be disturbed, but Martha had resolved that conflict by offering those folks a distant enclosed therapy area with comfortable chairs and couches, plus an array of free snacks.

The Jake Lawrence Band rehearsed a variety of partial numbers with different combinations of musicians while

Patrick Hurley adjusted the audio levels and moved around the hall to be sure all areas would have reasonably good acoustics. He decided to close the two doors closest to the building entrance to eliminate competing background noise as people arrived and left.

Midway through the preparations, Martha Callahan entered the dining area with Wally Sanborn trailing a few feet behind her, still self-conscious about people linking them as a couple. Martha beckoned Patrick Hurley and Jake Lawrence to join her so that she could give each of them a copy of the event program and review it segment by segment.

The nurses and other staff members began to accompany wheelchair patients into the open area reserved for them inside the semicircle of tables, while other patients drifted in to sit at those tables. Public and staff attendees would occupy folding chairs Patrick had rented to fill the rear of the hall.

Jeremy, Debbie, and Wally took their ushering positions at two of the doorways to the hall and started to guide arriving guests and staff members to their seats. It would soon be show time.

Martha Callahan entered from behind the stage and took her place at the microphone in front of the seated band members to slightly more than polite applause from the audience. "Good afternoon ... I want to welcome you to an interlude of festivities, and I want to introduce you to our special guests, the Jake Lawrence Band. First, we have our leader on alto sax, Jake Lawrence. Bob Bryce is on the piano; Buddy Wilks plays string bass; and Peter Sazan is the drummer. Please give them a welcoming round of applause."

After the applause settled down, Martha said, "I have another surprise for you. After the band plays its first set, they'll take a break, and during that interval we'll be entertained by Ragbo the Clown, who will make balloon animals and do magic tricks for you."

One of the older patients shouted out, "I love clowns!"

Another yelled, "Clowns are creepy. I hate them."

Irma leaned over toward Arthur. "There's no neutral ground with clowns. They have a long history of being both funny and creepy."

Arthur said, "Sometimes the funniest ones appear to be pathetic and inept."

Martha continued after the interruptions. "I'm sure you'll like Ragbo, but first we'll be entertained by the Jake Lawrence Band. Take it away, Jake."

On cue, the band launched into its first series of jazz classics - *Bluesette*, *Tenderly*, *Night Train*, and *What a Wonderful World*. Then, as the applause filled the room, Jake Lawrence approached the microphone. "Thank you so much. You're a great audience. I see that Martha Callahan has left the room, but please convey our thanks to her for all her preparations prior to our appearance. You didn't come here to listen to me talk, so, let's get back to music.

With that, the band continued their concert with *Misty*, *Fascinating Rhythm*, *Lullaby of Birdland*, and *In the Mood*. When they heard the familiar opening bars of *In the Mood*, a male orderly and a female therapist stood and started to dance. Two other couples from the public area of the audience joined them. The audience directed some of their subsequent applause toward the dancers.

The band's energy had increased with each additional song. After a brief pause and a few jokes by the drummer at the microphone, they continued with *A Kiss to Build a Dream on*, *Satin Doll*, *A Foggy Day in London Town*, and *Easy to Love*. Then they completed their first set by playing and energetically singing: *When the Saints Go Marching in*.

Richard Davidson

The musicians placed their instruments where they would be ready for the second set. Then all except Jake walked off the rear of the stage for a break. Jake paused at the microphone to announce that people should stay in their seats because Ragbo the Clown would soon take the stage to entertain them during the band break. Then Jake turned and left the rear of the hall to join his fellow musicians.

The audience members exchanged quiet conversation while they awaited the clown's entrance. After a few minutes, the sound level increased, indicating the audience's irritation at the delay. One of the older patients yelled out for the clown to get on with it. Arthur and Irma exchanged significant glances and left their seats to determine whether there was a problem.

In the hallway outside the rear exit from the dining room, they saw Detective Hank Robbins. Arthur gestured for him to come closer.

"Hank, have you seen that clown, Ragbo? The audience in there is getting impatient."

"I saw him about ten minutes ago, heading for the parking lot. He said he'd be right back. I assumed he was going to his car for some of his show supplies. I thought he had come back inside, but I didn't actually see him again. I'll go out there and look for him."

Hank went out through a rear door, while Arthur and Irma separated to check different hallways. As Irma approached Martha Callahan's office, she noted the closed door. Martha normally kept her door open, but Irma attributed its closure to possible concern about audience members walking off with something. When she got close to the door, Irma saw a streak of blood on the doorknob. She saw Arthur at the end of the hall and called out for him to join her. Then, Irma put on a pair of vinyl gloves she carried in her purse and turned the knob while holding it between her gloved thumb and forefinger to avoid smearing the blood streak or any possible fingerprints. As she entered the office, Arthur reached the open doorway. Observing Irma's caution and gloved hands, he avoided touching anything as he followed her inside. The outer room appeared normal as they passed through it and turned right to enter Martha's private office.

Martha's inner sanctum was anything but normal. Papers and books randomly covered the floor, while Martha sat with her head and arms on her desk. She had a bloody wound on the rear of her head and red marks on the sides of her neck. Irma checked for a pulse and nodded to Arthur when she found one. He called 911 to summon the paramedics and then left the office to find Bobby Andrews and his detectives. Along the way, he found Jake Lawrence and told him to return to the dining hall and play some soothing music to keep the audience under control during the emergency.

By the time Arthur and Bobby returned to Martha's office after a preliminary search of the building for the clown, the paramedics had arrived and bandaged Martha's head wound. They hoisted her onto a wheeled stretcher. She had not yet regained consciousness. Wally Sanborn hovered above Martha, looking for her first indications of awareness. When the paramedics took her away, he went with them, saying he wanted to be present when she opened her eyes.

Bobby, Arthur, and Irma examined the scene to reconstruct what had happened. During the process, Hank Robbins entered.

"I couldn't find that clown. It looks as though he attacked Martha, and then drove away before we could discover what he had done. He may have thought he killed her."

Irma said, "Her pulse was relatively strong. I think she'll recover and will be able to remember what happened. Did anyone see that clown without his makeup? Do we know who he is?"

Bobby said, "We don't even know whether the clown is a he or a she. Bulky clown costumes and makeup conceal gender. Hank, go find Patrick Hurley and see whether they have a tape of activities in the parking lot. I thought I saw a camera on the side of the building when I came in. The only way we'll find that clown is if we can track his or her car. I doubt that Ragbo will appear in public again. Slight changes in name and makeup convert a clown into a different character."

Hank left the office, and Bobby turned to Irma. "You took a good look at Martha's injuries before the paramedics came. Should the assailant have expected the attack to kill her?"

"That's a shrewd question. That's what bothered me when I first examined her. We didn't interrupt the attack, so the assailant had plenty of time to complete his or her objective. Martha received a head wound sufficient to make her lose consciousness and lose some blood, and the marks on her neck looked more like abrasion than choking. I'd say that the clown's objective was to scare her and to demonstrate that he or she could have killed her"

Arthur said, "Let's drop the ambiguity about the clown's sex, at least as a working assumption. Hank said that the clown told him he'd be right back when going out to the parking lot. If Hank heard the clown speak and judged the voice to be male, we should follow his lead."

"Follow my lead where?" Hank Robbins re-entered the office.

Bobby said, "Never mind that, Hank. What did you find out about the surveillance camera? Do we have footage of the parking lot?"

"Afraid not, Chief; Patrick said that he had the camera working during his earlier tour of duty here, but it conked out while he was unemployed, and he hasn't had time to fix it since he returned to the staff."

"I'll put out a bulletin for all departments to watch for a driver in clown makeup, but I'm sure this Ragbo character will stop and clean up as soon as possible. I doubt that we'll catch him without a tip from someone he knows."

Arthur said, "In the meantime, we'll have to finesse the end of the concert and party, by saying that Ragbo became sick and had to leave. Then we can let the audience have their refreshments and depart. I think they should have as satisfying an experience as possible. We owe Parkville Rehabilitation Home that much, so that it can continue to operate on a normal basis. Is that acceptable to you, Bobby?"

"It would be, if I thought we were ready to close at least some of our murder investigations."

"I think we are. We'll tackle that analysis after the public goes home – we're near enough to completion to reveal our thinking. I'll give you a list of the people I want to remain in the dining hall after everyone else leaves."

CHAPTER 100 – ASSEMBLY

The police and Patrick Hurley had rearranged the tables from a semicircle into a tighter U-shaped pattern in front of the stage. Arthur sat at the base of the U, along with Irma and Police Chief Bobby Andrews. Seated at the tables to Arthur's right were Jeremy Hadley, Debbie Danforth, Noel Burnside, and Esther Ramirez, the latter individual looking very nervous. Seated at the tables to Arthur's left were Patrick Hurley, Hank Robbins, Jake Lawrence, and Shirley Hadley, who looked across to the facing table and decided that Debbie would be a better match for Jeremy than Michelle would have been. Noel looked pleased that he had a seat next to Debbie, but he tried to avoid Jeremy's glances. Patrick had closed and locked all but one of the room's exit doors. Detective Gene Murphy sat next to the open door, prepared to stop anyone who might decide to flee before the end of the meeting.

Arthur stood to open the meeting. "Thank you all for attending. This has been a very puzzling investigation. Several times, we've had to modify or reverse our theories of the underlying motives and the perpetrators involved. Now it's time for us to assemble this jigsaw puzzle so that we will be able to view its picture. You probably noticed the video camera on its tripod. Jeremy Hadley will be recording our discussions so that we may later share them with Martha Callahan, now undergoing treatment for her injuries at Parkville Care Center, and with Wally Sanborn, who accompanied her there."

Jake Lawrence gestured for attention. "I don't know why I'm here. I don't know anything about your puzzling case. My band and I have only been here today to play music for the party."

"Yes, but during your performance, another crime occurred, the assault on Martha Callahan, who arranged for you to be here. Tell me, Mr. Lawrence, who initiated this concert date, you or Martha?"

"I don't know. Our business manager arranges our schedule. He couldn't be here today."

"We'll return to that point later. This case has involved several major crimes: the murders of four female patients here at the Rehabilitation Home, The Murder of Pastor Rebecca Klingham of the Parkville United Methodist Church, drug dealing involving high-potency pain killers on these premises, and the attack on Martha Callahan that occurred today. It has been difficult to put the puzzle pieces together because we now know that more than one villain has been involved."

Shirley Hadley said, "Then the rumors weren't true? This wasn't a situation where Pastor Klingham committed suicide from remorse after she somehow caused the deaths of those four patients?"

"Pastor Rebecca Klingham was completely innocent of any wrongdoing, and she did not kill herself. Even though all four of the patients who died at the Rehabilitation Home attended our church, their deaths had nothing to do with that affiliation."

Arthur turned to face Esther Ramirez. "Esther, you said that the painkiller pills you distributed continued to be stocked in their hidden container even after Joanna Diaz quit and went to Las Vegas. Is that correct?"

"Yes it is, but I'm not a drug distributor. I simply moved pills from one location in this building to another."

Bobby Andrews said, "When you move those pills to a place where they get picked up in exchange for money, that's distribution; but play it cool, they haven't decided to prosecute yet."

Arthur approached Esther. "Think carefully, Esther. This is a key question. Have you continued to find pills in that source container recently?"

"No, there haven't been any pills for the last two weeks. I did check, because I was curious about how they got there."

"Bobby, how long has it been since you arrested Quentin Edwards for attempted rape?"

"Just about two weeks ... I think we have a new topic to discuss with him. As the attorney representing the ownership trust, he would have had free access to all areas of this facility. Thank you for that information, Esther. I'll report your cooperation to the people who will decide about prosecution. It will help your case."

Arthur said, "Having identified Quentin Edwards as the probable source of the illicit painkiller drugs, let's examine his actions a little further. I'll guess that he and Joanna Diaz had a romantic relationship until she quit and went to Las Vegas. That's why she handled the painkiller deliveries earlier. He was the attorney representing the hidden ownership trust and had access to deliver the drugs after Joanna left town.

Irma looked at Noel Burnside, seated at the right-hand table. "Noel, you told us earlier that management had you include those insurance application forms with the standard legal forms that those three patients had to sign. Who, specifically, was the management person who did that?"

"That would have been Martha Callahan, but she may have received her instructions from Quentin Edwards, the lawyer."

"And who signed the orders for the insurance policies on behalf of Parkville Rehabilitation Home?"

"That would have been Martha. She's Vice President as well as Administrator, even though she doesn't publicize that title. It's a unique setup because the ownership trust is the true chief executive, but stays hidden, and Edwards, as the lawyer who represents the trust, doesn't hold a title because of possible conflict of interest. Anyway, the orders for insurance require an officer's signature to guarantee premium payments."

"Thanks for that information, Noel. I'll call Wally at the hospital and have him ask Martha for the details as soon as she's well enough to talk." Irma left the table and went to Martha's outer office to place that call with privacy.

After Irma left, Arthur said, "It's time to talk about the ownership trust. I've revealed what I'm about to say to Irma, so she won't feel left out if we discuss it during her absence. The identity of the person or persons behind the ownership trust has been a mystery up to this point. Now it becomes important to remove the secrecy. Would you mind contributing to this discussion, Patrick?"

Murmurs greeted this question as everyone looked at Patrick Hurley.

"You're right Arthur. It is time for me to be open about my ownership of the majority of the stock in this place. I protected my investment while doing services I enjoyed, by being on the staff where I could see how efficiently the business operated. I thought Quentin Edwards gave me honest representation. I see now that I had too much faith in him. You've said that he attempted rape and that he supplied painkiller drugs for distribution. Did he get involved in the murders you mentioned?"

"For a while I thought he did, but I now think he only profited from them. Did you know that the last three female patients who died had signed applications for life insurance with your trust as the beneficiary?"

303

"No, I didn't know that. Before you ask the obvious question, I never received any payoffs from an insurance company."

Bobby said, "We know that, because we checked your accounts as well as those of Quentin Edwards. He never told you about those policies, and he diverted the benefit payments to his own accounts."

Arthur addressed Patrick Hurley regarding ownership. "I have two questions, Patrick. First, you said that you are the majority owner. Who else owns part of this place? Second, given the fact that you will no longer have the luxury of playing the staff technician who has nothing to do with ownership, will you continue the ownership trust arrangement?"

"Arthur, you take all the fun out of my pretend games. No, there are no other owners. I own one hundred percent of this place. As to the future, I'll wait until you finish solving our mysteries before I decide on my ongoing management approach. I certainly wouldn't have committed crimes that could only ruin my business."

"I appreciate the logic of your statement, Patrick, but those insurance policies on the murdered women are the key to solving our puzzle. Did Martha as administrator initiate that procedure, or did Quentin Edwards instruct her to have those women sign the papers? Who signed the orders for the policies as an officer of the corporation? We'll soon know. I see Irma coming back from her telephone conversation. Irma, was Martha able to answer the questions Wally relayed?"

She stood next to Arthur as she answered. "Fortunately, Martha is conscious and responding well to her treatments. She said that she received a text message from the lawyer, Edwards, requesting the application procedure in each of the three cases. She also said that the instances of insurance applications were the only instructions from him she ever received as text messages.

She indicated that she had forgotten about those instructions and the applications until we mentioned the policies after those women died. She also said that she never signed the paperwork to order the policies as an officer on behalf of the Rehabilitation Home."

Arthur said, "If that were the case, then the lawyer, Edwards, would have had to sign those forms, representing the trust. Bobby can check with Edwards as to whether he signed the orders, but Noel Burnside stated that Martha signed them. How could that be, Noel?"

"Martha obviously isn't remembering clearly. She was hit on her head, and it may have affected her memory."

Arthur said, "There is another possible interpretation. You forged her signatures. You didn't receive instructions from anyone to order and guarantee those policies, Noel. The insurance policies were your own idea, and you sent the text messages to Martha, supposedly from Quentin Edwards, to initiate the process. I'll bet that Edwards will say that he knew nothing about the policies prior to receiving the insurance benefits after the women died. I also suspect that Bobby would like to have your cell phone examined by an expert to see whether there's a record of sending those text messages."

"That makes no sense. How would I profit from policies that benefitted someone else?"

"You were attempting to take over this institution. Parkville Rehabilitation Home would be discredited and available for purchase at a very low price once the public learned that the ownership trust had been the beneficiary of life insurance proceeds on three patients who had died within a short period. The greed of Quentin Edwards in grabbing the benefits for himself wrecked your original plan, because it made the ownership appear blameless. You wouldn't achieve a bargain purchase based on the crimes of a crooked lawyer."

"You have no proof of any wrongdoing on my part."

"When Quentin Edwards denies sending those text messages, we'll check your phone for them. If we find those outgoing message records, we'll have proved that you initiated the insurance application events. We can show that you had access to the three deceased patients and their causes of death. We can also show that, shortly after the last of the three women died, you arranged for a large line of credit with your bank based on your intention to make a major business investment."

"None of that means anything. It's all circumstantial. Obviously, it's legal to save money and make investments. Entrepreneurship is the driving force underlying the American economy. Dozens of other staff people and visitors had access to those patients' rooms. I didn't profit from the life insurance on Janet Cuspin, Mary Welker, or Beverly Mandow. I have done nothing at all criminal, and I'm going to leave because I don't like your accusations."

Everyone turned to look at the door where Sergeant Al Gomez of the Parkville Police had entered and stood talking with Detective Gene Murphy.

Bobby Andrews rose and joined them. "Did you find anything, Al?"

"We sure did, Chief." He showed Bobby a list of items.

Bobby nodded and returned to his place at the table, motioning for Al to follow him.

"Noel, please return to your seat. Everyone, Sergeant Al Gomez here led a properly authorized and warranted search of the home of Noel Burnside in connection with our discussion of crimes at this rehabilitation facility and elsewhere. We timed this search to coincide with the festivities here because we expected Mr. Burnside to be here and the house to be empty."

Noel said, "You should have asked, and I would have given you permission to search my house. I have nothing to hide."

"That's an interesting comment, considering what we found at your house. We have a printout from Wells Fargo Bank discussing the use of a trust as the beneficiary on a life insurance policy. The printing date on this document is one month prior to the earliest application date for our three insured and deceased patients. We also found a membership directory from Parkville United Methodist Church showing checkmarks next to the names of the insured women from that church who died here, but no mark for Phyllis Landholm from that church who died here before the first insurance application. That same directory had Pastor Klingham's parsonage address circled."

"Those documents are meaningless. I study insurance procedures and other administrative matters regularly and frequently print the results. As to the directory, someone left it on a table in the lobby, and I checked and circled familiar names. That's hardly evidence that I did something criminal."

"I didn't complete my list of items we took from your house, Noel. We also found a roll of the same duct tape that Pastor Klingham's killer used to attach a hose to the exhaust pipe of her car, and the end of that tape had a cut that matched the angle on the tape that we retrieved from that hose. You also would have had access to the shop vacuum hose that came from the Rehabilitation Home."

"Many people could have taken that hose. The technician's area is never locked."

"I didn't say where the shop vacuum was kept, but you had that information. Getting back to our search of your home, we discovered a container of assorted prescription pills that don't match any of your labeled prescription bottles. Some of them may match the prescriptions of the deceased victims. Finally, we found in your possession a pair of scissors that had disappeared from the garage where Pastor Klingham died. It belonged to Arthur Blake when he lived there, and had his initials, AKB, scratched into one of the blades. Al, please arrest Noel Burnside for the murders of Janet Cuspin, Mary Welker, Beverly Mandow, and Pastor Rebecca Klingham."

Sergeant Al Gomez led Noel away, reciting his rights as they left the room.

Jeremy waved to get Arthur's attention. "I'm confused as to why Noel would murder Pastor Klingham at the parsonage when he wanted the ownership trust to be held responsible for the patient deaths."

"He wanted the trust to be accused of profiting from the deaths. I don't think he knew Patrick Hurley was behind the trust. Noel hoped to buy and continue running this business, so he didn't want to scare away potential clients. He hoped to disgrace the trust, otherwise known as Patrick, for profiting from the deaths, but to convince the public that Pastor Klingham had committed the murders and then took her own life in an admission of guilt."

Irma said, "We still have the murder of the first patient victim, Phyllis Landholm, to solve. Her death came before the insurance scheme."

Arthur nodded. "Debbie, I believe you have some research results for us to discuss."

"Yes, Arthur, one of the final three victims, Mary Welker, was a former Broadway musical performer who had been married to a musician named Larry, or Lawrence, Jakes. That name sounds very much like an inverted version of Jake Lawrence, who is sitting with us at this table. Would you like to respond, Mr. Lawrence?"

"I confess. I am both Jake Lawrence and Lawrence Jakes. Mary Welker and I loved each other very much. For various reasons, we got divorced, but we caught up with each other after some years and continued to stay in touch after that point. Mary was on her way back to normal health when she died here, and I arranged today's concert in the hope of finding who caused her death. You have arrested Mr. Burnside, so that removes any need for my taking any action against him, legal or otherwise. I hope he gets the death penalty."

Arthur looked at Bobby, and received a gesture to continue the discussion. "Let's get the names back to normal. Larry, we have a few more legal matters to cover, and they involve you. Isn't it true that you and Mary Welker during recent years were partners in some businesses? Were they what you meant by keeping in touch?"

"We rarely saw each other. She was here, and I was on the road with my band or living elsewhere. I moved around a lot."

"You moved around to operate short-term businesses that were resurrected versions of dormant firms. Mary selected inactive businesses and handled the paperwork to reopen them with you in charge of their operations. Then, you fraudulently purchased large quantities of goods and closed each enterprise without paying your bills. That's fraud, and it's illegal. Would you like to comment?"

"I'm not saying any more until I have a lawyer to guide me."

Bobby said, "That's your right, Mr. Jakes, but we'll have to examine whether you might be involved in another murder."

"I never had anything to do with a murder."

"Phyllis Landholm, the patient who died here prior to initiation of Burnside's insurance scheme, just happened to have been a retired investigator of fraudulent businesses for the state of Indiana. She likely became suspicious of Mary's activities with you in these short-term businesses. We suspect that Mary killed Phyllis and that Noel Burnside later killed Mary. What do you know about the death of Phyllis Landholm?"

"I never even heard that name before today. If Mary did that, she's beyond prosecution now. She never said anything to me about that Landholm woman. If Mary had felt threatened by Landholm, she might have acted against her. That's what happened at the end of our marriage. Mary felt inferior to the younger performers who challenged her, so even before a youngster beat her out for a part, she told me she couldn't remain in our musical world without being top-rated, and she divorced me. Fortunately, we got back together on an informal basis over the years. I came here prepared to take revenge for Mary on her killer, but you've arrested him, so I don't have to cross the line and get violent."

Irma said, "If what you're saying about the way Mary reacted to threats is true, Phyllis Landholm may not have even suspected Mary of a crime."

Arthur asked, "Was the attack on Martha Callahan part of your revenge for Mary's murder?"

"I had nothing to do with that. I was performing with my band when it happened. Go find that clown."

Bobby said, "We'll be trying to do just that, Mr. Jakes, but I hope we won't find that he works for you. You may yet be facing increased charges."

CHAPTER 101 – PATRICK

When Wally Sanborn accompanied Martha back to the Rehabilitation Home after her release from Parkville Care Center, they found her office neatened up, slightly rearranged, and occupied by Patrick Hurley. As they entered, he rose and greeted them.

"Welcome back, Martha. It's good to see you Wally. I see you're no longer hiding your relationship. I hope that you've heard enough about events here to understand why I'm in your office."

"I'm glad I always appreciated your skills while you were an employee, Patrick. I don't think I did or said anything that will cause me grief now that you're my boss."

"We'll continue to work together well, but remember that I always was your boss. You just didn't know it. Tell me about that clown attacking you."

"He pretty much took me by surprise. It's hard to read a clown's painted-on expression. He definitely acted on orders from someone else because he minimized the injuries he gave me. If he had been enthusiastic about hurting me, I might not be here now."

Wally said, "Maybe the person that hired him wanted you scared but not permanently damaged. We'll never know for sure, but I'm glad you came through it in one piece."

"Are you taking over this office, Patrick? I won't mind having a different one."

"No, Martha, this is too big for me, and I'd rather avoid being in the front-office section of the building because I need a little clutter around me to feel comfortable. This office is big enough for two. How would you like to join our staff, Wally? You could help Martha run this place."

"That would be different. Let me think about it for a while. I will say that it's good to see you operating out in the open, Patrick. I guess this means I won't be calling on you in your neighborhood Irish pub again."

"I'll still have my reserved table at Murphy's. I pay them a little extra each month for that. Decide to join us here, and we'll make it a regular event. I do my best thinking there."

Martha said, "Don't count me out of that arrangement. I am a Callahan, after all. I still find it hard to believe that the snake that tried to ruin this place was Noel Burnside. He always seemed to be energetic and content."

Wally laughed. "Once again, St. Patrick has chased the snake out of our midst."

"I didn't do the chasing, and I'm no saint. I extend many thanks to you and your associates, Wally, especially King Arthur, if we're going to attribute legendary names to those around us."

"I can see that this place is going to be a lot more fun than it was in the past. I guess I've thought about it long enough. Make me an offer I can't refuse, Patrick."

CHAPTER 102 – SANDLEY AGENCY

Debbie refilled Arthur's coffee mug for the second time, added a small amount to her own cup, and then returned the pot to the kitchen after Irma and Jeremy declined refills. She returned to the dining room table in time to hear Jeremy speaking.

"This is the best part of any case, when you've reached the main conclusions and can relax a bit while cleaning up details."

Debbie said, "Jeremy likes to pretend he's older and more experienced than he really is. I believe this is the end of our first case, even though he helped you occasionally in the past. I suspect he pretends he's had more experience with women than he can prove too. Anyway, he's not a complete amateur in bed."

Arthur said, "I think that was more information than we really needed, but I'm glad you two are continuing to get along well. Jeremy, are you going to keep the Sandley Agency name, now that Wally is joining Martha and Patrick at the Rehabilitation Home?"

"I think we'll keep it, at least for a while. With Wally on board, it was easy to decipher the source of the two halves of the name, Sanborn and Hadley, but now we'll be able to keep people guessing. Otherwise, we could switch off with Debbie's name as Danley or Hadforth. Would you like that, Debbie?"

"Let's keep it Sandley. I'm hoping to change my name to the last half of that anyway."

Jeremy blushed slightly. "Don't rush. All good things come with time."

"Irma and Arthur, did you hear that? Jeremy, I have witnesses. You just proposed but gave it a long timeline. I accept." She leaned over and kissed him on the cheek.

Arthur patted Jeremy on the shoulder. "Don't say anything. You'll get into more trouble no matter what you say. Getting away from the romantic side of your relationship, are you wanting to continue working with us when we have suitable cases?"

They looked at each other and nodded. Then Jeremy said, "I majored in Criminology at UW-Platteville. I consider working with you folks my post-graduate education, so Debbie and I definitely want to remain part of the team. We're getting closer and more in tune with each other because we've been working together. She's no longer the weird girl in the library stacks."

Irma said, "Enough frivolity – I'd like some opinions or more discussion regarding Rebecca Klingham's death. We concluded that Noel Burnside killed her and made it look like a guilty remorseful suicide to blame her for the deaths at the Rehabilitation Home. Earlier, the police held the theory that the person behind the drug sales killed her because she had detected that operation. If Noel hadn't killed her, would she still have been in danger because of the drug angle?"

Debbie said, "It's possible that Quentin Edwards would have wanted to kill her to protect his drug business. Based on the way he tried to rape me, I'd say that he wouldn't have attacked Rebecca Klingham unless he could minimize risk to himself. He came after me because he thought I had succumbed to his drugged wine. He didn't want to take the chance of being openly aggressive. My guess is that he would have hired someone else to kill Rebecca if he had wanted to go after her. He doesn't like to take chances."

Jeremy continued her thinking. "That suggests Quentin Edwards as the person who hired Ragbo the

Clown to attack Martha. I had attributed that deed to Larry Jakes. We'll probably never solve that one. Does it bother you, Arthur, when some aspect of a case remains open?"

"Like anyone else, I prefer to have all the loose ends neatly tied up, but I can live with some unfinished business. If an individual who escapes us continues to commit crimes, he or she will eventually face arrest by another agency. Larry Jakes is a good example. Bobby Andrews and his Parkville Police have neither the jurisdiction nor the inclination to go after Larry for running up unpaid bills at rejuvenated inactive companies and fencing the purchased items. If Jakes stays out of trouble in the future, he's not likely to face prosecution. I'm not bothered by that."

Irma asked, "How did Joanna Diaz fit into the drug dealing?"

"Bobby confirmed my speculation that she had been Quentin Edwards' girlfriend while she worked at the Rehabilitation Home. She handled the drugs for him inside the facility until she quit and went to Las Vegas. After that, he had to deliver his own drugs and pick up the proceeds during his visits representing the trust. They used a hidden drop-box container for deliveries and pickups to avoid detection by staff members. Bobby also said that they won't prosecute Esther Ramirez at this time, but they'll watch her for possible criminal activities in the future."

Debbie said, "I have one loose end I'd like to discuss, Arthur."

"What's that?"

"What happened to Jeremy's old girlfriend, Michelle Caspar, and will I have to worry about her in the future?"

"Michelle has gone through a rather unique self-evaluation program. I can tell you that she's not planning to return to this part of the country except for occasional family visits. Her outlook has changed in many ways, so she's not likely to be your competition."

Jeremy said, "My outlook has changed too. You're stuck with me."

Irma nudged Arthur. "That's our cue to leave and give these lovebirds sole possession of the apartment."

CHAPTER 103 – MICHELLE

Irma finished wiping the surface of the rugged old kitchen table after a session of cookie baking. Their Queen Anne home made her feel as though she were in an older era, so Irma always baked using individual ingredients rather than modern mixes. It took longer, but it was far more satisfying. Arthur had gone off to a church conference on *Tailoring the Message to Multiple Age Groups*, so she had plenty of time for her own hobbies and interests. She set up a gate to keep Rex out of the kitchen while she baked so that he wouldn't get flour in his thick hair and shake it all over the house. When her baking and cleaning were complete, she let down the barricade. Rex bounded into the kitchen and jumped up on her. She hugged him and scratched his back. As Rex settled back onto the floor, the doorbell rang, and he ran out of the kitchen toward the front door. Irma followed, after wiping her hands on a towel.

She opened the door to find Michelle Caspar facing her, carrying a gift-wrapped box.

"Hi, Irma; I stopped on my way back from visiting my folks in Iowa. This is a small token of my thanks to you and Arthur for tracking my second life memories. Is Arthur home?"

"He's off at a church conference. He has to wear his other hat from time to time. Come on in. I just cleared the kitchen table, so we can settle down there. I noticed that you said second life memories instead of prior life memories, the normal university term."

"That's because that guy who gave me his memories was still alive during part of my life. They say I'm a very unusual case, and I believe it."

"I have freshly baked oatmeal raisin cookies for you, but let's open your gift first. Thank you so much for your thoughtfulness."

"It was also an excuse to see this amazing house. I'd heard so much about it."

"I'll give you a tour after our cookies and conversation." Irma unwrapped the carton, being careful to fold the silver-colored paper after removing it.

"Oh, how special! It's an old-fashioned German cuckoo clock."

"I wanted to give you a gift from my Kurt Linser side. It's supposed to be almost as old as this house."

"I love it, and I'm sure Arthur will too. I'll hang it in a place of honor next to the living room fireplace. Now, let's sit and chat."

They settled at the kitchen table after each collecting a plate of cookies and a mug of coffee from the long counter.

Irma said, "Since you like our house so much, please consider visiting and staying with us whenever you're passing through Illinois."

"I'll take you up on that sometime, but we're not that far from the family home in Monticello, Iowa, so I won't want to slight my folks too frequently. Besides, I may not be around much at all, because I've decided to move to Charlottesville, Virginia. I'm joining the Division of Perceptual Studies at the University of Virginia, so that I'll be able to study other examples of my own phenomenon."

"I'm sure they'll also want to use you as an example to show others."

"I won't mind being used. I'm enjoying the way that my uniqueness has turned into a career."

"Have you had any additional memories of Kurt's life?"

"That's the most interesting development, Irma. Once you and Arthur confirmed my memories and traced Kurt's history, my memories of him started to fade. It felt as though he had commissioned me to discover his message, and then he released me when the job was complete."

"Wow! You really have had a special experience. As one who has performed a large number of autopsies, I'd like to learn more about people whose memories live on in others ... let's start that house tour."

CHAPTER 104 – DREAMS

When Arthur returned from his church conference, he called out for Irma, but didn't receive a response. He saw the basement door open, so he figured she was down there working on something. Undeterred, he entered the kitchen to get coffee and cookies. Irma had promised she would make him some of his favorite oatmeal raisin cookies while he was away. The surprise came when he found only two of those treats in the cookie jar. As he sat enjoying them with his coffee, Irma joined him, carrying a book on self-hypnosis.

"That looks interesting. Are you working on a new hobby?"

"I found this at a used book sale, so I thought I'd give it a try. I went down into the back end of the basement so that I'd have complete quiet. That's why I didn't hear you when you came home."

"Do the self-hypnosis techniques work?"

"Only one does so far ... the book is so boring in discussing technical aspects of the mind, that it put me to sleep."

"That's funny. How much company did you have while I was at the conference?"

"And how do you know I had company?"

"You told me you were baking cookies for me, and there were only two left when I arrived – none now. Therefore you had unexpected company arrive right after you finished baking. Am I correct?"

"Yes, while I was in the middle of cleaning the kitchen, Michelle Caspar stopped in on her way back from her family's home in Iowa. I knew you wouldn't mind my sharing your treats with her."

"That's fine with me. How is she coping with being the subject of psychological studies? She'll always be viewed as someone unusual and special."

"She's coping in a very healthy way. She's joining the team that studies past life memories. She'll be making a career of it."

"I guess that falls under the category of: *It takes one to know one.* That's an interesting development. I would have welcomed memories of a prior life as a child. I think I told you about my déjà vu experiences back then, of frequently doing things that I felt I had done before, but couldn't have."

"I remember that conversation, Arthur. The unique things about Michelle's memories are that they came to her as an adult and that the person whose life she remembered was still alive during part of her life."

"That's a challenge to some of the earlier research results, but it's exciting to learn that every case is singular. These studies show that the mind and the soul are different. Everyone has a mind; everyone has a soul; but only a few people have the experience of having a second person's soul interact with their own."

"Is that your interpretation of what's going on in these cases?"

"I don't see how it could be the mind of a dead person that is interacting, so I choose to believe Christian doctrine about the immortality of the soul and assume that if souls are immortal, they can interact with each other."

"I'm not at all sure I agree with that, Arthur, but I can't disprove it either. How do dreams fit into this philosophical structure?"

"They're something separate, because waking thoughts and sleeping thoughts are the experiences of an individual living person. They're more like alternate universes. Dreams are patterns of thoughts unfettered by logic and the physical laws of nature. That's why they frequently make no sense when you look back on them, even though they flowed freely during your sleep."

"That brings us back to the dreams you had, Arthur. They disturbed you at the time. Do you now feel clearer about their significance?"

Arthur tilted his kitchen chair backward, enjoying Irma's expression of cautious warning as he did so. "I actually do, but not because of any philosophical thinking. My original dreams were alarms about the difficulty of responding to and satisfying everyone wanting my assistance. While I was away at my conference, I had another dream. In this one, I was using a tall stack of video recorders to duplicate my thinking and pass it on to others. The column of recorders collapsed, breaking all of them. At that point, I felt completely free. I've interpreted this most recent dream as telling me that I don't have to convince others of the merits of my thinking. I can forge ahead on my own without telling anyone to follow my thoughts and interpretations."

"Does that mean you've decided what to tell Bishop Chandler?"

"It does. I'll tell him I want to make my leave of absence a long-term thing. Irma, you and I should be free to tackle any challenge we want and go wherever the road takes us. My church background should empower me, but not entangle me in a structural relationship."

- END –

ACKNOWLEDGEMENTS

The analysis of Michelle Caspar's unusual memories is based on work performed at the actual University of Virginia Division of Perceptual Studies by Jim B. Tucker, M.D. and his associates. His books on this subject include *Life Before Life: Children's Memories of Previous Lives*, and *Return to Life: Extraordinary Cases of Children Who Remember Past Lives*. The latter volume was a great resource for me, as were answers to questions I put to Dr. Tucker during several exchanges of emails.

Certain details and scenes included in Michelle's memories of the youthful Kurt were based on actual events included in a memoir by my close friend, Peter Slonek, *Who Stole My Father?* Peter graciously agreed to my use of the Austrian scenes, and I suggest that my readers will gain a better understanding of the pleasures and difficulties of growing up in Austria before and during World War II from reading Peter's book.

The childhood déjà vu incidents described by Arthur Blake were my own, and perhaps because of them, I found myself quite open to exploring investigations of memories of prior lives. If you have experienced such memories, your current life may be proof of life after death. It's worth discussion and consideration.

Richard Davidson

Richard Davidson

ABOUT THE AUTHOR

Richard Davidson is the author of the self-help guidebook: *DECISION TIME! Better Decisions for a Better Life.* He has written the five-novel Lord's Prayer Mystery Series: *Lead Us Not into Temptation, Give Us this Day our Daily Bread, Forgive Us Our Trespasses, Thy Will Be Done,* and *Deliver Us from Evil.* He has edited an anthology, *Overcoming: An Anthology by the Writers of* OCWW. His latest two novels, *Implications* and *Impulses,* from his new Imp Mysteries series, continue to chronicle the exploits of Arthur Blake and the investigative associates who aided him in the earlier mystery series, taking their interests in new directions. Mr. Davidson is Past President of Off-Campus Writers' Workshop, the oldest ongoing group of its kind in the U.S. and is the founder of the ReadWorthy Books Book Review Blog. He is the founder of the Independent Mystery Publishing Society (IMPS). Mr. Davidson is a Certified Lay Servant Speaker and a former Lay Leader in the United Methodist Church. He is also an aeronautical & astronautical engineer and a businessman.

WORKS BY THIS AUTHOR

NONFICTION:

DECISION TIME! Better Decisions for a Better Life, VBW Publishing, Inc.
ISBN 978-1-60264-063-4 (paperback)
RADMAR Publishing
ISBN 978-0-9829160-7-0 (2nd edition paperback)
ISBN 978-1-60264-064-1 (hard cover)
ISBN 978-1-4581-8395-8 (Smashwords eBook)
ASIN B0052GOZEO (Kindle Edition eBook)

Where you are in life today is the result of all of the past decisions you have made or which have been made for you in response to the various situations and events that have impacted your life. The decisions that you will make from this point forward will determine the degree to which your future will be positive or negative. *DECISION TIME!* gives you insight into the subjective decision-making process as applied to both small and large choices you will face. It includes dynamic aspects, cultural effects, and morality as applied to decision-making for individuals, teams, corporations, and societies. *DECISION TIME!* prepares you to face the continuous impacts of decision situations confidently and without hesitation.

FICTION:

Lead Us Not into Temptation (The Lord's Prayer Mystery Series, Volume I),
VBW Publishing, Inc.
ISBN 978-1-60264-407-6 (paperback)

Richard Davidson

ISBN 978-1-4581-7381-2 (Smashwords eBook)
ASIN B0052MGI6Q (Kindle Edition eBook)

Arthur Blake, former NASA engineer turned minister, receives an emergency appointment to be pastor of the United Methodist Church in Parkville, a distant suburb of Chicago, following the bizarre sudden death of the church's unusual former pastor. Pastor Blake's attempts to unravel the mystery that shrouds his predecessor become involved with tracking the child of a possibly bigamous soldier in World War II England, art and jewelry treasures plundered by the Nazis and their sympathizers, and the eventual results of childhood sibling conflicts in combined families. Arthur's allies in his investigation include Parkville Police Chief Bobby Andrews, County Medical Examiner Irma Custis, and the married team of Penny and Joe Gonzalez who work for a clandestine government agency. During the course of *Lead Us Not into Temptation*, the reader discovers how seemingly minor historical events lead to major present-day dislocations in church, village, and family relationships.

Give Us this Day Our Daily Bread (The Lord's Prayer Mystery Series, Volume II)
RADMAR Publishing
ISBN 978-0-9829160-0-1 (paperback)
ISBN 978-0-9829160-5-6 (2nd edition paperback)
ISBN 978-1-4580-6717-3 (Smashwords eBook)
ASIN B0052MQI66 (Kindle Edition eBook)

Arthur Blake, Pastor of Parkville United Methodist Church, has to deal with the aftereffects of a traumatic communion incident. He works to assist the authorities in investigating the cause while doing his best to convince members of his congregation that it is safe to return to church. Working with the police and federal agencies, he discovers that the terror of the initial event is minor compared with the potential chaotic impact of future disasters being planned by the perpetrator. The investigation is interwoven with several relationship situations that affect the final outcome.

Forgive Us Our Trespasses (The Lord's Prayer Mystery Series, Volume III)
RADMAR Publishing
ISBN 978-0-9829160-1-8 (paperback)
ISBN 978-1-4657-3739-7 (Smashwords eBook)
ASIN B005SULQ6Y (Kindle Edition eBook)

Arthur Blake, Pastor of Parkville United Methodist Church, tries to assist his father to resolve his trauma after learning that his best friend, recently killed in a car accident, may have been an imposter with a heinous background. The investigation reveals that the presumed accident was but one link in a chain of murders. Blake works to determine the true identity of his father's friend, while also discovering the man's past activities and affiliations. Arthur works to solve the murders in conjunction with his colleagues at ABC Consultants. He also draws on assistance from associates at a covert government agency with which he has worked before. The coordinated effort to solve the puzzle examines incidents that span the period between World War II and the present in order to defuse the personal, national, and international dangers resulting from them.

Thy Will Be Done (The Lord's Prayer Mystery Series, Volume IV)
RADMAR Publishing
ISBN 978-0-9829160-2-5 (paperback)
ISBN 978-1-3013-4293-8 (Smashwords eBook)
ASIN B009JU6EZM (Kindle Edition eBook)

Richard Davidson

The sudden death of a young woman attending Parkville United Methodist Church infuriates her brother and leads to congregational outrage over his outburst and subsequent murder. The investigation of that slaying by Pastor Arthur Blake and his associates leads to revelations of a previously undetected criminal organization operating in the area. Unraveling the mystery and scope of this group entangles Arthur and his associated investigators in a web of conspiracies extending from Illinois to both U.S. coasts and through Mexico to Guatemala.

Deliver Us from Evil (The Lord's Prayer Mystery Series, Volume V)
RADMAR Publishing
ISBN 978-0-9829160-3-2 (paperback)
ASIN: B00EBDUXFY (Kindle Edition eBook)

Arthur and Irma's wedding day has finally arrived, but an unexpected interruption leads to their need to investigate a possible murder committed by someone close to them. With the aid of friends and federal agents Penny and Joe Gonzalez, they follow a series of clues, crisscrossing the United States to learn more about the murder, related subsequent events, and the significance of a rare object brought home by a veteran of the Iraq War. A second murder close to Pastor Arthur Blake's church involves them in a new investigation, assisting Parkville Police Chief Bobby Andrews. Are these murders and the tracking of that strange object connected? Will marriage deteriorate or improve the relationship between Arthur and Irma? Character flaws in many relationships color the outcome.

Overcoming: An Anthology by the Writers of OCWW

Impulses

Edited and with an Introduction by Richard Davidson
RADMAR Publishing
ISBN 978-9829160-4-9 (paperback)
ASIN B00E80NN4I (Kindle Edition eBook)

This anthology covers many aspects of overcoming
life's problems, obstacles, and challenging developments.
The contributing writers have used fiction, non-fiction,
memoir, poetry, historical chronicle, and drama to
highlight our continuing need to overcome our problems,
rather than dwell on them. The reader will learn from
many talented writers the skills needed to respond
constructively, energetically, and sometimes humorously
to whatever obstacle bars one's path. Apply their lessons
to your own needs and to those of others you cherish.

Implications: An Arthur Blake Mystery Novel
RADMAR Publishing
ISBN 978-0-9829160-6-3 (paperback)
ASIN B00LY9IBWK (Kindle Edition eBook)

Bishop Howard Chandler has assigned Pastor Arthur
Blake to investigate the burning of a church in the small
city of Amboy, Illinois. He learns from that church's pastor
that she had to overcome past improprieties by former
members. During the investigation of the fire's cause,
Arthur and the other state fire investigators uncover
disturbing aspects of the ninety-year-old church's design
and history. Arthur calls on his federal associates for
assistance, as the investigation of a local church fire
expands to seeking solutions to related crimes occurring
from the present to recent years and back to the
Prohibition Era. Progress in the investigation intertwines
with new developments in Arthur's family life.

Impulses: An Arthur Blake Mystery Novel

Richard Davidson

RADMAR Publishing
ISBN 978-0-9829160-8-7 (paperback)

Several disturbing dreams cause Arthur Blake to wonder whether he is trying to do too much for the many people who seek his services. These qualms are complicated by Bishop Howard Chandler's suggestion that Arthur temporarily set aside his official duties and take an extended sabbatical leave. His resulting internal debates about career moves are set aside when the pastor who replaced him at the Parkville church dies in an apparent suicide possibly linked to several deaths at the Parkville Rehabilitation Home. The bishop assigns Arthur to determine the circumstances behind the new pastor's death, while Arthur and Irma, his wife and constant investigative partner, also study a mysterious shipment at his father's antiques shop. The sudden disappearance of a young associate provides another mystery and leads to questions of life after death and reincarnation. Events that initially appear simple become increasingly complex as the true natures of many people come into question.

Learn more about the writings and random thoughts of Richard Davidson at: davidsonbooks.blogspot.com davidsonbookshelf.com betterlifedecisions.blogspot.com and at the Independent Mystery Publishing Society (IMPS) https://www.mysteryimps.com
Richard Davidson's author page on Amazon is located at https://www.amazon.com/author/richarddavidson
Follow and *Like* Richard Davidson, Author on Facebook at https://www.facebook.com/richarddavidsonauthor?ref=hl
Follow him on Twitter @mysteryimp